Darklands Online

By: David J. Bushman

Prologue

"This is Sedona Chen of Tech Talk Live coming to you from day three of the Electronic Gaming Expo. I'm here with Oliver Crist, Founder and CEO of Wave Interactive," the smiling woman said warmly looking into the camera. The man standing next to her looked like he'd be more at home in Napa Valley than Silicon Valley. "Mr. Crist you have delivered what many analysts are saying is the most anticipated keynote of this year's expo. Care to tell us a little bit more about your company's new Wavegear Immersion Technology and the recently released Darklands Online?"

"Let me start out by saying thank you for the kind words Sedona," Crist smiled looking into the camera with a practiced ease. "At Wave it's been a very exciting year for us. We launched Darklands Online as our pilot program for the Wavegear headset. In the first quarter and the game really took off. For us though this is just the first step. The video game is set to act as our test bed for the hardware."

"Now during the keynote you mentioned some very lofty plans for your hardware beyond just a game system," Sedona explained. "Can you elaborate on those for the audience at home?"

"Absolutely, the video game is only the beginning for our plans at Wave. It is our proof of concept for completely immersive virtual environments. While the Darklands video game is exciting, the possibilities for real life applications is what really excites me about our technology. With our technology medical students can gain first hand experience in high pressure situations. Imagine being able to experience hundreds of heart surgeries without ramifications for your mistakes. A student can experience some of the most complicated procedures an operating room can offer without leaving the classroom. Instructors can present an infinite number of complications and variables to challenge even the best doctors in the world all from the comforts of their own home. The technology serves as a tool for teaching, long distance communication and experimentation."

Smiling and nodding Sedona went on amidst the flurry of activity surrounding the expo's main floor. "Now during your keynote, you noted that Wave Interactive would be working very closely with FEMA for the next generation of disaster relief and training. While this news wasn't the biggest aspect of your talk it seemed like a portion that you were really excited about."

"Yeah that partnership wasn't something we expected a lot of people to get excited about. For us it goes back to training. We can get firefighters and other emergency personnel training in dangerous situations without putting them at risk. Beyond that FEMA will serve as another testbed for us. Beyond working in virtual environments, our second major function for the Wave headgear is remote piloting of unmanned robotics. With our partnership with FEMA the idea is piloting small drones in real time into places people cannot otherwise access. Most remote-controlled devices lack a certain perspective from the operators. I want to take that to the next level. I want drone pilots to feel as if they are driving the robot as if they were the robot. It's this kind of bridge between a virtual space and the real world that we are striving for."

"And that is your goal when it comes to Wave's involvement in space exploration? I think that was the largest head turner. While it was known you had big plans for your immersion technology, I think most people were expecting a talk about the future of video games."

"I really don't want to downplay our plans for Darklands Online," Crist chuckled. "The game really had been a large focus of what we've been doing at Wave for a long time. It is really our playground for testing the limits of the technology we've been developing. As far as space travel goes, we're still in the infancy of what we have planned there. Our hope is to take what we plan to learn with FEMA and expand that to space travel. One of the biggest hurdles, humans have encountered, while venturing beyond earth is how to do so safely and efficiently for the people manning our ships. While we don't have a solution for this, we are hoping that what we learn with FEMA can be expanded to a new more sophisticated unmanned drone that can change how we explore our universe. If we can mine asteroids, ferry supplies and venture further into our own solar system with a newer more advanced unmanned solution, we feel at Wave that this will be a massive step forward into this still developing frontier."

"As exciting as these new ventures are, I'm sure there are still a lot of people who are eager to hear about your future plans for Darklands," Sedona smiled. "While developing your hardware you've managed to stumble upon a runaway hit in the world of online gaming."

"We knew we had something special with Darklands online," Crist began thoughtfully. "I don't think any of us were surprised that people would be interested in entering a new world. The sheer excitement surrounding the game since day one is what has really floored us. To us what started out as a proof of concept has really become a cornerstone of our business. Right now, it is our most financially solvent property surpassing even the hardware itself. I cannot get into too many details, but we have some really big things planned for the game. Our main goal right now is to make the world as realistic as possible. Players will tell you that it is the most realistic game they have played. To us that is not good enough. We want our virtual world to be indistinguishable from reality. Even since launch our developers have made great strides in the sensations experienced in everything from the weather to eating and drinking. We have been ambitious with the size and scope of the world we've created. I think in the coming months players are going to be pleased with how we begin to really fill that world. Like I said I cannot get into too many details on what we have planned. We have some really good things lined up so I would just say stay tuned."

"Well thank you very much for your time Mr. Crist. On behalf of everyone at Tech Talk Live, I can say we are excited to see what exactly you have planned."

"Thank you, Sedona," Crist smiled before the camera cut away.

Chapter 1

Rain drops from outside the cart felt so real as they pelted Kurt's neck and back through the iron bars. The sounds of horse hooves on broken cobblestones rhythmically sounded with the gentle rocking of the wagon. He pulled hard against his bonds only to have the same jarring message appear in red script in front of his face.

You Are Restrained

"It'll only be a minute bro. Just hang in there. This is going to be so cool, I promise."

"You've been saying that for twenty minutes now, Greg."

"Just wait it'll be totally worth it. You're going to be awesome at this."

Kurt's little brother had been bugging him for months to try out Darklands Online. Greg was a good kid but he had been putting it off. Videogames were fun and all but he just had other interests. Once everything had gone to Fully Immersive Virtual Reality, he really had to make a choice. So while Greg spent hours flying internet spaceships and fighting cartoon goblins in the virtual world, Kurt continued to wrestle. Practices, weight training, clinics, meets; the list went on and on with his obligations. So yeah he had been putting this off.

"Like I said this one doesn't use special attacks and stuff. What you can actually do is what makes you good. Even getting to level two is a huge deal. There's no need to catch up with my character because I'm going to be starting from scratch too. This is going to be awesome."

"Okay okay, I'm playing alright." The words bit a little more than he intended. He was only a day removed from the Ohio High School State Wrestling Tournament. As Roseville's best wrestling prospect in a long time, he flamed out on day one, dropping two matches by decision in a row. Even thinking about it now seemed unreal since he hadn't lost two matches all season long. He pulled up hard on his manacles feeling the tight pressure on his wrists.

You Are Restrained

You Have Been Invited to a Party by ???
    Accept   Decline

"I just sent you a party invite, bro," Greg whispered to his brother. "Just concentrate on the 'Accept' option."

"Okay," Kurt said, focusing on the option in front of him.

"Pipe down in there!" a gruff voice shouted. Something blunt knocked his head forward causing the periphery of his vision to redden. It wasn't painful per say but more like a heavy pressure that hinted at damage. Almost like having someone slap him in the back of the head without the impact. It was a surreal experience to say the least. He brought his eyes up and saw the bristled snout of a rat man sticking out from under a rain soaked hood. Kurt couldn't tell for sure but he thought there was a satisfied grin on the thing's ugly snout.

"Don't get crazy, bro. If you get killed you're locked out for twelve hours before you can reroll. We'll be out of this in a minute. Oh man here we go get ready!" Abruptly the cart stopped as the large horses whinnied in protest. Kurt turned his head in curiosity to see what had happened. Almost on cue the storm picked up in earnest, drenching everything inside the cart.

Greg bounced excitedly in his seat across from Kurt. "Ok as soon as we get free, book it down the hill behind you and get some distance from these guys. Don't worry about the handcuffs. I found a place where we can get them taken off so we don't need to waste time trying to figure out which of these guys has the key."

Kurt felt a little confused but Greg had been playing this game non stop since it came out. He probably knew what he was talking about. The commotion outside drew away his attention when the lead guard began to yell. "Get him out of the road and put him in the back! We have a schedule to keep." Straining to see in the dim torch light, Kurt could barely make out a cloaked figure as two of the guards advanced down the center of the road. Brandishing cudgels the two ratmen seemed eager for a bit of fun with the newcomer. Their easy nature was short lived though as a horizontal streak of light bisected the both of them abruptly dropping them in gruesome fashion. In one deft move the man threw off his cloak and swung his now radiant greatsword in a vertical arc. A wave of white energy sheared the wagon in two, freeing their bonds from the floor as the two wagon halves fell away from each other.

"Time to go," Greg smiled as he bounded over the wreckage toward the muddy slope beyond.

Kurt sat dumbly as the cart toppled over dumping him into the road. The world around him devolved into chaos as some people scrambled away while others took up the fight alongside the man with the glowing sword. Ratmen shouted as some fell quickly while others brutally beat prisoners too slow to escape.

"You won't get away, pink skin," came a shout from behind. Kurt looked up just in time to see a familiar guard's cudgel coming down toward him in a high arc. On instinct Kurt rolled to his side catching the blow on his arm as he struggled to his feet. Heavy pressure let him know that he took damage as he numbed on that side. Another wild swing came but this time he was ready as he moved up to a crouch. Shooting forward he took the guard off of his feet and crashed to the ground on top of him. In a panic he tried to grip him around the waist but his manacles limited the use of his arms. The guard struggled frantically to bring his weapon to bear but in close contact it was proving a useless gesture. Kurt wormed his way up the rodent's body wrapping his manacles around its neck. Realizing what was happening the guard dropped his weapon and clawed at the ground in an attempt to escape. When he did he left his back exposed and Kurt's training took over. It was over in a second as Kurt readjusted his grip with the chain and hauled up hard. There was a pop and the guard went limp. In the bottom right of his vision a notification scrolled.

You Have Slain - Rattling Guard Level 1
You Have Acquired - 1 Silver and 3 Copper

Frantically Kurt looked around as slowly the guards were turning the tide and regaining a measure of order. "Come on Kurt get out of there," came a shout from the other side on the embankment. Greg's voice brought him back into the moment as he found his footing. He was about to run when he saw the cudgel laying next to the body. Picking it up another notification came up in the same place as the other.

You Have Acquired - Soldier's Cudgel

The weapon disappeared from his hand. Confused, Kurt looked to see if he had accidently dropped the weapon when his brother's voice rang out again. "Now Kurt! I don't want to have to wait for you to reroll."

8

Not wasting anymore time, Kurt gave up on the weapon and sprinted for the muddy tract his brother was waiting on. Angry shouts sounded behind him but soon faded as the brothers moved off into the nearby woods.

Stamina Depleted

The notification flashed across the center of Kurt's screen as the two boys bent over with their hands on their knees, breathing hard.It was uncanny how real the exertion had felt. The dead sprint from the fight felt as real as any conditioning workout he'd endured in the real world. Another notification popped up in his bottom right.

Maximum Movement Speed Decreased by 30%

Almost on cue Greg chimed in. "Don't worry about the debuff. It'll clear in a minute. You always get one when you completely deplete your stamina. In combat it sucks but those guys won't leave the road."

"How many times have you played this game?"

"That event is the game intro. It's the same every time. Since Darklands uses permadeath, I've seen it too many times."

"Doesn't that get boring?"

Greg just shrugged his shoulders. "The good part comes later. Once you get to Silent Grove the different paths really open up. We'll get there soon. Let's get these handcuffs off first."

Kurt thought it was a good idea and followed his younger brother deeper into the trees. This was his world anyway. Following his lead only made sense. The brothers walked in silence for a time and their stamina completely refilled while the debuff dropped away. The rain had either stopped or it was being blocked by the canopy overhead. Either way the night took on a much more peaceful tone as moonlight began to filter in through the branches above.

"So did you get anything good off the guard?"

"Um I got some money. I tried to grab his weapon but it disappeared."

"Really that's weird. Is it in your inventory?"

"Uh I don't know. How do you check?"

"Well there are no buttons like the old games you're used to. Instead you need to concentrate on the icons at the side of your vision. Try it on the one that looks like a bag."

Kurt found the icon in the top right and focused on it. A small grid opened in front of him. The square in the top left had something in it. "Ok I see something."

"Concentrate on it."

Kurt followed his brother's instructions and two buttons appeared in the center of his vision.

Equip. Examine

Focusing on the Examine button, Kurt's button was replaced with a block of text.

Soldier's Cudgel

Damage: 1-3

Quality: Normal

Requirements: None

"Yeah that's it. I have it."

10

"You have to equip weapons and armor to use them. Go ahead and equip it."

Kurt went back to his inventory this time concentrating on the Equip button. Abruptly he felt a weight on his hip as the Soldier's Cudgel appeared in a loop off of his belt. Kurt picked it up and gave it a swing. It felt solid and real.

"It's only a starter weapon but we're both going to need something."

"I'm not going to be able to do much with it if we don't get these handcuffs off."

"I got that covered. Come on."

Kurt broke into a run to match pace with his brother as the trees thinned giving way to another steep embankment. Scrambling upward on hands and knees, the night opened up around them. Stars became visible through the clouds cover as it dissipated. A small swift moving creek churned not far in front of them as Greg pointed out a building on the opposite shore.

"There it is. That's where we can get these things off. Just follow me."

Kurt watched as his brother set off down the hill for a fallen log caught amongst some large rocks a little further down stream. As he caught up Kurt could only groan while his brother broke into a reckless run across its soggy trunk. When Greg appeared to run out of room he startled his brother by leaping out into open air before splashing and disappearing beneath the dark waters. In a panic Kurt scrambled out onto the log only to watch as his brother appeared in the waist deep current half walking and half swimming onto the opposite bank.

Cupping his hands, Greg yelled back to his brother. "Your turn bro. Get as much distance as you can then just keep fighting forward."

Heart racing Kurt nodded and backed up to build up his speed. In two quick, easy strides he was on the log moving fast. He could feel the leather shoes slip and threaten to dump him over the side but he ignored it and charged forward. Once he reached the point his brother had made it to, he let loose with everything he had and hurdled outward trying to cross the distance to the bank. He wasn't sure how far he'd made it when the frigid weather rushed up to meet him. The world went dark as the icy depths pulled the air from his lungs. Struggling to find purchase he pressed his feet down into the soft river bottom only to feel them slide away from underneath him. Kurt lost all sense of direction as he could feel the current spin his body around and drag him away. Flailing wildly Kurt tried to pull himself up to the surface. He felt his hand break through only to be spun around again. As he tumbled he felt his feet drag the river bottom. Desperately he kicked up hard. Briefly his head came above the water but not long enough to see where he ended up.

Just as he felt himself dip under again something caught the chain between his hands. With a sudden jerk his head was back over the water. Greg was standing up to his armpits in the creek and tugging for all he was worth on his brother's bindings. The resistance against the current and being able to reorient himself was all he needed. Kurt was able to dig in and find his footing in the bottom struggling upright. Once he accomplished this the two brothers carefully found their way to the muddy bank.

"Man you almost made it all the way across," Greg laughed. "But I think you landing needs some work."

Kurt could only nod in between coughs. Adrenaline pumped through his veins still as he was still trying to come down from the experience. "That was nuts."

"I told you man this is the most real game I've ever played. We haven't even got to the good part yet. Come on!"

Greg was back up and moving. It was all Kurt could do to keep up with his brother again. He could honestly say it was the first time he had to work to keep pace with Greg. Kurt was skeptical about playing this thing with him but he had to admit he could see the appeal. It wasn't everyday he could do this kind of stuff. Then again maybe that's why his brother logged in everyday.

The two brothers came to the long abandoned building at the edge of the water. A large wooden wheel sat motionless half submerged in the creek. Its ramshackle door rested partially on its hinges until Greg threw it open detaching it completely. Moving inside the moonlight illuminated the decrepit building through sizable holes in the roof and walls. The level of detail was incredible. Even though he knew it wasn't real, Kurt couldn't help but feel a strong sense of foreboding from the inky shadows that danced along every surface. Greg busied himself with a rope and a lever toward the center of the building but Kurt couldn't help but gawk at his surroundings.

"You sure it's safe to be in here?"

"Yeah, man. This is the easiest way to ditch these restraints. I've done it like a million times. I don't think anyone even knows about this place. Most people just fight at the caravan until they can get a key to drop off of a guard."

"That's not really what I meant."

Having freed the rope, Greg pulled down on the lever and a loud clang resonated through the building as a cloud of dust coated everything. Kurt stifled the urge to cough and was once again amazed by the realism. Slowly a large shaft running down the center of the building began to turn and the mill came to life raining dust and grime down throughout the mill.

"At first I thought I would have to cut these things away from my hands or have a blacksmith break them apart for me." Greg moved over to

13

the giant spinning blade on the other side of the workshop floor. Thrusting the chain of his manacles into its path a shower of sparks followed by a small cloud of smoke. His manacles disappeared. "It turns out though that if you do enough damage to them, like any other item, they just disintegrate."

Kurt forcibly closed his mouth as he regarded his brother's casual attitude around the blade that was larger than either of them. "It's just a game," he reminded himself as he walked to the saw. He moved in close as the chain caught slamming both of his wrists down on the belt leading up to the blade. In an instant the manacles were gone in an explosion of sparks and smoke. Kurt couldn't help but grin as he rubbed his wrists and stretched his arms. The freedom of movement felt amazing with the virtual weight gone. "My wrists don't hurt but it's good to get the pressure off of them."

"Yeah no one would play if there was real pain involved. The stuff they do with hot, cold and pressure go a long way toward simulating it though. I spent most of my first day just walking around town barefoot feeling the grass and cobblestone road. It was crazy."

Kurt really couldn't say much so he just smiled and nodded at that. "I guess plugging a game straight into my brain is a little more than I'm used to."

"You're going to be addicted soon, bro. I can see it already and we haven't gotten to the real fun stuff yet."

"We'll see," he said as a low thrum sounded from somewhere overhead. Greg clutched at his chest straining to pull out the arrow shaft. Spinning and searching on instinct, Kurt barely ducked in time when the second arrow caught his brother in the stomach. With this Greg fell backwards onto the ground unmoving.

"Keep standing still so I can save some arrows," a voice laughed

14

from above. "I can't believe you noobs aren't even wearing armor."

Rage bubbled up from somewhere inside as he scanned the patchy roof. Another arrow came down clattering on the floor in front of him before disintegrating. The near miss shocked him into action and he bolted for the door. Kurt moved toward the opposite end of the building as two more shots sank into the soft dirt where he had just been standing. Staying close to the wall to cut off the archer's line of sight, Kurt desperately looked for a way up into the roof. He nearly circled the building avoiding shots when he saw the water wheel and had an idea.

Drawing fire for a moment, Kurt dove out into the water. The current threatened to sweep him away again but this time he moved with purpose. Staying under the surface, he watched in the top left as his stamina slowly drained. Searching by feel rather than sight he soon found the water wheel at its lowest point. He had to force himself to stop as the wood brushed his fingers. Maneuvering around to the back side he could see that it was time to move. He allowed the turning wheel to pull him out of the water. He quickly climbed up the improvised moving ladder. Another pair of shots sank into the wood harmlessly. As he had guessed his assailant did not have a decent angle. Reaching the top of the wheel, Kurt sprang onto the roof as the man's name tag came into view.

Killa420 | The Undertakers | Level 3

He took two steps toward the shooter before darting out at an angle. Another arrow flew wide into the night as Killa420 had not been expecting the move. Undaunted Kurt continued to close, running erratically. The next shot that came grazed his cheek and felt as if someone rubbed it with a piece of ice. A third shot sailed wide and then he was on him. Ignoring the man's weapon, Kurt shot in low catching the man just

15

behind the calves before pulling him in tight. Dumbfounded Killa420 flailed with nowhere to go as the two rolled. Connected in this way, they slid toward the roof's edge. It was only a moment and then Kurt instinctively let go as the two fell out into the open air. He felt as if someone hit him with a heavy pillow the size of his entire body while his vision tinted red. He stole a glance at his health bar while scrambling to his feet. It was just over halfway depleted but that really didn't matter now.

Killa420 had managed to hang onto his bow and was moving to get some distance. In doing so he turned his back to Kurt giving him the only opportunity he needed. Closing quickly Kurt wrapped his arms around Killa420's waist. The archer tried to pull away but Kurt had done this exact move too many times over the years. He locked his wrists and placed both of his feet behind his opponent's own feet rocking back with all his weight. His training did all the work as he landed on Killa420's back driving his face into the ground. Panic gripped the player as he tried to squirm away. It was then that he had attempted to say something but Kurt had already heard enough from him. He spent the next few seconds raining down fists and elbows onto the back of his opponent's exposed head. Kurt could feel the man struggle but he already knew he had all the leverage. In a matter of moments it was over. A new notification appeared in his vision at the bottom right.

You Have Defeated - Killa420 | Level 3

Kurt pulled himself upright still sitting on the other player's back. He let out a long breath that he didn't realize he'd been holding in. When he killed the guard before it had been different for some reason. Despite the realism in the game the guard was just a thing. It had been fairly predictable. This had been a living breathing person that had attacked him and his brother. The thought suddenly occurred to him, his brother.

Sprinting back into the mill, Kurt scanned the room and found his brother where he had left him. Two arrows bit deeply into Greg's chest. He tried to check for any signs of life but ultimately he had no clue how to do that. Resigned to the fact they'd have to try again tomorrow Kurt searched for the menu icon. He found the gear icon and concentrated on it. The background greyed and the world went silent. In front of him a small menu appeared.

Settings

FAQ

Submit Ticket

Logout

Chapter 2

He was about to select Logout when a small, quarter sized orb of light began to bob up and down in front of his face. Unable to tell what it was he dismissed the menu and the world came alive around him once more.

"Wait! Don't quit. Wait a second bro."

Kurt was confused as the small orb of light sounded just like his brother. "Greg?"

"Yeah man don't quit out."

"I'm really not looking to play by myself. We can try again tomorrow. No big deal."

"Hang on. As long as you stay logged in I can still play."

"Um you look pretty dead to me," Kurt goaded as he looked at his brother's avatar lying motionless on the floor. "I thought you said you were locked out for twelve hours."

"Yeah I am. I can't make a new character but that clock is running. As long as you stay logged in I can haunt you."

"What?"

"I hadn't had a chance to try this yet but when you die while in a party there is a random chance that you can stick around and haunt them. There are a couple different forms you can take that have drawbacks and advantages. Like a ghost can't be seen but it can only speak slowly and be heard by everyone. Vengeful spirits can help someone fight but cannot communicate and can be killed. It looks like I rolled wisp. Everyone can see me but I can only talk to you and no one else can hear. That's handy because I can still get you to the starting town and we'll be able to meet up after I can restart."

"I guess that's better than your day being done," Kurt shrugged.

"What attacked us anyway? Did you see where it went?"

"It was another player. I killed him."

"Oh nice. Did you get any good loot? What about his bow?"

Remembering how he had received the money and cudgel from the guard, Kurt opened his inventory. There was nothing new added since the last time he had looked. "I'm not seeing anything in my inventory so he must not have had anything I could take."

"You have to loot players manually. There is no auto loot for them like the trash mobs. Take me to him and I'll show you."

Kurt shrugged and walked outside with his brother the wisp circling. He kinda reminded Kurt of a white overgrown firefly. It would probably only be a matter of time before his brother's new form became irritating. Following alongside the building they moved to the grassy patch where the fight had taken place. The body was where he had left it.

"Whoa Kurt this guy's not dead! Did you use your cudgel on him?"

"No. It was a little crazy. I just used my hands."

"Ok, no problem. You can still loot him but you need to hurry before he wakes up. Just concentrate on him to examine and then select loot all.

Kurt bent over the fallen player and concentrated like he had before when going through his inventory. A prompt appeared before him.

Killa420 | Level 3 (Incapacitated)

Examine

Loot (Select)

Loot (All)

He selected Loot (All) and a number of notifications scrolled in the bottom right. Kurt ignored these for the moment as the body in front of him physically changed. Armor and weapons disappeared leaving a different looking player in plain clothes. In that instant the player's eyes opened and a hand darted to his belt for something. Killa420's eyes grew wide with realization. " Oh you son of a…"

Kurt cut him off quickly slamming his fist into his face repeatedly before the initial surprise had worn off. Killa420's eyes rolled back and he slumped back to the ground. The shock of him waking as much as anything had caused him to react. Even now he could feel his heartbeat in his ears as his nerves were on edge. Until Greg had pointed it out he thought the player was dead.

The wisp spoke up snapping him out of his thoughts. "You need to finish this guy off or he's going to kill you. If not that his guild mates will find us if we hang out too long. Better make it quick too so we can get moving."

That made sense to Kurt. He didn't need anymore trouble now that he was on his own. Crouching over the body Kurt gripped the unconscious player by the collar and belt. It took a couple tries but he got him up into a fireman's carry over his shoulder. "This guy didn't look that heavy," he rasped, struggling to get the weight adjusted evenly.

"That's because you're still base 10 across the board. Humans might be the meta but you haven't put any points into power yet. You're still pretty weak right now," Greg explained as he watched his brother struggle. "You could have just finished him with the cudgel, you know."

Kurt knew he was right but that seemed too good for a guy who wanted nothing more than to try and ruin a couple other people's day. Wading out as deep as he dared, Kurt hoisted the body off his shoulder and into the center of the creek. The current was strong and soon swept the body away and out of sight.

"I thought you were going to force him under or something."

Kurt only shrugged.

"If the river doesn't kill him, I'm sure that guy is going to come looking for you. He will probably have some buddies next time too," his brother added.

"I'm sure if I killed him with the cudgel, he would be coming after me too."

"True but at least you would know he wouldn't be Level 3 then."

That thought hadn't occurred to Kurt.

Greg must have seen him considering what he had said because he spoke next. "There's nothing you can do about it now. Did he have anything good on him at least?"

Kurt looked to the list of prompts in the corner of his view.

You Have Acquired - 1 Gold, 12 Silver and 7 Copper

You Have Acquired - Hunter's Leather Tunic

You Have Acquired - Forester's Padded Pants

You Have Acquired - Worn Leather Boots

You Have Acquired - Cadet's Belt

You Have Acquired - Simple Green Cloak

You Have Acquired - Fine Recurve Bow

You Have Acquired - Basic Quiver

You Have Acquired - Hunting Arrow x17

You Have Acquired - Steel Dagger

You Have Acquired - ??? Ring

You Have Acquired - ??? Charm

Kurt recited the list of prompts to his brother who floated around him aimlessly in his new wisp form. He wasn't sure how far the money the player had on him would go but it was better than what he'd started with. "What do you think?"

"It sounds like some pretty normal stuff. This guy wasn't really pushing through any special dungeons. Unless he had a hidden stash someplace, he was probably playing it fairly safe up to this point. You should get those last two examined by someone just to be sure. They are probably minor magic items but you never know. All of this stuff will be upgrades for you since you're running around with a bunch of open slots."

Kurt opened his inventory and started equipping the armor and weapons. With each item he watched in amazement as, one by one, they appeared on his person. Most of it simply appeared over his clothes but his old belt and shoes were moved into his inventory. When he tried to equip the ring he found it to be greyed out. "So can I not use the ring?"

"Once you get it examined you'll be able to use it. I mean unless it has a requirement you don't meet," his brother explained as he flew in circles around Kurt. "The charm is active as long as you are carrying it. Figuring out what that does will be important since it's always on whether you want it or not."

"At least I'll be harder to hit with the armor now."

"Not exactly," Greg corrected.

"What do you mean?"

"Well do you remember how I said this didn't play like any game you were used to? How what you can actually do in real life matters."

"Yeah, okay." Kurt thought that sounded familiar.

"There are no stats to hit or miss. There is no armor class. Everything in this game is a skill shot. If you want to shoot a bow, you better know what you're doing or learn through practice. Same thing with any of the other weapons. There are no class restrictions because there are no classes. It's all about what you can do."

"So what's the point in wearing armor if it doesn't make me any harder to hit?"

"Well when I said there were no stats it wasn't completely true. Armor soaks up damage before it gets to your health. You have your basic stats which determine things like how hard you can swing that cudgel or how long you can run. They even factor into things like balance and magic use. They just have nothing to do with hitting something. Right now your stats are tens across the board. Everyone starts out that way as a human. Look at your character sheet and you'll see what I mean."

Kurt concentrated on the silhouette icon at the edge of his view. Instantly a translucent character sheet overlapped his view of the world.

Character Sheet

Character Name: ???

HP 100/100   MP 100/100

Level: 1

Power: 10

Agility: 10

Endurance: 10

Mind: 10

Moxie: 10

Luck: 10

Affinities: None

Triumphs: None

"Okay you're going to have to break this down for me. Some of it looks pretty straight forward but some of it not so much. Did I miss something? Why don't I have a character name?"

"Yeah there really isn't a point to looking at your character sheet at level one. Let me start from the top. Once we get to town you'll get to name your character. Since the game uses permadeath it kinda keeps people from sitting on names. You have to play in order to become named. Then when someone dies their name gets thrown back into the pool of available names. It's a little weird but I've always had good luck naming characters because of it."

"Okay that makes sense. Being level one does too but I don't see where my experience is tracked."

"Well that's because there is no experience to track. You only level up through triumphs. Once you do something that is considered meaningful for your level you will advance and get a point or two to put into one of your stats. Sometimes you get an ability too or some other reward. That doesn't happen easily. I've never made it past level three and like ninety percent of people in the game are under level ten. When you dropped that dude you really ruined his day. Level three was probably months of work for him. It can go faster with a guild's help or if you want to take some big risks but there is no fast track to leveling."

"That sounds pretty harsh."

"Well, yeah but it also evens the playing field. With the player base within striking distance of each other most people get to do everything in game. Only the very top end players have a significant advantage. They are kinda like Demi Gods in game with so many points in their stats."

"What about affinities?"

"Those are different traits or perks you might pick up along the way. A lot of them have to do with magic and casting but some are just random things. I once had one called Nature's Friend. I constantly had animals following me around even in the city. It was cool at first but it ended up getting old fast. Affinities are probably the thing the devs mess with most in game. People are constantly posting about new ones they've found and some that were around in the beginning but no one has seen since."

Kurt watched the wisp bounce as his brother's voice explained everything. It was good information but he couldn't help but feel a nagging in his mind. They had just been jumped. His eyes darted from shadow to shadow searching for would be assailants even as he listened to his brother. "Think we should get moving? Is there pvp in the starting town?"

"Yeah Silent Grove isn't too far from here. The town and the nearby quest areas are all safe from other players. Most towns are pvp zones but that one is not. If we had finished out the event and stuck to the road, we would have been safe from players too."

"Are you kidding me? Why didn't we just do that then?" Kurt turned exasperated.

"Easy man. Usually players don't come out this way. The event is dangerous too. You can still die from the rat guards. That and it takes forever. It's quicker to just cut through the woods," Greg stopped and thought it over for a moment. "You're right though. We should get moving. Head east."

Kurt moved away from the old building and back into the woods. A cool breeze brushed against his skin causing him to shiver. He had to tell himself it was still just a game because the sensation felt all too real. Clouds continued to thin allowing moonlight to filter in around them illuminating their path. The added visibility encouraged Kurt to quicken his pace as he moved into an easy jog. He noted as his stamina bar slowly increased its depletion but it was at no where near the rate it had during his earlier flight.

25

Another small hill stood not far ahead of the brothers as the wild undergrowth of the forest faded. Kurt could tell the settlement wasn't far off as the torch light could be seen even before they made their way over the final elevation. It was then something caused him to stop short. "Did you hear that?"

Greg did not answer initially but then quickly agreed, "Yeah just ignore it so we can get to town."

"Is someone there? Someone please help!" A woman's voice called out in the night.

Kurt peered out into the darkness trying to locate the source.

"It's just a quest man but not worth your time," Greg answered before Kurt could ask the question. "I've done it. You won't level or anything."

He ignored Greg's voice as he swatted at the wisp bouncing in front of his face. Hundreds of times before he had played older MMOs with various quests. Sometimes you would find an item that would start a quest line while other times an NPC would be waiting patiently for someone to start a conversation triggering the quest. This felt different somehow. It seemed more real.

Kurt approached as the underbrush cracked beneath his feet. Entering a small clearing he could see a heavily trafficked dirt road that was momentarily quiet. A woman desperately searching for something looked up as he approached. "Please sir, please help me."

"What's wrong?" Kurt called out cautiously walking forward.

The wisp bouncing around his head answered first, "Well you see she has this find a needle in a haystack quest that will reward you with a couple coppers and her digital gratitude. Remember there is no experience in this game so since it won't level you it's just a waste of time."

She said something but Kurt had missed it. Staring at the wisp he tried his best to hide his annoyance, "Dude you wanted me to play. This is me playing. Just relax a minute." Turning back to the woman he tried again as he continued to approach, "I'm sorry ma'am. I didn't hear what you said. What is your name?"

"My name is Mabel, sir. I am in need of help. My grandfather has lost his pocket watch. We were traveling up the road to Silent Grove. When we arrived we couldn't find it. He must have lost it on the way. It's so very important to him. Will you help me find it?"

A translucent prompt filled the center of his screen. This felt familiar to the old games he had played years ago.

Will you accept the quest, "Time to Help?"
YES
NO

Kurt concentrated on the YES option and the prompt faded away leaving Mabel looking at him expectantly. Shaking himself back to attention he answered,"Uh yeah. Of course. Let me see what I can do."

Mabel rose to her feet and threw her arms around him. The embrace took him aback with its realism. He could feel real pressure from the young woman's embrace and her warm breath on his neck. The sudden unexpected sensation caused a visceral reaction. It was all Kurt could do to separate her from him.

"Thank you. Thank you! Please find me at my grandfather's house in Silent Grove when you find it. It's the white cottage with blue shutters. You can't miss it!" With that Mabel quickly ran down the road toward the lights of the village, seemingly unconcerned with searching further herself.

Kurt was left scratching his head as Greg began. "The whole purpose of the quest is to get you to town. If we would have stuck around at the escape event we would have come up this road. She will literally accept any pocket watch you give her. We can grab one from a vendor in town or find one on a random mob. You actually get rewarded less than the purchase price. There is no real reason to do the quest."

"Fine, whatever man." Kurt said, trying to placate his brother. "I just don't want to rush through the whole game ignoring all the story trying to get to the next thing. You can't respawn for a while so I might as well get my feet wet and figure some of this stuff out. We can go to town next and you can show me around."

Greg seemed to calm down a little at that. "No biggie. Let's go. We need to get your character name and get you onto the main quest line since we skipped the first event."

Kurt turned and followed the road into town that Mabel had just taken. He had forgotten just what it was like to play an MMO with his brother. He would need to pump brakes a little more if he was going to have any idea of what was going on. Greg would have them fast tracked to endgame if he left it up to him. If that was the case, he really would have no clue why they were doing anything along the way.

Chapter 3

The road to Silent Grove appeared to be a well traveled one. Hard packed dirt had been smoothed under many boots and wagon wheels over the years leaving a remarkably level surface. Trees and overgrowth had been cut back somewhat regularly leaving enough room for at least two wagons to run abreast. The darkness of surrounding wood encroached but was stopped short by the moonlight from the open sky above. Despite this, however, strange sounds echoed on either side of Kurt. Oftentimes it would be something small like an animal running through the foliage or the distant howl of a wolf. Hooting of owls and the wings of bats also sounded overhead periodically but these were not the sounds that gave Kurt pause. At times stranger noises would abruptly resound in the quiet of night. It was hard to place exactly what they were. Once it was the sound of something heavy falling onto soft earth. Another time a bit later it was the low whimper of a wounded thing. The most alarming came when the walls of Silent Grove were just coming into sight. The noise was shrill and abrupt. It cut through the night and was gone just as quickly as it came. At this both boys went silent while Kurt quickened his pace.

Bright lights illuminated the cleared land that hosted the starting village. Rough cut timbers had been buried at regular intervals making up the backbone of a wall that appeared to be more than equal to the task of thwarting the various denizens of the forest. Perched on either side of the town's open gate stood a fierce looking man in chainmail under the tabard of a golden sunburst. Each sentry held a heavy crossbow easily but at the ready. The wall itself stretched out in either direction before him as far as he could see always at least thirty yards away from the encroaching wild. Regular torches set along it's top told him that the structure was well garrisoned as dark forms marched regular paths well into the distance.

"Okay get a good name ready, bro. We're coming up on that."

Before Kurt could react, a voice called out from just ahead. "Oye who goes there? I don't think I recognize you."

"Huh?" Said Kurt obviously perplexed.

"You there boy. I'm talking to you," shouted the guard in an authoritative but still relaxed manner. "I like to know just who I'm letting into my city. Isn't that right, Rocco?"

"Quite right," the other guard answered absent-mindedly as he continued to survey the tree line.

"So as I said before who goes there, boy?"

"This is where you pick your name so think of something good." The wisp pleaded as he bounced around Kurt's head.

Swatting at his brother like an annoying insect was a bit odd Kurt thought but oddly appropriate. "I got a good one, Greg. Just let me do this." Kurt stepped forward to address the guard. It was a unique way to go about character creation. He really hoped the rest of the process was just as interactive. Drawing up to his full height he shouted back to the guard in the wall embracing the moment. "Well met good soldier. I apologize for the confusion. I am new to these lands. I am Galahad. What be your name?"

"No, no that won't due. I met Galahad already and that's not you. Isn't that right, Rocco?"

"Quite right," the other man answered.

"Alright, out with it. What's your real name?"

"The name's taken Captain RP," Greg needled. "Maybe you should lay it on a little thicker. I think there's a renaissance fair coming up and your game needs some work. Besides if you keep having this conversation and I can get a new character and meet you back here."

"I can always log off for the night," Kurt whispered. Once he was satisfied Greg was done he spoke up again. "I am Percival."

"No, not you," the guard answered back.

"Arthur?" Kurt ventured.

"Definitely not."

"Maybe you should try something not in King Arthur's Court," Greg chuckled. "I would also probably stay away from Lord of the Rings, Dungeons and Dragons and I don't know any other reasonably popular work of fantasy that every nerd in game has heard of or used some variation of at least a hundred times. Just an idea I had."

Kurt knew it wouldn't take much to log out right now and knock his brother out of his chair and onto the floor while he was still plugged into the game. He would be completely justified in doing it too. No one would blame him. Instead he just stared at the wisp floating mere inches from his face. Without blinking, without taking his eyes off of that annoying wisp, he answered again. "Turk."

"Ah now there's a name! I don't believe we've met him," The guard said thoughtfully. "Isn't that right Rocco?"

"Quite right," his partner said, still paying more attention to the tree line than the gate.

A translucent prompt filled Kurt's vision.

Is the name TURK correct?
YES
NO

"What kind of name is that?" Greg asked haughtily.

"It's an anagram. Look it up." Kurt settling into his new name walked forward through the gate as his brother floated behind frantically trying to catch up.

"I know what an anagram is you know."

"Good then I won't have to explain it to you. If you want to go by DragonSlayer32 or MafiaDude that's on you. I want a halfway decent name," Kurt grinned having his fun at his brother's expense.

"Take it easy bro," Greg said defensively. "I was just giving you a hard time. It's a good name."

Kurt couldn't hide the smirk on his face. He wasn't really mad at his brother but sometimes he needed to be kept on his toes. He did have to admit, Greg picked a really realistic game to get into. Just walking into the town proper, Kurt was amazed by the level of detail in the world around him. Numerous buildings lined the main thoroughfare but no two were very similar at all. They were nothing like the cookie cutter buildings from the old MMOs they played growing up. Each building had different spots of wear in seemingly random locations. Peeling paint and rusted metal work gave everything a very lived in quality. Some steps to a building might slope to one side as if from years of use while another set had a railing missing the middle strut causing it to wobble. Even the cobblestones under foot did not feel completely level as he walked toward the center of town. "Alright man. What's next?"

The wisp bobbed up and down in front of his face. "I would say blacksmith but everything you have is better than what you could buy right now. We could start the main quest line. We'll need to repeat it when I reroll but it's the best way to start getting light points and get raid ready."

"What else can we do? I really don't want to start the game doing quests twice."

"Well light points are kinda the big thing. They let you get faction gear and are required to get into higher end dungeons and events. We won't even be able to go into certain zones without light infused gear. Quests are the best way to accomplish that until you get some points under your belt. Once you get some faction gear we can grind more points out through dungeon runs or hunting in special zones for drops."

"Are there any quests we won't have to repeat then?"

"Not really. I want credit for any of the quests that are worth doing. I mean you could go buy a pocket watch at the general store and complete the quest you have. I won't do that one again."

"Is that the only way to complete it? It doesn't really seem in line with the quest."

"No it's just the easiest way," Greg repeated wanting to be done with the quest. "She will literally accept any watch you give her. Some monsters drop watches that are just vendor trash. She'll take those too. All you'll get is a hug and a few coppers for your time."

"Is there anything else to do?"

"You haven't tried to eat in game yet. That's pretty cool the first time you do it."

"Really?" Kurt asked in disbelief.

"Oh yeah it's one of the most realistic things in here. Come on I know a good place"

Kurt shrugged, falling in behind his brother's wisp form. The road into the center of town wasn't overly crowded but there was enough traffic to make the environment feel alive and occupied. While most people had nothing over their heads many had names of players, guilds and levels. These people seemed to shy away if he looked at them for long but it was nice to be able to easily tell the difference between players and NPCs. Soon Greg stopped before a squat building that sprawled across two lots. A freshly painted, wooden sign hung over a set of double doors facing the street depicting a pair of bucks with antlers locked in combat. In block letters it read, "The Twin Stag."

"Yeah man, this is the place," Greg said excitedly. "Come on let's get a table."

Kurt pulled open the door allowing the raucous noises within to flow out into the night. Inside a room packed with players who gamed, drank and sang along with a minstrel near a fireplace made of river rock. Busty maids buzzed from table to table with trays of meats, sweets and drink as players pawed for any bit of softness that came too near. Weaving through the press, Kurt found a quiet corner along the back wall and slid into a chair facing the rest of the room just taking it all in. He wasn't even really paying attention when he barely heard his brother.

"Are you ordering anything man?"

Kurt turned his head with a start as a busty brunette stared at him expectantly. Kurt cleared his throat seeing her for the first time. "Umm I'm sorry. I didn't catch that."

"What can I get ya hun?" the waitress cooed leveling the practiced smirk of the service industry at him. Kurt's eyes darted up noticing he was talking to an NPC.

"What do you recommend?" It was the only thing he could think of without a menu.

"The special is beef and potato mash. It comes with a piece of pie. We also have a number of other selections if you are looking for something in particular," she rattled off in a practiced manner. The waitress nodded down to the folded menu that lay untouched in front of Kurt and looked at him.

"No, the special sounds good."

The waitress wrote his order down before sweeping toward the kitchen. Kurt couldn't do anything but shake his head as he watched her move away. It would take him a while to get used to the idea of talking to

NPCs like real people. The idea that they could just come up and start a conversation without a player triggering it was a bit jarring. If it wasn't for the fact that players had tags over their heads, Kurt could see getting the two confused.

"Oh yeah, smooth man," Greg said, starting in on his brother again.

"Hey, I'm not used to talking to these NPCs yet. I can't believe how realistic they are."

"Yeah, the realism really got ya, bro," Greg mocked.

"Greg..." Kurt began but was quickly cut off by a notification in his bottom right.

You Have Lost - 4 Copper

"Hey I just lost some money!"

Greg was nonplussed as he answered. "Yeah money is handled automatically if you don't actually hand it over. You don't have to physically hand it to vendors if you don't want to. The same goes for quests and looting too. Stuff just kinda moves in and out of your inventory. As realistic as this place is they still have to automate some stuff. The actual handing items back and forth thing is a newer feature. I think devs are trying to move that way with everything but it's not quite there yet."

"Makes sense," Kurt said thinking back to the gear he took from the player who'd attacked them not all that long ago. He looked at his silhouette icon again bringing up his character sheet. He then concentrated on the bag icon pulling up his inventory interface beside it. The two snapped together into a single interface and a prompt appeared filling his vision.

Do you wish to use the combined interface?

YES

NO

Kurt thought for a moment and then concentrated on the YES button. His vision was filled with a new style of character sheet.

Character Sheet / Inventory Combined View

Character Name: Turk

HP 100/100   MP 100/100

Level: 1

Power: 10

Agility: 10

Endurance: 10

Mind: 10

Moxie: 10

Luck: 10

Affinities: None

Triumphs: None

Head -

Neck -

Waist - Cadet's Belt

Body - Hunter's Leather Tunic

Back - Simple Green Cloak

Legs - Forester's Padded Pants

Hands -

Feet - Worn Leather Boots

Ring 1 -

Ring 2 -

Melee (D) - Soldier's Cudgel

Melee (O) -

Pouch 1 -

Pouch 2 -

Range - Fine Recurve Bow

Container - Basic Quiver

Ammo - Hunting Arrows x17

Starter Backpack (5/20)

Wallet

     1 (G)   13 (S) 6 (C)

Steel Dagger

??? Ring

??? Charm

Refugee Belt

Simple Hide Shoes

He sat for a moment taking it all in when Greg brought him back to reality. "Hey what are you looking at?"

"Sorry man I'm just trying to sort out these new menus. It put my character sheet and inventory together. It seems a little more streamlined but it takes up a lot of my view."

"Combined Interface is the way to go for sure. I guess at higher levels though people separate them back out once the information gets a little more cluttered. I've always liked it though. The HUD in the game is really unique. It kinda changes and adapts as you play. It adapts and puts information where you need it. There are a couple options to use like Combined Interface early on but eventually the game kinda learns where to put things. You looking at the stuff you got off that guy?"

Focusing on his new belt a familiar prompt with a pair of buttons appeared.

Unequip.   Examine

Kurt focused on the Examine button and a text box appeared..

Cadet's Belt
Weapon Slots - 2
Pouch Slots - 2
Quality: Normal
Requirements: None

"Okay, so I'm looking at the belt," Kurt explained. "It has weapon and pouch slots. The weapon slots make sense. I have my cudgel in one."

"Yeah you should fill those up in order to have easy access to weapons in combat. Same goes for the pouch slots with small items like potions. It's better to have a potion handy instead of going through your pack looking for one. The pouches can help you save inventory slots in your bag too. Having a whole bag slot used for a small item can be a waste when you start running out of room."

"That makes sense. I can put the ring and dagger on the belt and that will save some room." The interface was becoming second nature now and Kurt was able to quickly swap around his inventory. Like before the dagger magically appeared at his other side and he checked his updated status page. Kurt had a thought and tried to move his charm into a belt pouch. He was met with a prompt.

This Item Exceeds Current Pouch Capacity

It was worth a shot, he thought. He wasn't hurting for bag space yet anyway. Instead he continued examining his gear.

Steel Dagger

Damage: 2-4

Quality: Fine

Requirements: None

Hunter's Leather Tunic

Defense: 1

Quality: Normal

Requirements: None

Simple Green Cloak

Concealment - 5%

Warmth - 15%

Quality: Normal

Requirements: None

Forester's Padded Pants

Defense: 1

Quality: Normal

Requirements: None

Worn Leather Boots

Defense: 1

Quality: Subpar

Requirements: None

Fine Recurve Bow

Damage: 3-5

Quality: Fine

Requirements: None

Basic Quiver

Capacity: 30

Quality: Normal

Requirements: None

Hunting Arrow

Damage: 0-1

Quality: Normal

Requirements: None

"I'm not sure why this guy didn't have better stuff," Kurt wondered after reading the gear off to his brother. He wasn't familiar with the gear in Darklands yet but it looked like pretty normal equipment. "I mean how did he destroy you like that. I'm not seeing anything special here. Where's all the good stuff?"

Greg bobbed in the air for a moment. "Sorry man but I'm not surprised. That guy was out hunting for people just starting out. He probably has his real gear stashed somewhere when he rerolls. Guys that hunt noobs don't need anything special to grief them. Just a couple levels would be more than enough with low end gear."

"Sure but this stuff only does a couple points of damage. You have a hundred hit points and he dropped you with only two arrows. What am I missing? I don't see damage numbers or a combat log. The only reason I know how many hit points you have is because it says I have a hundred at level one."

"The game interface is really simple. There isn't really a combat log like in the old MMOs. The idea is that it's more immersive since there isn't all the extra information. If you look on the wiki though you can see how damage works and some of the other mechanics. Damage is pretty simple though. Your weapon has a damage range. That's the number you start with. If you make a melee attack you take the Power stat into account. If your Power is one higher than your opponent then you add one damage to that damage range. If it is one lower then you subtract one damage from that range. After that you subtract the armor rating from the damage."

"That still doesn't add up. He couldn't have done more than ten points of damage with an arrow. You should have been able to take a couple more hits."

"That formula only gives you the basic damage," Greg continued. "There are other things that come into effect. This game is all about what you can do so there are no hit modifiers but there are still critical hits and damage multipliers. If you shoot someone in the heart it's not the same as shooting them in the leg. If you hit a critical area on a person or monster your damage can be multiplied by a factor of ten or more. So a well placed arrow could kill someone in one shot under the right circumstance. That doesn't even get into magic enhancement or Affinities he may have had. You'll get used to it. Almost everyone playing has had to reroll a few times. The game is brutal."

"One special, hun." Kurt's head jerked up from the interface he'd been pouring over as he willed it away. The barmaid slid a pair of plates in front of him with a practiced deftness slipping away before Kurt could respond. Anything he was going to say was immediately forgotten as the rich, savory scent of roasted beef wafted over him.

"Is this for real?" Kurt asked, inspecting the plate.

"Just taste it bro," Greg said buzzing around the table.

Snatching up his fork, Kurt took a large bite letting out a satisfied grunt.

Greg's wisp form swayed side to side as he let out a chuckle. "You enjoy that. It's the most real thing in game. Early on they had food that gave you a little bit of sensation but it was largely forgettable. After a couple patches they got it down to the point you could forget you really need to eat. Well you forget until real life reminds you. They've been steadily improving the sensations of the world. The weight of items, the feel of stones under your toes and the wind on your face have all come a long way since they opened up from Beta.

"I'm sold man," Kurt mumbled between bites as he loaded up his fork again with potatoes and brown gravy. It only took a few moments and he was onto the piece of cherry pie oozing out onto the edge of his plate. To his surprise a prompt quickly flashed onto his screen.

You Are Well Fed

The prompt faded and an icon of a stick figure holding his stomach appeared in the top right corner of his screen.It was simple but got the point across. He was about to ask Greg what it meant when he saw the notification in his bottom right corner.

Focusing on the icon a countdown ticked away from sixty minutes as long as it held his attention. It was the first time he noticed the feature when it came to a buff. Only now did he recognize a second icon of a pair of crossed swords counting down from ten minutes next to it. "Hey, what's the crossed swords buff that comes with eating?"

"Crossed swords buff?" The wisp was confused. "What are you talking about?"

The room quickly grew silent as a figure stood silhouetted in the tavern entrance. "Oh hell no! Turk you're a deadman.' Grabbing a nearby chair, the hulking man launched the piece of furniture across the room effortlessly.

Chapter 4

Clumsily Kurt fell to the floor while wood splintered behind him. The sounds of moving feet and chairs accompanied the fleeing of players and NPC alike. Glancing at the player's tag he struggled to find his footing while keeping his head down.

Thicc Rick | The Undertakers | Level 8

"Uh time to go, Kurt," Greg said in a panic.

"I thought you said town was a nonPVP zone," Kurt growled.

"It is if you aren't already flagged for PVP."

"What?"

"Yeah you have the debuff from killing a player earlier. Remember?"

"You told me to kill him!" Kurt protested a little louder than he'd intended.

Patrons scurried away as a large table was upended while Thicc Rick stalked forward. "You said you were giving up on Darklands when you left the guild and now you're out here ganking our guys. Bitch move, bro."

"Yup time to go." Kurt darted toward the bar taking the hurdle in a single leap. Glass crashed around him but he ignored it as he half crawled, half ran through the door into the kitchen. Confused cooks and waitstaff dropped trays of plates as Kurt pushed past to the door he'd hoped would be there. Slamming the door, he staggered into the alley. The gloom hung heavy with the noisy tavern now behind him. Walking toward the street,

Kurt craned his neck to find the point of light that was his brother's wisp form.

"Hey over there in the alley, get him!" a new voice shouted.

Wrecklord | The Undertakers | Level 2
Demonborne | The Undertakers | Level 4

Seeing the tags made Kurt turn on heel and dart for the opposite end of the alley. In front of him the door crashed open breaking one of the hinges free of the door jam. A meaty hand reached for him as he careened past at a full run. He evaded his grasp but even the glancing blow was enough to spin him sideways into a stack of crates nearly sprawling onto the ground.

"Go go go!" This wisp shouted as it zipped past in a blur.

"Oh now you show up!" Anything else Kurt wanted to say was cut off abruptly as something metallic clanged off of brick just overhead. The alley gave way to a side street as shouts rang out from behind. "Where do we go?"

"This way," his brother shouted.

Pushing himself, Kurt strained to keep up with the wisp as a heavy pressure slammed into his shoulder nearly taking him off his feet. Sparing a glance to his health bar he inhaled quickly as nearly a third of his bar disappeared. Reaching back his fingers grasped at a hilt protruding upward. With a quick jerk, Kurt nearly lost his footing as the knife failed to come free.

"Aren't there guards or something here?"

"There are a couple not far behind them but if they catch you It's not going to matter," Greg shouted. "Take a right up here. We're going to make for the wall."

"Sounds good," Kurt puffed anxiously. Stealing a glance at his stamina bar, Kurt was dismayed to see it sliding below the halfway point. If it wasn't for the food buff he would have already bottomed out. Seeing the alley coming up Kurt stepped out to his left and rounded hard to his right to widen his angle. The knife thrower must have anticipated the maneuver because as he cleared the entryway pressure lanced across his back and his health bar degraded further. Steps echoed not far behind him but he didn't dare spare the time to look back. Another knife flew wide as he pushed himself into a sprint. The glowing projectile mesmerized Kurt for a moment as it lodged into the wall a few feet ahead.

"Look out!" Greg pleaded but the warning was too late as the glowing blade exploded filling Kurt's path with wood and stone shrapnel from the ruined wall. The concussive force flung Kurt hard into the opposite wall as dozens of pin pricks of pressure dotted his body. He didn't even have to look at his health bar to know more damage had been done. Surprisingly through it all Kurt was able to go into a crouch using the opposite wall for balance. With closed eyes he forced himself ahead into the next street.

Carts and tents lined either side of the street as players and NPCs milled about. Barkers shouted various deals and promises with the hope of luring the next customer to their stall. Smells of freshly baked bread mixed with the tang of newly forged iron all while the din of commotion drowned out the otherwise peaceful nighttime sounds of the forest. "Which way now?" was all Kurt could get out before a wall of golden energy crackled into existence before him. The inevitable impact threw Kurt back onto the cobbles and pushed the wind from his lungs. To his dismay he watched as his stamina all but bottomed out and his health bar began to flash in alarm now that it was below a quarter of its maximum. Kurt tried to sit up and the world swayed back and forth. It was all he could do to keep his head upright as a debuff of three stars spinning in a circle counted down in the corner of his vision.

"I don't know what you thought was going to happen, Turk," Thicc Rick menaced unsheathing a large two handed blade that lacked a cross guard. With a flick of his wrist the blade ignited in a similar crackling energy as the thrown knife and the magical wall had been. Rick's cronies fell in step behind him, fingering their own weapons eagerly. "It's one thing to gank one of your own but then you're dumb enough to run around wearing his gear. You think no one was gonna notice?"

"Hey asshat you owe me a new cart!" Kurt was only vaguely aware of a number of apples rolling on the ground near his head as he stared at the warrior clad in hides stalking forward toward him.

"Pipe down bitch," Rick growled, not looking away from Kurt who watched his debuff flash and fade away bringing his world back into focus. Bewildered he looked on as Thicc Rick's guild mates began to back away. Laying back Kurt found himself staring at a dark pair of legs wrapped in hide strips leading up to a tunic made from some sort of wolf or bear. He wasn't really sure which. She moved directly over him as if he wasn't even there loosing a large axe from across her back with ease. Her athletic frame dwarfed Kurt's own in game character. He could easily see her playing basketball or volleyball in the real world. Looking at her tag he had no idea who she was but he was happy to see her.

Bhae | The Premade | Level 6

"Oh bitch is it? I'll show you who the bitch is," she growled icily through gritted teeth.

Furious, Thicc Rick didn't hesitate swinging his massive blade in a baseball style arch right through the woman. His momentum carried him

47

past both Bhae and Kurt while his strike failed to find any purchase.

"Rule one of world PVP is to make sure your target is flagged, you moron." Before Rick could gain his footing the woman swung the axe in a sweeping backhand scoring diagonally across his back and shoulders sending him sprawling. Instantly her name tag changed from bright green to deep red.

The one named Wrecklord spoke next as he began casting, "Dude she's part of The Premade. I'm not looking to lose my gear over this!" His spell flashed and a bubble surrounded Thicc Rick as he struggled awkwardly to his feet under the weight of his heavy armor. In a fluid motion she grabbed a smaller axe from her belt, squared on the caster and buried it in his center of mass dropping him to his knees. He made a sick gurgling sound as he slumped forward onto his hands

Demonborne muttered, "Nope," before turning at a full run back down the alley.

"Damn it, she's only level six," howled Thicc Rick, igniting his blade again." He launched into a series of wild heavy swings sending up sparks when it came into contact with the wall of energy surrounding them with every miss. Time and again each strike was deftly parried or dodged by the more agile warrior sending Rick into a fit of rage. "Stand still!"

At this point, Kurt scrambled back out of the combat and wanted to help in some way. The dude was a real douche but he was beyond outclassed by the PVPer at this point. As he considered it he noticed his PVP debuff blink and finally fade away. With the debuff gone he was even more at odds with himself. His experience with old school MMOs told him nearly any action he took would put him back into PVP and in imminent danger. Reaching back in disgust he wrenched the throwing knife free and jammed it into his pack. "I have to do something," he muttered to himself.

"No you don't. She's got this. Her guild is one of the top PVP guilds in game if not the top one." Greg's wisp form bobbed up and down in front of Kurt's face as if to try and drive the point home. "You literally have to do nothing."

"Well you're already reported but that's okay because I'm going to vendor that scrub gear you're wearing." Kurt felt the chill come off her words as she launched into her offensive flurry. At first Thicc Rick managed to raise his blade using its energy enhancement to parry the warrior's axe. Despite her lack of magical enhancement, Bhae's skill was more than a match for Rick's level advantage. The duel looked to be moving toward a stalemate when Bhae let out an unearthly howl. The already muscular woman strained against her hide armor as her body shifted and bulked before his eyes. Froth sprayed from her mouth as she rejoined the fight with renewed aggression. Now each strike pushed Thicc Rick back further and further. When her attacks finally broke through, Thicc Rick's face blanched. The sounds of rending metal filled the street and Rick's body flew nearly fifteen feet before skidding to a halt. To Kurt's amazement, Thicc Rick found his feet. For a moment, it looked like he might try to continue the fight but instead he turned into a full sprint pushing through the amassed crowd.

Bhae swept her gaze over Kurt and looked at him with wild eyes. Forgotten was the fact that his PVP debuff had expired. Real apprehension filled him when she regarded him. Instead her attention snapped to Wrecklord. Poor, poor Wrecklord Kurt thought to himself. Still consumed by her anger, Bhae walked over to her prey as he still tried to crawl away with what was surely a mortal wound. In an almost careless swing she removed the player's head from his body in what Kurt almost thought to be an act of mercy. Violently she flipped the player over and wrenched her throwing axe free before putting it back on her belt.

"My kill, my loot," she grated. Her lean, hard face wasn't

unattractive but her cold stare added the menace of a woman who didn't mince words. The warrior finally seemed to deflate a bit as she bent down to claim the corpse's belongings..

"Yeah that seems fair," Kurt stammered unsure if he should laugh or run.

In agreement Greg bobbed up and down. "More than fair really."

With the caster finally dead the energy barrier bisecting the street finally winked out of existence. The crowd gathered amongst the carnage began to disperse. Kurt could now see the extent of the wreckage and a number of players trying to salvage what that could from the stalls destroyed by the barrier. The guards that had been in pursuit finally arrived on scene. Briefly looked around and left without saying a word since the players who had aggroed them were long gone. Once finished collecting her new belongings, Bhae moved to leave pausing for a moment as she considered something. Turning to Kurt she only had one thing for him. "A word of advice...Turk." She appeared to notice his tag for the first time. "Be careful where you go to quest. You can end up ganked and starting over if you run into dickbags like them."

"Thanks. I'll…"

"Yup," she interrupted with a dismissive wave walking into the busy market that even now resumed business as usual.

"Well that was fun," Greg beamed. "What should we do now?"

Kurt, still sitting on the ground in the middle of the street finally found his footing. "Well my health doesn't seem to be regenerating so I guess I'm going to need healed?"

"Yeah that's a thing in Darklands. You can gain health back slowly by camping in an inn or a home instance. Otherwise you need healing items, potions or spells. In town you can also get healing at a Temple of Light for a few silver. We should probably get that done before we do too much exploring. Maybe if we get those items identified one of them will be a healing item."

"How do we do that?"

"You either need a spell or a scroll. Luckily I know a guy." Hearing this Kurt felt he could almost see his brother's self satisfied grin. "Actually it's not far from here. Come on."

Kurt followed as the wisp struck out ahead down the bustling street. While a variety of vendors existed, most of the player run stalls appeared to carry similar trade goods for crafting and food stuffs. It made sense for people trying to profit from their crafting professions or make money from the raw materials those same crafters needed. Kurt had often made money in games by selling the same kinds of crafting components. The NPC vendors on the other hand dealt in border line useless equipment like most other MMOs he'd played. The stuff was typically a step better than his starting gear but paled in comparison to even the most basic of dropped gear from monsters. To be honest he had never known anyone to seriously use the stuff when leveling a character. I mean there was the one time his brother had used a katana from a junk vendor to duel people as a gag. He'd won some fights but by and large it was just to stunt on people. They had always called the NPCs junk vendors because their sole purpose was to off load useless drops for what pocket change they could.

After a few minutes of meandering, the wisp stopped in front of a simple trading post. A wooden sign hung next to the door reading, "Slay-a-Lot a WGD Company." Greg stopped abruptly in front of his brother. "This is the place. It's a guild run store." Entering the shop was a bit underwhelming as Kurt noticed many of the same goods for sale in the various stalls on the walk here. A buxom NPC in a very anime inspired uniform stood behind the counter at attention as he entered. In a practiced manner she turned her attention to her only customer. "Welcome to Slay-a-

Lot! How may I help you today, sir?"

"That's just the guild leader's wai fu. Let her know we're here to see Therin."

"Yeah um I'm here to see Therin," Kurt mumbled, still trying to get used to the idea of carrying on a conversation with an NPC.

The clerk giggled, "Right this way, sir!" Walking to the end of the counter she opened a door leading into a back room and gestured for the players to proceed. Kurt felt he had to pass uncomfortably close to her to pass through the door but no one really seemed to notice. The room within was slightly larger than the shop's main showroom. In the corner a gnome repeatedly slashed at an armored training dummy with a saber while holding some sort of curved knife in his off hand.

Tallorder | WGD | Level 12

In the center of the room, two dwarves stood over a book. One dressed in casters robes studied the book through an ornate looking monocle while noting something on a piece of parchment next to him. "Yeah it's a fake," he said, putting the eyeglass on the table.

Therin | WGD | Level 10

The second dwarf in full plate armor gestured wildly with a stone mace as he spoke. "Oh man you gotta be kidding me, how much did he pay for that?"

Zeklor | WGD | Level 12

The conversation cut off abruptly as a slightly annoyed Therin noticed Kurt for the first time. "Can I help you?"

Greg realized something for what seemed to be the first time, "Tell him Wheeler sent you."

Kurt's head snapped around at his brother. "Wheeler? Seriously that's the name you chose?"

"There's nothing wrong with it," Greg argued.

"Again, who are you? Why are you here," grumbled the dwarf while the other two stopped what they were doing to turn their attention to Kurt.

"My name is Turk and my brother...Wheeler sent me." He shot a cockeyed glance at the wisp that only hovered as if oblivious to the whole thing.

"Great. Why are you here?" Therein asked, still somewhat annoyed.

"Oh sorry. He said you could identify some things for me," Kurt explained.

"Sure. You got money, Turk?" Pushing the book aside, Therin gestured at a chair next to the table.

Accepting the seat Kurt began to dig in his backpack producing the unidentified charm. After a moment he realized he had put the ring in his belt pouch and removed that as well setting both on the table.

Thoughtfully Therin examined the two items before scratching his chin and saying, "Fifty silver..."

"Fifty silver?" Kurt blurted aghast.

"Fifty silver, each." Therein repeated.

"Man that's almost all my cash. Are you kidding me?"

"Therin looked to the other two in the room before continuing. "Look you must be new to the whole magic item thing. It takes time and money to obtain the spell and get the proper appraisal skills to properly identify something. These low level items will do nothing to help me improve my skill so that's the going rate."

"He's not lying," Greg chimed in.

Begrudgingly Kurt fished his only gold piece out of his coin purse and placed it on the table. "Let's roll the dice, I guess."

"Awesome." Therin laid a hand on the ring first, murmuring words of power, while studying the piece carefully. "It looks like a Silver Ring of Unencumbered Movement." Immediately a prompt filled Kurt's vision.

Therin has identified your ring as a Silver Ring of Unencumbered Movement

Silver Ring of Unencumbered Movement

Effect: This ring allows the wearer to pass through rough terrain with ease and without increased stamina usage. Duration of slowing effects are also reduced by half.

Quality: Uncommon Magical

Requirements: None

Will you accept this identification?

YES

NO

"What's with the prompt?"

Therin looked confused for a moment before realizing what Kurt meant. "You must really be new to magic items." Therein said genuinely surprised. "When someone IDs something for you, the result can be rejected in case you think someone can give you a better result. On high level items it could mean different stat points or effects. Once you accept an identification the results are locked on the item and the item is usable. This is a low level item so I can tell you you're not going to find a better result. Do what you want though. I'm keeping the money either way."

Kurt selected "YES" and the ring shimmered for a moment before the name locked in on the item. Amazed by the process Kurt looked at the ring for a moment before equipping it. Therin had already moved onto the charm repeating the process. And soon a second prompt filled Kurt's screen.

Therin has identified your charm as a Dwarven Dowsing Rod

Dwarven Dowsing Rod

Effect: Carrying this item in your inventory gives you something of a sixth sense when it comes to finding ore veins.

Quality: Extraordinary Magical

Requirements: Novice Miner

Will you accept this identification?

YES

NO

"Now that is interesting," Therin mused to himself as much as he spoke to Kurt. "I haven't seen one of those for mining before. The Elven Herb Finder is much more common but I figured there was one for mining too. This one is a little higher level than I first thought. You can do what you want about the identification but I think it looks like a good one."

Noting the dwarf's interest Kurt did not hesitate in selecting "YES."

Their business concluded Therin picked up the gold piece and quickly stashed it away in a pouch. He regarded Kurt thoughtfully. "We do run a business here. I'm assuming that's Wheeler floating around you, listening in on our conversation, so he can vouch for what I'm saying. We buy and sell trade goods here so if you need a place keep us in mind. We can also sell more… interesting items on consignment if you have a need as well."

Seeing where the conversation was going Kurt only gave a wry grin. "I think I'll hang onto the charm for now."

"Ah you can't fault a guy for trying. Still keep us in mind. Here's a bit something extra in good faith." With a quick waggle of his fingers and a word of power, yellow energy washed over Kurt before he could object and his health bar refilled before his eyes. "It'll save you the tithe at the temple. Like I said keep us in mind."

With nothing more to say, Therin went back to what he was doing pouring over the book. Awkwardly Kurt looked to the other two guild members who only stared back at him. "Right. Um nice meeting you guys." Backing toward the door Kurt almost ran into the clerk who appeared to be in the same position he'd left her in the entryway. Quickly he turned and let himself out of the store shaking his head the whole way.

"I thought you said there were no skills in Darklands. I thought it was based off of what you could actually do. Care to elaborate Greg or is it Wheeler? What the hell is up with that name anyway?"

"Dude easy. It doesn't bother me so it shouldn't bug you. I never said there were no skills in game. I said there are no combat skills. There isn't a Shield Bash ability or a Backstab. I mean nothing would get enchanted if it relied on people actually knowing how to use magic in real life," Greg protested with his older brother on the offensive.

"Okay Greg so what do I need to know?"

"The game has skills. Think of them as knowledge skills. It's how you know things like History and Lore. You can up those skills by reading books in game or studying under an expert on a subject. A couple like Cooking can be found just by using what skill you already have," Greg continued seeing his brother was becoming mollified. "Some are useful and some just add backstory. The different trades also use knowledge skills. Those are a bit more useful for making money or improving your gear. Crafting really isn't a dead end but it can be a money sink."

"So how does that even work?"

"It depends on the skill. If you're smithing places will light up to hit with your hammer. The areas get larger or smaller spending on the skill level of the smith and the difficulty of the project. It acts like a guide. It's a little more complicated than a mini game but not quite actually forging something."

"What about regular knowledge skills?"

"Those are a little different. You might remember reading something naturally or in the case of identifying an item you might just kinda know. You could be reminded of something else that is similar. They can be kinda eerie really. I'm not sure how they do it but when you're in game there are things you just kinda know. Like the game puts the information into your head."

"I'm not sure how I feel about that," Kurt grimaced. The thought of people rummaging around in his brain was a bit unnerving. Unfortunately it was already past that point when he decided to plug his brain directly into a video game. Compared to the games he'd grown up with everything about this game was a bit unnerving when you really thought about it. When sitting at a computer or with a controller in your hand you had a certain amount of disconnect from the world you were in no matter how immersive the game. This, however, took things to an entirely different level. While pain and harm were sheltered from the player, all other sensations were uncanny in their realism. It made sense why his brother was so drawn to it from day one.

"Well since you're waiting for me to do quests for reputation with Silent Grove or The Order of Light, we could try to get you a knowledge skill so you can see what that's all about."

"You want to float around and watch me read a book?"

"No, not really," Greg said, amending his thought. "I was thinking about trying that mining charm out unless you want to sell it. We can at least go out into the world a little bit then. I still have a while to go on my reroll."

"Yeah, we can do that." Truly Kurt didn't know how much he could get for the charm but gathering skills in other games he'd played gave him a decent income while exploring and completing other objectives. Sometimes rare crafting components could really be worth the time to hunt up if the crafting part of the game wasn't a dead end. The way Greg was talking it was at least worth looking into.

Chapter 5

The two doubled back the way they had been walking and made their way back through the market stalls. At first the layout of Silent Grove confused Kurt but now that he had crisscrossed the main thoroughfare which led into the market district. In the distance he could see the main gate and they veered off onto a side street which brought them into a more industrial looking section of the town. Carpenters and leather workers worked in front of their workshops paying little heed to the passersby. Trade and business went on here as well but this appeared to be more of the sort that happened between merchants and suppliers rather than the general public. These streets were crowded with wagons and crates of raw materials rather than people. Workers carried specialized equipment and finished products to and from various carts stepping deftly around obstacles and each other. The press of congestion was no less than the market district but has its own feel.

A large stone building billowed smoke down the street and Kurt knew it was his destination as soon as it came into view. Pangs of metal ringing on metal resounded from two squat buildings that flanked the main domed structure. Pulling open the reinforced door caused a wave of heat to wash over Kurt forcing his eyes to tear up. Rubbing his eyes he walked in as a voice off to his right caught his attention.

"May I help you?" asked a voice devoid of emotion.

"Yeah I'm looking for," the words caught in his throat as he stared dumbfounded at the fair complexion of a slender elf holding a ledger. The man wore the clothes he would expect in the mining trade but this man looked more like a clerk than what he'd expected. "I'm looking for the Mining Trainer."

"My name is Master Smith Alen. How may I help you?" Kurt hesitated and the elf picked up on it. "Let me guess you were expecting a grizzled dwarf with a drinking problem? Maybe a bare chested human with skin scarred from a lifetime of working in the forge? I'll have you know that many of the most sought after blades in history started out in the forge of an elven smith."

"Hey, okay, I just need someone to teach me how to mine. I meant no offense."

"Indeed," the elf answered, looking more put out by the second.

Greg floated next to him giggling. The fact that only he could hear his brother made this all the more irritating. "I was told I needed to seek you out to gain the mining skill."

No less annoyed the elf considered for a moment then sighed heavily. "Fine. If you haven't noticed this is a busy place and I'm a busy man. If I'm going to take you on as an apprentice miner, I'm going to need you to prove I'm not wasting my time. Head out of the Crafter's Gate and into the surrounding hills. Bring back ten good sized chunks of coal and ten pieces of copper ore. Do that and I'll take you on as an apprentice and reward you for your time." A translucent prompt filled the center of his screen.

Will you accept the quest, "Not Wasting the Man's Time?"
YES
NO

It wasn't the worst job interview Kurt had ever had. He concentrated on the "YES." An icon of a scroll on the right of his screen

60

flashes when he did so. He hadn't really looked at it before but he was pretty sure he knew what it meant. He concentrated on it anyway to take a look.

Accepted Quests

+ **Time to Help**
- **Not Wasting the Man's Time**

> "Fine. If you haven't noticed this is a busy place and I'm a busy man. If I'm going to take you on as an apprentice miner I'm going to need you to prove I'm not wasting my time. Head out of the Crafter's Gate and into the surrounding hills. Bring back ten good sized chunks of coal and ten pieces of copper ore. Do that and I'll take you on as an apprentice and reward you for your time."

Satisfied that the quest tracking worked as he expected, he closed the window with a thought. Kurt turned to depart when something else occurred to him. "I'm going to need a mining pick for this job, correct?"

Alen stared at him blankly for a moment. "Yes. If you have a need, speak with the provisioner next door."

Greg chuckled again and Kurt made his way to the adjoined building where a human woman poured over a ledger that took up most of the counter. Relieved he decided not to make the same mistake. "Hello you must be the provisioner?"

With a smile she greeted him. "Yes, my name is Floria. How may I help you?"

"Well Floria I'm in need of a mining pick. Whatever the entry level model is will do. I don't need anything fancy." He shot his brother a self satisfied glance after he had so much entertainment at his expense already.

She turned and looked under the table for a moment before

producing a large pick with a heavy thump. Looking up expectantly she recited, "The basic mining pick is fifteen silver."

Kurt's breath caught. A quick count of his coin pouch confirmed it. "Umm I'm a little light." The wisp next to him erupted into raucous laughter that only he could hear. He could feel the heat rising up his neck to his ears but he pushed it down. Thinking quickly he produced the cudgel and laid it on the counter. "How much for a slightly used cudgel?"

"She looked at it a moment before responding, "I can take that for three silver."

"Deal." Kurt laid the rest of the needed silver on the counter and scooped up the Basic Mining Pick. He examined it.

Basic Mining Pick

Effect: Using this pick allows the miner to excavate the most basic materials.

Quality: Common

Requirements: None

"Dude that had to bottom you out on cash," Greg chimed in alarm.

Kurt ignored him moving his dagger to his dominant hand equipment slot. He tried to equip the pick to the other belt slot to no avail. He pulled up his character sheet to see where he stood.

Character Sheet / Inventory Combined View

Character Name: Turk

      HP 100/100   MP 100/100

Level: 1

Power: 10

Agility: 10

Endurance: 10

Mind: 10

Moxie: 10

Luck: 10

Affinities: None

Triumphs: None

Head -

Neck

Waist - Cadet's Belt

Body - Hunter's Leather Tunic

Back - Simple Green Cloak

Legs - Forester's Padded Pants

Hands -

Feet - Worn Leather Boots

Ring 1 - Silver Ring of Unencumbered Movement

Ring 2 -

Melee (D) - Steel Dagger

Melee (O) -

Pouch 1 -

Pouch 2 -

Range - Fine Recurve Bow

Container - Basic Quiver

Ammo - Hunting Arrows x17

Starter Backpack (5/20)

Wallet

    0 (G)   1 (S)   6 (C)

Basic Mining Pick

Dwarven Dowsing Rod

Refugee Belt

Simple Hide Shoes

Shadow Tainted Throwing Knife

    The pick must be too big for his belt was all he could reason. Since it wasn't a weapon he supposed it wasn't too big of a deal to have to take it out of his pack to use it. Removing the belt and shoes from his inventory he asked the provisioner, "How much can you give me for these?"

    She wrinkled her nose before answering, "Four copper?"

    "Deal!" It wasn't much but they were just taking up space. After making the exchange Kurt waved goodbye as he exited into the street. Stepping back outside a cool breeze picked up as the last of the clouds moved on illuminating the world in a bright moonlight. It wasn't like being out in the day but it was the most detail he had seen in the surrounding town since entering the game. Holding his head high, Kurt took a deep breath and surveyed his surroundings. "Okay, which way to the Crafter's Gate?" Kurt was certain that Greg was giving him some sort of look. They stood there in silence for a moment before Kurt spoke again. "I'm not sure your facial expressions are coming through on your new look."

    "It's back this way." Abruptly the wisp took off down the street deeper into the Crafter's Quarter. Chuckling Kurt fell in behind his brother. "What?"

    "Oh I was just thinking since you don't want me progressing

without you, we've turned you into a living breathing tutorial."

"Ha.ha," the wisp mocked sarcastically.

"Hey listen," Kurt exclaimed in a high pitched voice. He paused for a moment letting a grin stretch across his face. "I appreciate everything you're doing out here but you sure you don't want to call it? I know watching someone else..."

"No, it's fine," Greg barked a little too quickly. "The gate's this way."

The Crafter's Gate was less impressive than the town's main gate but was still large enough for suppliers to bring wagons in and out of the city. A guard on the wall faced outward but paid the two little mind as they passed out into the night. Within a moment of exiting the gate the sounds of the city faded and the world came alive with the rustle of leaves and the chitters of various unseen woodland creatures. While not as dense on this side of the town, the trees still cast shadows in the moonlight adding a sense of foreboding. In the distance the terrain visibly sloped upward in the direction Greg led them.

"So what do these ore veins look like?" Kurt asked, feeling a little guilty for needling his brother. "Are they just rocks sticking out of the ground or something?"

"Well if we are lucky enough to find a surface vein, yeah. Surface veins are kind like rare spawns and they get picked over quickly once they turn up. We'll have to go underground a bit to find veins that respawn more often. Don't worry, I know a place."

"So how often can you farm them?"

"It all depends on the vein. Some have daily resets. A lot are weekly but the really good ones are longer. Where veins spawn is randomized too so no one really knows exactly how they work. It's a lot of guessing but that's part of what makes it profitable."

Eventually after a bit of walking a Kurt noticed a notification scroll in the bottom right of his view.

Slipwater Foothills (PVE Zone)

"So this isn't a PVP area?" Kurt asked, a bit surprised.

"Nope. A lot of areas close to town aren't unless you get flagged somehow. It's usually a good thing to keep an eye on when you go into a new zone though. Sometimes you'll be out running a quest and cross into a new zone without realizing it and then all of a sudden you are flagged for PVP. The game really doesn't beat you over the head with it so you really need to stay on your toes."

"Otherwise you'll run into a PVP guild?"

"Well yes and no. The Undertakers look like they get off on ganking lowbies. Guys like that will be the biggest danger to you out in those zones but if you can get a few levels they will be less likely to come looking for you. They don't want to lose any gear they don't have stashed to permadeath."

"What's the no part then?"

'Well guilds, like The Premade, largely do instanced PVP. They play games like Capture the Flag and Arena. In those instances death isn't permanent. You can get some nice gear. Some of it has a good amount of dark resistance too for raiding and high end dungeons. We'll get a little bit of that once we start building reputation and working down the main storylines."

"So you want dark resist for PVP then?"

"Nah you want Light Resist gear for PVP or at least a mix. Most people have big damage spells from leveling and light enhanced weapons. Those are needed to even damage monsters as you progress. Since people that run PVE have a bunch of Light based attacks many PVP only people don't even bother going that route. Instead they just get the Light Resist gear from PVP and farm out big damage non aligned weapons favoring their increased stats."

"Does anyone run Dark Magic?"

"No. Well there is some gear out there that drops like that throwing knife you caught in that back. That's a common one. It gets used because it bypasses Light Resist but it can't take any enhancement from Light Magic. I think the weapons were put in game for PVP but without the use of light enhancement most of them aren't even usable.

Kurt rummaged through his bag and pulled out the throwing knife turning it over in his hand as they walked. It didn't look overly special despite the dark appearance. "How did you know what it was?" He asked while examining it.

Shadow Tainted Throwing Knife
Damage: 1-3
Quality: Fine
Requirements: None

"Like I said they are fairly common especially in story quests. Usually Rattlings like the ones from the intro event will use them. They get some use in PVP since they are not affected by light resist but they also can't be charged up with light magic so it has its drawbacks. They can be nice for spell interrupts or dropping someone trying to run away."

Kurt equipped the throwing knife in his open belt slot. Better to have it at the ready in case he wanted it. "But could I get dark magic and charge this with it?"

"Nope. Dark magic is only for the bad guys. We get light magic along with the good guys in game. Didn't you watch the trailer or read any of the background stuff I sent you"

"Yeah I read it," Kurt protested unconvincingly. "Well I skimmed it."

"Uh huh." The two walked in silence for a time ascending and descending small rolling hills. Occasionally a player would run in one direction or another occupied by one task or another. The night had turned almost peaceful with the worry of PVP well behind them. Eventually they approached a larger series of hills more thickly dotted with trees and overgrowth. As Kurt climbed a particularly steep hill the terrain became more stony than earthen. "It's just up ahead bro," Greg said breaking the silence.

Kurt nodded while trying to catch his breath. Gradually the slope leveled and a plateau became visible ahead. Greg zipped ahead excitedly as Kurt scrambled after him. Where the hill continued upward a doorway had been cut into the rock supported by rough hewn timbers. Iron cart tracks exited the cave but sat rusted from long years of disuse. "Anyone else know about this Greg?"

"I'm sure some do. It's not very well hidden and people are all over these hills farming and completing some of the zone quests. I doubt the mobs are farmed out of here though."

"Right." Sliding his dagger from his belt Kurt edged forward through the entrance. The wisp bounced up and down a few feet ahead illuminating something hanging from the wall.

"Twist the bottom until it clicks," Greg explained.

Greg's wisp form only gave off a faint light so it was hard to see what he was talking about at first. As his eyes slowly adjusted to the gloom, he could make out a black steel knob at the bottom of a hanging lantern. Following his brother's instructions, Kurt found the lantern's ignition and turned it. After a couple clicks a wick inside caught and the tunnel was bathed in a dim orange glow. Kurt lifted the lantern off the hook with his off hand and brought the light into the center of the walkway. He was surprised by its heft as he tested the weight. Changing his grip Kurt found a comfortable way to carry the lantern and peered further into the cave. The tunnel itself stretched down and out of sight. While the ceiling hung low enough to give a mild sense of claustrophobia the width gave enough room that three people could comfortably walk abreast. Greg moved ahead bouncing from wall to wall looking for something. Kurt followed quietly.

"Check this out over here." Kurt looked at the spot in the wall next to his brother. "See the tool marks around this divit? Someone mined something out here. I'm not really sure what but we're going to have to go deeper to find anything if someone was here recently." Greg continued on checking the walls as the two wandered forward. Periodically he would stop but the results were always the same. They continued like this for the better part of an hour. Eventually the brothers came to a fork in the shaft and to the left sat an abandoned cart that had been moved just off the track enough to be immoble.

"Anyone ever found anything in one of these?" Kurt wondered aloud sifting through the top of the cart's contents with the blade of his dagger.

"Not sure. Might be worth a look," Greg said.

Setting down the lantern Kurt stowed his dagger back into its place on his belt. He lifted the first heavy rock from the cart placing it off to the side. Greg buzzed around the cart's interior checking the rocks while Kurt removed the next large one. "Looks like there might be some in here, bro. Bring the lantern in here. I think some of this in the bottom is coal."

Moving the light into the cart Kurt could see what his brother was talking about as some of the rocks in the bottom appeared to be darker than

69

the others. Grasping a piece of the dark rock he was met with a notification.

You Have Acquired - Lump of Coal

The baseball size rock disappeared from his grasp and he knew already that it had moved into his inventory. Digging through the bottom of the cart he found four more such pieces adding them to his inventory. There were other pieces there but to Kurt's dismay they were too small to register as pieces for the quest. "Well we're halfway home on coal. Think these bigger rocks have anything in them since they were in the cart?"

"Get your pick out and check."

Kurt set the lantern aside so as not to accidentally knock it over and pulled his pick from inside the bag. It would have made more sense for it to hang on the outside of the pack but he chalked it up to video game logic. The weight of the pick was solid in his hands like a heavy axe. Bringing it down on the basketball sized rock was met with a loud clang as tremors resonated up the handle and into his hands. His stamina dropped noticeably but not enough to stop him outright. Twice more he struck the rock before a large size piece came off. Three more strikes and the rock gave cracking in half. Moving in closely to examine the rock, Kurt found it to be just that, a piece of rock.

Kurt lurched forward as something heavy fell down on him from above. Something cool and clammy scurried off of him as he was sent sprawling. The mining pick flew from his hand knocking the lantern on its side throwing odd shadows across the corridor. Opening his mouth to call out Kurt was met with a slimy bitter taste as muscle tissue wrapped around his head dragging him across the ground. Vaguely he heard his brother somewhere as his vision went dark. "Shit, shit, shit!"

Despite his vision being compromised, Kurt could still see his

70

health bar was slowly chipping away. Reaching over his head he found what had him and gripped it with his left hand. Searching with his right, he found his dagger at his belt and cut furiously just over where he had the creature gripped. On the first slice he was jerked across the stone floor violently. After a second cut he stopped moving instantly and what had his face went slack. Awkwardly Kurt worked at unwrapping his head while Greg continued to shout. "It's trying to eat you bro. Get up, get up!"

Finally pulling his head free, Kurt oriented himself and found his assailant flopping its head from side to side violently. A severed length of pink tongue hung limping from the grey lizard's mouth. Concentrating on the creature added a tag above it.

Rock Gecko | Level 1

With the initial shock wearing off, Kurt shuddered involuntarily. In the moment the rattling guard had been a monster but everything had happened so quickly he hadn't had time to process it really. Now staring at a thirty pound lizard, he was hesitating. It wasn't long and the respite was over. With its tongue immobilized, the gecko was forced to charge, jaws wide. It was all Kurt could do to throw himself to the side to avoid the attack. From instinct more than intention he lashed out with his foot at the passing creature staggering it. The gecko's next lunge was not so easily dodged as Kurt was forced back onto his back with the full weight of the monster on his chest. Dislocating its jaw the lizard slipped its mouth over Kurt's face. Pressure increased on his head and Kurt started stabbing wildly at any part of the monster he could find.

"Kurt you got him. Kurt. Kurt snap out of it!"

He wasn't sure how long he'd been screaming but now he was aware. The thing had stopped moving and he saw the familiar notification in his bottom right.

"I need a second man. Can you just fly around and make sure nothing is going to jump out and kill me?" Kurt breathed heavily.

"Sure no problem," his brother answered sincerely.

Kurt just laid back and closed his eyes. He concentrated on his health bar. Doing so brought the numbers into view.

Health: 83/100

He hadn't brought up the specifics before but it made sense. Things all seemed to work the same. Concentrating on something brought up more detail. It was still a game. He'd felt no pain but the panic was real in the moment. Greg had been playing this for a while now. He was handling it. There was something to be said for that.

"Uh you okay. Bro?"

Kurt opened his eyes and sat up. "Yeah. This shit is just really realistic."

"Yeah well it's going to get a lot more real. We got another one coming."

Kurt's heart started pumping and he staggered to his feet. Looking down past the wisp, Kurt watched as another gecko started on the floor and moved up onto the wall as it progressed toward him. Putting away the dagger an idea came to him. "Light him up, Greg."

The wisp buzzed close to the lizard while it continued up onto the ceiling. Drawing his bow, Kurt pulled an arrow from his quiver and let out a breath. He had used a bow in real life. It wasn't completely foreign to him.

72

He could do this. Pulling the string taut he peered down the arrow shaft concentrating on the gecko's head. Loosing his shot Kurt watched as the arrow shattered against the rock nearly a foot to the left of his target.

Wasting no time the gecko launched into its tongue attack. Muscles shaking Kurt found he was relieved to see it coming. Stepping to the side, he watched it fly past harmlessly as he pulled a second arrow. Going for the head was a mistake. He knew that now as he aimed for the creature's center of mass. Letting his next one go he was relieved to see it strike home dropping the creature from the ceiling. This time it was his turn to charge. Moving quickly Kurt stood over the prone creature letting a third arrow go.

You Have Slain - Rock Gecko | Level 1
You Have Acquired - Torn Gecko Hide

"You handled that one better," Greg said inspecting the body.

"Thanks," Kurt said, feeling an odd sense of pride.

Kurt stood with another arrow ready as Greg patrolled the surrounding area. Fearing to take his eyes too far away from the dark tunnels, Kurt moved to the lantern and righted it off to the side giving himself room to work. It looked beat up and some oil had spilled out but other than that it seemed to be in remarkably good shape. Minutes passed and the cave remained silent. Satisfied that they might finally be alone, he stowed his weapons. Cautiously Kurt recovered the pickaxe and moved back toward the cart. There was another large basketball sized rock he'd removed from the cart. Centering it up he went to work. After a handful of strikes this one split as well. This time however both halves produced something different. An off colored strip snaked through each piece.

"Alright now wait a second. You can still ruin the ore. Concentrate on the vein. You are still considered unskilled but you should still get a faint aura from it. Do you see it?"

Kurt concentrated for a second but then he saw what his brother was talking about. A ruddy red light seemed to shift and fade around the vein. It never stayed for long but he could see it. He shook his head in ascent.

"Cool. It will get easier to see the more you level this skill. Now carefully strike around that aura and have the rock around it fall away. This will come easier too as you level the skill. It's like the exact opposite of how they handle combat in this game. You are literally learning the trade now."

Kurt took his time with the first half of rock striking only when he saw the aura. It took time with the big pickaxe. In time he was left with only a chunk of pebbled ore. Picking it up he found the expected notification.

You Have Acquired - Chunk of Copper Ore

A new icon appeared in the periphery of his vision and he concentrated on it.

Skills

- **Mining**

    Novice Miner - Level 0 (25/500)

It was a start. He dismissed the screen and turned to the second half of rock. Nothing had changed from the first to the second but knowing failure was an option, Kurt took his time. The same red aura flickered in and out around the ore in different spots highlighting where he could safely strike. Sharp pings of metal on stone echoed throughout making him wince with each swing but after a couple minutes it was done.

74

"Okay that's two down. Hey, you see that?" Looking up from the spot he'd been working, Kurt noticed several small motes of red light drifting lazily down one of the unexplored paths. They were slightly smaller than Greg's wisp form but still visible outside of the lantern light.

"See what?"

"Those   red   lights," Kurt   said   curiously. "I don't see anything."

"Come on." Still holding the pickaxe in one hand, Kurt retrieved the lantern and fiddled with the knob on the bottom. After a moment he figured out how to dim the light source enough so he could see the dots of light amongst the light pollution. Curiosity getting the best of him Kurt moved out past his brother venturing deeper in.

"Hey where are you going?"

"I want to see where those lights are coming from."

"What lights?" Greg shouted exasperated.

Kurt ignored him, having a guess as to what he was seeing but didn't want to get too far ahead of himself. The tunnel meandered and turned back onto itself as they descended further underground. Small puddles pooled in low spots of the floor as the walls became noticeably more damp. In time the number of motes increased before bringing Kurt to an otherwise nondescript rock wall. Holding the light up to the wall nothing was readily visible but when he brought the light down he could see the red specks of light moving in and out of the surface. Putting the lantern aside he took a moment to make sure there were no monsters in the immediate area.

"So what's all this about?" Greg asked, somewhat annoyed. "I don't see any lights."

"Just let me know if you see anything coming." Kurt removed his pickaxe from his pack and began working on the otherwise smooth wall. Greg flew back and forth down the cavern. After a minute of this Kurt noticed his stamina dipping lower than he'd like and stopped. He raised the lantern up to the hole he'd just made. Flying over to see what was happening Greg bobbed up and down excitedly.

"How did you know to dig there?

"I think the light I was seeing was from the Dwarven Dowsing Rod. It led me to this wall."

Greg pressed in closer on the hole before zipping out and around Kurt. "Yeah man it looks like coal. You're probably right about the charm. That's badass man. Might be a decent vein too."

Satisfied that his stamina had refilled enough Kurt set to widening the hole. Now that he had a starting point progress came more quickly. Soon he could see the flickering red aura outlining what appeared to be a large deposit of coal. After making noticeable progress again, Kurt set down his pick and listened for any noise from the corridor. Letting his stamina recharge again, he began to clear away loose debris when a prompt surprised him.

You Have Acquired - Block of Usable Stone

"Hey I found some usable stone. Is that for crafting too?"

"Yeah you can get some of that with mining too," Greg explained as he flew over the debris. "You might want to check the rest of this on the ground just in case."

Sifting through the remnants of what lay on the ground to his surprise there was another piece he would have otherwise missed. His mining proficiency had not pointed these out as useful but as soon as he touched it he looted it.

You Have Acquired - Block of Usable Stone

Clearing away the rest of the hole his stamina had recharged enough to continue. Using his proficiency aura to guide him he began extracting his first piece of coal. It only took one bad miss hit though to shatter the chunk he'd been working on. It was his first real mistake doing this and he winced watching the valuable resource crumble.

"Don't sweat it man it happens. Just wait until you do it with something really valuable like a gem or mithril. That will be really painful."

Brushing more debris away he went back to work. Carefully this time he progressed trying to keep himself from getting overly eager. Periodically he had to work on the stone itself to allow more room to work. The process was becoming time consuming especially with the frequent breaks to regain stamina. Kurt shattered at least one more piece but he tried to not let it bother him. When he was done he had a small pile of resources sitting before him.

You Have Acquired - Block of Usable Stone
You Have Acquired - Lump of Coal x4

Kurt stood facing the dark and waited. He'd hoped for a repeat performance from his charm but it wasn't looking promising. "Looks like you're going to lead the way again." The wisp took off into the dark once again. They hadn't gone far before they found another harvestable piece of copper. Kurt was able to gather it with relative ease before they moved on. It was like this for the better part of an hour finding small single pieces of ore that had otherwise been missed.

"Getting close on that quest?"

"I still need four more pieces of copper," Kurt said as he did a quick check of his inventory.

Continuing on down the corridor, the two descended further as the grade decreased gradually. Greg continually darted from side to side searching for veins while Kurt followed with the lantern searching for any hints from his mining charm. As they progressed the hard stone floor gave way to a wet mix of stone and silt creating a slick soup that threatened to send Kurt sliding. He was ready to suggest turning back when his foot caught empty air abruptly. Everything slowed down as his plant foot slipped and the lantern flew backward from his hand. Slamming hard on the lip of the precipice, he felt the wet ground slide out from under him while his brother hovered over the gap high above him.

"Greeeeg!" Kurt howled as he fell down into the dark.

"Huh?" Greg said in surprise.

There wasn't pain per say but Kurt definitely felt the sensation of the air being pushed from his lungs. Shallow water soaked his clothes but failed to really cushion his fall. The light went out somewhere up on the path when the lantern had hit the ground. He wasn't even sure how far he'd fallen. Ten feet maybe? Further? Only the soft light from Greg's wisp form gave him any point of reference. Concentrating on his health bar did nothing to reassure him as he stared at his brother floating down to him.

Health: 57/100

"Dude you okay?"

"Ugh I think so," Kurt groaned, doing a quick pat down of his body. "I took some damage but I'm not seeing any debuffs or notifications telling me anything terrible."

"Think you can climb back up?"

"I don't know. How high is it?"

"Um pretty high, I guess."

"Maybe we should have a look around down here. If there's another way out, I'd rather see if we can find it instead of trying my hand at rock climbing in the dark. Just stay close so I don't fall off another cliff."

More slowly this time the two of them inched forward. Kurt held tighter to the wall in the hopes of having a hand hold if the ground fell out from beneath him again. Greg did his part as well staying closer instead of racing ahead to check for ore. He also hovered nearer to the ground in the hopes of illuminating the path. The wisp only gave off light equal to a candle at best but it was all they had at the moment. They walked for nearly half an hour and the slope had long since leveled off. Throughout the water remained about ankle deep and murky. Engrossed in watching their footing left Kurt's guard down when a familiar tongue shot down from the ceiling entangling him around the neck. A look up only alarmed Kurt further as he saw the creature's tag.

Rock Gecko | Level 2

Silently swearing for not having a weapon out, Kurt could feel his feet coming up off of the ground. Panicking he strained to find some hand hold on the wall as the giant gecko pulled him into the air. Kurt thrashed wildly as he was pulled back to the center of the chamber as he stretched for the wall. Swinging his legs back and forth. Kurt found he was now out of the water entirely and slowly ascending. His health bar was beginning to drain. With little else he could do, Kurt reached up with both hands grabbing the slimy tongue.

"Bro! Oh shit!" Greg screamed before Kurt lost all sense of what he was saying. He could still see the wisp flying around him ineffectually as the gecko's appendage continued to envelope his head as he was slowly reeled in. Desperate Kurt held on with everything he had beginning to kip back and forth in mid air. His eyes now covered, he felt his feet graze something. Swinging again he felt it again. It was the wall, a little more solid this time. A third time he kipped and his feet found it. Kicking off hard he jerked downward with both arms. Kurt dropped about a foot abruptly as the tongue partially unraveled. Wet popping sounds echoed high above as he made his way back to the wall. He nearly slammed into it but caught the rock surface with knees bent. Pushing off desperately he jerked down again for all that he was worth.

Unceremoniously he hit the shallow water. Kurt only had a moment as the large lizard crashed down next to him while he rolled. The rock gecko turned and flipped back onto its feet but Kurt seized his opportunity. Shuffling into a quick bear crawl, Kurt took the creature's back. The slick lizard squirmed and thrashed. Kurt gripped the creature as best he could with his hands while clamping down hard with his knees. Feeling himself already sliding free he risked loosening a hand hold long enough to grab his dagger from his belt. Trembling he rose up as high as he dared. The gecko began to buck but Kurt drove down hard to meet it lodging the dagger deep into its back. Kurt nearly fell as the gecko darted forward violently. He held tight grabbing the throwing knife with his opposite hand. He couldn't risk rising up again. Hugging the gecko he thrust the knife into its side. The lizard staggered and fell briefly. Seizing the moment he stabbed again. The monster had little energy and now strained to regain its footing at all. Kurt stabbed one final time and the monster collapsed.

You Have Slain - Rock Gecko | *Level 2*

"Hey Kurt you dead?"

Kurt tumbled off onto the ground still desperately clutching both of his weapons. His breath was coming in ragged starts and he could feel himself shaking as he stared at the ceiling. Concentrating on his health bar he was less than pleased.

Health: 31/100

"Not dead but getting close," Kurt breathed trying to calm his nerves.

"We gotta get out of here. The last one was higher level so we're going the wrong direction."

"Yeah sounds good. I think it's time I climb out of here. We can come back and get the rest of the ore after I get patched up."

Still laying back in the water, Kurt heard the sound of wet, sucking on rock. Hurriedly he sat up and stowed his blades. "We got another one coming. Go back the way we came in and check."

"Yeah okay," Greg agreed.

Scrambling to his feet Kurt concentrated in the darkness trying to pinpoint where the steps were coming from. Without Greg there the light had gone from barely there to nonexistent. As quietly as possible he reached back and unslung his bow, nocking an arrow. The steps were not coming quickly but they were not trying to hide themselves either. Maybe they didn't know he was here. Willing himself to be absolutely still he reached out with all his senses to take in any hint as to what was out there.

"They saw me! We gotta go." Greg's wisp form came rushing back into view flying quickly if not erratically. "There's two of them we can't go back," he blurted as he flew past Kurt.

With that the two brothers were running blind in the dark. Splashing water echoed throughout the tunnel as Kurt gave up on keeping his bow at the ready. He didn't dare to look back as something big hit the water in the darkness. Rounding a corner the sudden glare of moonlight reflecting off of the water nearly blinded him as if running into broad daylight. To his right a small waterfall fed into the widening cavern from an opening high above. Further out in the center of the chamber sat a small island where a horse sized gecko rested surrounded by dozens of smaller cat sized versions. The creature's tag had what looked like a metallic border around it as he looked at it.

Rock Gecko Matriarch (Special) | Level 3

"They can't be far behind," Greg shouted flying out over the water toward the light. "Make for the waterfall!"

Kurt only nodded as he darted off to the side watching with apprehension as his stamina bar steadily drained under the sprint. The water deepened coming up to his knees and then waist as he shouldered the bow and replaced his drawn arrow. A warmth ebbed from his hand and radiated through his body down to his legs as he cut through the water with ease. He would have to thank the Santa Clause Dungeon Master in the sky for the timely magic item.

"They just got into the cavern but I don't think the big one's seen you. Go!"

Reaching the wall, Kurt didn't hesitate grasping for the first handhold in sight. He never really did much in the way of rock climbing but climbing a rope was a regular activity in wrestling practice. The problem with the comparison was he wasn't fit in the same way he was in the real world. Struggling with his lack of strength and endurance it reminded him more of the first time he had ever climbed that rope. Something slapped the rock not far below him but he kept moving steadily. One hold at a time. Hand over hand.

"Looks like one lost interest but you got one on you still," Greg squealed in a panic.

Thrashing in the water neared the rock wall as Kurt willed himself up faster. He could see his stamina visibly draining but the ledge next to the waterfall wasn't far. The familiar sucking noise of a gecko climbing began behind him as he pushed himself to continue on. Greg was so excited to get him into this game because it was based around what you could actually do. His brother always looked up to him when it came to wrestling and thought it would make him good at this game. Climbing a wall was something he could really do. He knew that.

"Man you gotta go it's almost on you!"

A tongue lashed out and grabbed him by the ankle. The sudden jolt nearly pulled him free of the wall. Somehow Kurt held tight. Looking up he could see the ledge was just a little further. Only a couple more seconds and he could be there. Kurt's ankle was pulled hard and both of his feet came free at once. Somehow he managed to retain his grasp though and get his free foot back on the rock face. A quick look at his stamina told him he didn't have long. Pulling hard he brought the entangled foot back to the wall and slammed it against the largest protrusion he could find. The grip slacked for a moment. It was long enough. With the tension relieved he was able to move his leg back and forth against the rock face sawing at the tongue. It didn't take long for the creature to abandon its grip. In that instant he knew he had to go for it. Panting hard he pushed for the next hand hold and then another. His final move put him level with the ledge and he forced himself over the top. Rolling clear he felt the last of his stamina drain as much as he saw it. It was all he could do to draw his dagger and wait as his vision went hazy.

The pursuing gecko never came. Rushing water filled the middle three quarters of the tunnel. Moonlight filtered down through a large fissure that ran the length of the tunnel's ceiling reflecting from the surface. Kurt lay still for a while recovering his wits just watching the light dance along the walls. This game was terrifying. He wasn't sure what to expect when he started but a hyper realistic world complete with nightmarish monsters should have given him a clue. Fighting the rattling was bad enough but now he was coming up against creatures that didn't even resemble human beings.

"I'm not sure how you can even play this thing," Kurt confessed to his brother while he tried to calm himself. "It's a bit more intense than I thought."

"You'll get used to it. Eventually you'll start to see patterns and it will even be less realistic. I mean you'll still get your share of scares but after you go to the same zones a couple times you'll start to see things functioning in the same kind of way."

"We'll see," Kurt said skeptically. "Where are we anyway?"

"No clue. My guess is we are somewhere near the Slipwater Rush with all the water coming in. Either way we are close to the surface otherwise we wouldn't have light."

"Let's get out of here then." Kurt pulled himself to his feet and readied his bow. It felt like it was more for show than anything. His nerves weren't ready for another fight right now. Following the moving water back to its source only took a matter of minutes. The tunnel opened into a kind of natural spillway for a large river that thundered in the cool night air. Checking his bottom right he saw the notification confirming their location.

"You know how to get back to town from here?"

"Yeah I think we can manage," Greg said matter of factly. "The river runs on the other side of the foothills. Once we cross into those it's a pretty straight shot."

Chapter 6

Greg led the way down river a bit until they came to a rock formation he thought looked familiar. They turned from the shore and pushed into the hills. Small animals that might be owls and bats flew across the clear sky while larger animals like deer and wolves could be seen running from time to time. They were cautious of the latter but they were easily avoided at their distance. Players seemed to keep the animal numbers down as they hunted them for quests or just harvested them for pelts and meat. This was the first area of the game that really felt like an old school MMO.

"So it's always night time here huh?"

"Dude I thought you said you read the background I sent you."

"Yeah, I totally did. Well I mean I skimmed it like I told you. It's your standard two faction stuff, right?"

"Yeah if you mean the Order of Light is one faction and the Darklands are the other faction then sure standard two faction stuff. Yes it is always night time here. It's kinda the overarching theme of the main storyline. The Nightlord plunged the world into a state of eternal night and the Order of Light is trying to restore the balance. When we get to the main storyline stuff you'll get into more of the details if you decide to take in any of the flavor text."

"Hey man I said I read it, mostly. I just had a question is all."

"Sure bro," Greg said unconvinced.

Cresting a small hill the pair found a clearing nestled in a valley bisected by an old dirt road. A lone home, long reduced to rubble, sat overgrown with vines and tall grass as nature sought to reclaim it. A small flock of black birds took flight from the structure as Kurt approached. Within the sounds of small moving rocks were barely audible. Kurt readied his bow and moved to the door in curiosity. As he approached a handful of rats scurried out and past him. He let out a breath when he saw the one room structure was empty save for a collapsed roof that had long burned away into unusable chunks. Tumbled stone and mortar left the walls only partially standing in places.

"We should get back to town," Kurt reminded himself aloud as he glanced at his health bar. "I wouldn't mind checking this zone out though. It seems like a good one to run around."

"Yeah there are some quests over here. We can get you the cooking skill and maybe some gear. The stuff you're wearing is decent for starting out but exploration is a big part of this game."

The two turned to leave when more rubble cascaded down in the back of the structure. Kurt stopped moving abruptly. Waiting in silence, Kurt faced away from the door. He could feel something watching him. In one move Kurt turned pulling back the string on his bow. The arrow flew off into the shadows shattering against the crumbling structure beyond. To the right something moved dislodging more rocks and Kurt sprang. Shouldering hard into something unseen he heard a distinct yelp.

"The hell was that Kurt?" Greg flew around the room trying to find what his brother was shooting at. "I don't see anything."

Dropping his bow, Kurt ignored his brother, closing his eyes and listening. It was almost instantly he heard the shuffle of something trying to move past him. He went down to one knee in a lunge, dragging his trail leg behind him in a shot. He brushed something with his hands but it had lept back out of his range. Resetting himself he stayed crouched on the balls of his feet. The sounds of movement came again this time to his left. He shot on instinct. This time his left hand caught a clothed leg. He still couldn't see it but he pulled it in tight to his body. It was humanoid or at least it wore pants.

"Holy crap Kurt, you caught something!"

Jerking himself upright with a snap, Kurt clenched an ankle tight in his armpit. Whatever it was, it was light. The space around the creature shimmered as whatever magic obscuring it faded away. Kurt still wasn't sure what he was holding as he looked at the struggling child sized humanoid. It thrashed about upside down with short bristling fur that was colored either grey or light blue. He couldn't really tell. Long floppy ears like a dog hung limp while eyes, twice the size of a human's, bulged in wide astonishment at its predicament. If Kurt had to guess he would say the thing was male by its dress but it's high pitched voice made him question even that.

"I yield, I yield!" the creature yelled.

"Dude that's some kind of darkspawn! Kill it, maybe he'll drop some good loot."

"No, don't kill it! It's not darkspawn," the small creature pleaded in genuine alarm.

"Don't listen Kurt. He'll kill you the second you drop your guard."

"No he won't kill! He is unarmed. He has no weapon. He swears."

"Kurt don't let it…"

"Everybody shut up for a second," Kurt shouted, shocking them both into silence. Quietly he regarded the small creature that looked terrified more than anything and his brother who was little more than a ball of light. "Greg, cool the blood thirsty stuff for a second. I need some answers out of you," Kurt stated flatly as he held up the creature staring into its face.

"Oh anything but please do not kill me," the humanoid pleaded.

"What's your name for starters?"

88

"I am Wallo. Please set me down. I will not fight you. I promise."

"Kurt, be careful man. Look at your bar."

Kurt was well aware of his hit point situation and while his brother meant well. Kurt knew his brother was misreading the situation. Gingerly he sat Wallo on a nearby ledge so they were at eye level. Carefully but firmly he kept a hold of Wallo's arm just in case he did try something before continuing. "Ok Wallo, what exactly are you?"

"That's easy, I'm Rosharn!" He paused a moment but when Kurt didn't react he continued. "I'm one of the Night Folk."

"See I knew it! He's a Darkspawn. He's one of the Night Lord's devils."

"No, Wallo does not serve the false lord, I promise it!"

"Both of you quiet," Kurt growled. He took a deep breath and then another. The wisp was looking like he was going to say something so he shot him a glare and took a third cleansing breath. "Okay now Wallo, my brother the wisp here believes you are evil and a threat. I believe you are unarmed because you had plenty of time to attack me and didn't even though you're down here lurking about. What are you doing here?"

"The Night Folk need to scavenge. We don't go near the towns or the people but we take their discarded things. You throw out many nice things. Please let me go. I mean no harm. I am not here to fight. You attacked me and I was trying to hide. I was only looking for things here."

Kurt thought for a moment. He was the one who went on the attack first. Before he caught Wallo he wasn't even sure what he was. Honestly he still wasn't really sure what a Night Folk was. If truth be told though, Wallo did nothing to him.

"Kurt, don't even think about it. This thing will stab you in the back the first chance it gets," scolded Greg. "The Night Lord's servants are not without guile. That's an actual saying here!"

"Let me go and I will grant you a boon! I promise it. I have nothing of value to you. Please be reasonable," Wallo pleaded.

"I'm inclined to believe you," Kurt began.

"Excellent!" Before Kurt could go on Wallo reached up and touched the side of Kurt's head. Mumbling a word of power, Wallo discharged a small burst of purple light that seeped into Kurt's head and flared from his eyes. Kurt leapt back in surprise pulling Wallo from his perch before letting loose of him. The Rosharn fell unceremoniously but quickly turned invisible and scampered past.

"Thank you," Wallo shouted as he ran off into the night. "Always you will be a friend to the Night Folk."

Kurt reeled as the world came to light in bright relief. A new icon appeared in line with the others and notifications scrolled in the bottom right.

You Have Gained the Affinity: Shadow Sight
Reputation Gain plus 500 with The Night Folk
Reputation Level - Favorable 1 with The Night Folk
Reputation Loss minus 2000 with The Order of Light
Reputation Level - Unfavorable 3 with The Order of Light

Greg zipped after the Rosharn toward the door. "Wait a second, how can you hear me? No one's supposed to be able to hear someone in wisp form. Kurt there is something really screwy going on he shouldn't be able to hear me." Greg turned back to his brother but all thoughts of the creature were lost. "Oh crap man your eyes are glowing purple. I think you've been cursed."

A quick look at his health bar and debuffs showed nothing. "I'm not seeing anything man. There's no debuff and my health looks the same."

"Man your eyes are glowing purple. That's a sign of the Night Lord."

"It says it's an affinity in the notification. Those are good right?" He opened his character sheet and concentrated on the Shadow Sight affinity.

Spell - Shadow Sight   20 MP   Instant Cast
          Grants Dark Vision while Active
          Grants the Ability to See and Read Shadow Script
          Detecting Stealth Becomes Easier
          Side Effect - Eyes Glow Bright Lavender while Active

"Yeah affinities are good but I don't know about that," Greg trailed off.

"I mean it looks like good stuff when I inspect it," Kurt reasoned.

"We need to get it cleared off of you. It might even keep you out of the main quest line."

"Um well we might have bigger problems with that."

"Why?"

"Well it looks like I have access to reputations now. Mine with the Order of Light went down quite a bit," Kurt answered sheepishly.

"Oh shit, man how bad?"

"I lost two thousand points."

"Dude are you serious?" Greg was incredulous. "We can't just make that up. There's no way to just fix that. You might be killed on sight with them now. You need a good faction with them to progress at all. That's the main faction in the game. All your good gear and abilities come through that."

"Whoa, take it easy Greg. It's a game right. I wouldn't be able to get this without being able to progress.

"We need to get it cleared off," his brother answered stubbornly.

Moving back toward the door an odd purple outline caught Kurt's eye from across the building. On closer inspection the old brick chimney had a bizarre series of scratches that glowed just below eye level. Had the odd purple light not illuminated them they would have only appeared as wear and tear to the casual observer. He concentrated on them and a prompt appeared.

This chimney is always backing up when I build a fire. I really should look into that.

"If that wasn't video game logic, I don't know what is," thought Kurt before looking back to his brother.. "Can you see this stuff on the chimney Greg?"

The wisp flew over and scanned the area Kurt pointed out. "See what?"

"Shadow script," Kurt said to himself as much as anyone else. "You know Greg I'm not so sure this affinity is a bad thing." Kurt bent down and ducked under the hearth peering up into the chimney. With his enhanced sight, the shelf was easy to see just within arm's reach where a brick should be. Reaching up Kurt felt something smooth and metallic. Gingerly he removed it and brought it out to inspect.

Antique Pocket Watch

Quality: Rare

Shadow Script: Thank You for Your Service Dearest Edward

"Check it out Greg. You know Mabel's grandfather's name?"

"Uh no."

"I think I just found out. I bet this is the watch she's looking for on the road."

"She will literally accept any watch. You can probably vendor that for more than the quest reward. How'd you find that anyway?"

"I'm thinking the clue you can't see on the chimney is Shadow Script. You think this affinity is a bad thing but it's paying out."

"We'll see man. We should see if we can finish your ore quest quick before we head back to town. There are a couple rocky patches we can check on the way there."

"Works for me as long as we can avoid much more fighting." Keeping the affinity on just to mess with Greg alone would be worth it. The pair moved on to a couple above ground mining locations. Most of the monsters were being farmed out so the travel continued to be rather uneventful. The first two locations proved to be equally farmed out for ore. They were considering giving up again when Kurt's mining charm activated itself again leading them to a small natural shelf that was heavily overgrown. With a bit of clearing of shrubs and tall grass they found a respectable vein that netted him the rest of the needed copper ore and a couple blocks of usable stone as an added bonus. A notification scrolled in his bottom right.

You Have Achieved - Novice Miner - Level 1

"Okay I should be ready to turn these in now. Looks like I also upped my mining skill."

"Sounds good. After you get a couple levels you should be able to mine better stuff and mine more easily," Greg explained. "We aren't too far from town. The mining quest gives a good reward I think. I haven't done a lot with professions but from what I understand doing the starter quest is the way to go."

93

It was a straight shot back to the Crafter's Gate. Within minutes they could see the open doors where players streamed in and out of the village. It was a strangely welcome sight as the fatigue from days events finally began to set in. The stress of using up his stamina in large chunks and losing so much health was real. He could feel the aftermath of his exertion. Until now he'd been running on adrenaline but all he really wanted was to sit down for a minute. They came to within maybe a hundred feet of the wall when several crys went up.

"Guards to the wall!" A guard shouted.

"Crossbows at the ready!" Someone else answered further down.

"Bar the gate!" came a voice from ground level.

"Darkspawn spotted," still another person said.

Players and guards alike rallied to the defense of the village. Those outside the walls scurried about in a panic as news swept over the surrounding area. Kurt swung around trying to locate the danger. He was still a good distance from the wall when the first crossbow bolt landed well short of him.

"Uh Kurt I think you're the one they spotted. Your eyes stick out a bit in the dark."

A volley of bolts and arrows fired from the wall. The shots all fell short of the mark except for a few arrows. Kurt's luck held as these were fired by players and since he wasn't flagged for PvP. Those shots passed through him harmlessly.

"There's no telling how many of them are out there. Ready another volley!" Whoever took charge of the guard was getting them more organized. It hadn't occurred to him that they couldn't actually see him. He was already taking for granted the enhanced sight granted by his affinity. Concentrating on the icon for Shadow Sight in his buffs, Kurt found he was able to dismiss it. The world plunged into darkness instantly.

94

"Greg you're sticking out like a sore thumb too. Head around to the gate we came in first. I'll meet you there."

"Um I'm not sure how far away I can go from you," Greg protested.

"Well let's test it out. If nothing else try to lose yourself in the trees a bit."

An uproar broke out on the wall as Kurt and Greg split up. Shouts of confusion echoed through the night as projectiles rained down from the village wall sporadically. They still fell harmlessly to the ground but any semblance of organization the guard had evaporated. Orbs of light were cast out from the wall and more torches lit as the people prepared for the attack they were sure was on the way. Ducking into the nearest copse of trees, Kurt began circumventing the town.

Kurt pulled the hood of his cloak up over his head. Not wanting to appear hostile he made sure to stow all of his weapons before darting to the next clump of trees. He moved like this from one stand of trees to another keeping the village on his right. Dots of magical and mundane light multiplied around the village as more players came out to hunt for kills. Before long a pair of players spotted Kurt and called out to him.

"Yo Turk, you see any fiends out here?"

Kurt balked at the use of his game name for a moment since he hadn't really been using it. They must not have noticed as he stepped out of the trees though. Both players surveyed the area getting ready to jump at any shadow. He looked at their tags quick before responding.

Lassiter | Don't @ Me Bro | Level 2

2cuteCora | Makeshift | Level 3

"Uh you mean those wolves with the glowing eyes?" Kurt tried to

95

make up something generic. Most games had wolves, right? Did these guys not even know what they were looking for, he wondered.

"Oh no shit," Lassiter said, turning to give Turk his full attention.

"I didn't think Shadows Stalkers came out this far," Cora chimed in.

"Maybe it's some kind of event," Lassiter wondered, scratching his head.

"Yeah they were back there," Kurt bluffed pointing back in the general direction of the foothills. "I'm gonna go heal up then get back out there."

"Right on. Thanks man," Lassiter said waving as he broke into a jog.

"Yeah thanks, Turk. We'll see you out there." Cora gave a practiced wink.

As soon as they left Kurt took off in the other direction. Instead of going for more cover he cut across open ground making his way back toward the gate. Still people searched but no one else came up to him as he looked to be doing the same thing. Soon Greg was floating beside him again.

"Turns out I can't get that far away from you. I would have beat you to town if you hadn't stopped."

"Good to know. Let's go for the gate. I think we're in the clear."

Moving at a jog Kurt led them back to the city gate. Soon the guards manning the wall were within sight and peering off into the darkness. The way remained open as they approached and the NPCs paid them little heed as they passed within the wall. In mere moments they were walking the village streets as if nothing had happened at all. While the world outside of Silent Grove hunted for darkspawn, the people in town went about their business as if nothing was going on.

"Let's head over to see the blacksmith, Greg," Kurt suggested.

"Okay, I wouldn't mind seeing what the reward for that one is."

Kurt was finding himself more comfortable navigating the city streets now that he'd been down them a couple times. Greg still led the way but soon it wouldn't be needed at all. This was only a small village after all and while it was bigger than what traditional games featured there was still a logical order to things. The sounds of the forge came to life before Kurt spotted it. Jogging through the front door he surveyed the room and noticed a couple players had joined NPCs in their work since Kurt was last there. Upon entering Master Smith Alen looked up from the plans he was studying. He came to the door and greeted them.

"Ah Turk back so soon?" He wasn't overly warm in his manner but he was also intrigued. "Most people who come to me to learn the mining craft fail to return from their first task. What do you have for me?" A prompt filled Kurt's screen.

Will you complete the quest, "Not Wasting the Man's Time?"
Required Item - Chunk of Copper Ore x10
Required Item - Lump of Coal x10

YES
NO

Kurt concentrated on the YES. "I have the materials you requested Master Smith." A bag materialized in Kurt's hand. He nearly dropped it in surprise but instead he handed it to the blacksmith. Greg chuckled and Kurt did his best to ignore it.

"Excellent, thank you Turk. Come with me."

You Have Lost - Chunk of Copper Ore x10
You Have Lost - Lump of Coal x10

The elf walked from the table leading Kurt toward the back of the forge. The other players largely ignored him which made sense if this was a common quest. The chunks of copper ore were placed into a small cauldron and slid into a furnace.

"Watch here," the smith said pointing to a small gap that allowed him to see the contents of the cauldron. The smith moved to a great billows and stoked the furnace. The wave of heat that flooded over Kurt made his eyes water. "You must heat the furnace evenly to ensure that the metal melts evenly and remains usable." In time the smith moved the cauldron over to a series of molds and poured the molten metal. The ten chunks of ore was enough for five ingots. Calling to an assistant to mind the molds, he beckoned for Kurt to follow.

Numerous weapons and tools hung on a nearby board in various states of completion. Removing a small copper pickaxe from the wall he presented it to Kurt. "Turk, you have proven your worth as a miner. The materials you have brought me will help us train our apprentice smiths. As a token of my thanks, I present you with this pickaxe."

You Have Acquired - Portable Copper Mining Pick

"Thank you Master Smith." The elf nodded his acknowledgement before returning to his work. Wasting no time Kurt examined his new toy.

Portable Copper Mining Pick

Effect: The quality of this pick will allow you to mine slightly better materials..

Quality: Uncommon

Requirements: Novice Miner - Level 1

"Well how is it?" Greg asked.

"It says it will allow me to mine better materials so I guess that's good."

"Skill levels and gear combine to help you in crafting. So it's probably a decent reward."

"I think it's time we stop next door and get some money back on the other one," Kurt suggested strolling off in that direction.

Alen didn't acknowledge Kurt's wave as they left the building. He held his hand up there a little too long but he was in a good mood nonetheless. Floria was right where he'd left her next door. She was talking to another player who looked to be selling her a pile of useless scrap. He'd never had to wait for a vendor before but he guessed this was more realistic. It only took a moment but it seemed like a nice touch toward adding immersion. Soon the customer was on his way and Kurt stepped up to the counter.

"Good evening, Floria," Kurt said with a cheesy grin.

"Dude you hitting on NPCs now? That didn't take long," Greg chuckled.

"Shut up, Greg." he growled. "I'm working a little RP here."

"Excuse me?" Floria said grimacing.

"Oh I mean my wisp here not you." He glared at Greg.

"How may I help you?"

"Well I'd like to return this mining pick. It's just not for me."

"Hmm, I can give you three silver for that basic mining pick."

Kurt wasn't sure he had ever truly heard someone guffaw before but that is exactly what Greg did in that moment. People talk about a robust belly laugh but mostly they just laugh normally but not Kurt's brother. He laughed like it was the funniest thing he'd ever seen.

"Well you see I bought this here and would just like to return it. Not sell it to you. I paid fifteen silver not a couple hours ago." Kurt tried to haggle but the NPC just stared at him blankly.

"Dude you can only resell stuff for like twenty percent of their sell price. The game is realistic but they are pretty firm on that one. This isn't Costco."

"Three silver will be fine," Kurt grumbled trying not to look at his brother who was still chuckling.

You Have Lost - Basic Mining Pick
You Have Acquired - 3 Silver

"Is there anything else I can help you with today?" Floria asked in a tone Kurt thought was a little too chipper.

"No thank you," Kurt moped as he turned to the door.

"Dude did you really think that was going to work?"

"It was worth a shot."

"You're going to be the first MMO Karen."

"Dude really? One log out and you cease to exist until you reroll remember?"

"Easy bro I'm just messing with you," Greg backpedaled with a real sense of panic in his voice. "I would have been impressed if that would have worked."

"Let's just go turn the other one in."

"Sure man but don't get your hopes up. I'll get us over there."

Chapter 7

Greg took off out the door and Kurt had to jog to keep up. Once outside he slowed to a more comfortable pace but soon they found themselves out of the Crafter's Quarter and passing through the Marketplace. They weren't here long either as they moved into a new section of town. The Residential District wasn't overly impressive but it was alive with players and NPCs alike.

"If you get enough gold you can buy your own place over here. There are areas like it in other towns that you might like better but having your own instanced home can be nice. You also don't lose it or the things you have stored there when you die. That's the real important thing."

"Good to know," Kurt said looking around at the homes.

"They are a bit pricey so you'll have to play for a bit to afford one but yeah they are totally worth it. It's one thing I really want. They are great if you have to reroll because you can store some gear for rerolls."

"So that's the stash you were talking about before?"

"Well it's the most common kind of stash. Guys that gank or do world PvP are most likely using an instanced home or guild hall to secure their good gear. You can also ditch items somewhere in a pinch and come back for them but that's not very secure. There are things in the world like chests in dungeons that can hold items in the same way. Some are secure and some are not. I don't have a lot of experience with them. I only got in at the very end of beta."

True to the description Greg eventually stopped at the end of a small lane leading to a humble white cottage with blue shutters. Well maintained flower gardens ringed the home and an air of country pride surrounded the property. They had only entered the front gate when Mabel came running from the house.

"Here we go," Greg chuckled. "Don't get your hopes up."

"Turk, I knew you'd come back! Did you find my grandfather's pocket watch?"

Kurt shuffled through his bag and produced the Antique Pocket Watch. He handed it to Mabel and her face immediately lit up. As she reached out a prompt appeared.

Will you complete the quest, "Time to Help?"

Required Item - Antique Pocket Watch

YES

NO

"Just remember man she will literally accept any watch for this quest. It'll net you a small amount of cash but we can probably sell that watch for more."

"Dude I don't need you backseat driving in this game. You don't even know if we can sell this I'm sure. Just let me handle it," Kurt growled before turning to Mabel. "I hope this is what you were looking for." With that he concentrated on the "YES."

You Have Lost - Antique Pocket Watch

Mabel put her hand to her mouth in stunned silence. Her eyes began to well with tears before she threw her arms around Kurt. "Thank you, Turk! You have no idea what this will mean to my grandfather. Please come in so you can meet him." Immediately she spun on heel and began to walk briskly toward the house.

"Wait what?" Greg blurted in obvious confusion.

"Was I supposed to get the reward before going in the house?"

"No, she never invites you in. You get a brief hug and she presses some coins into your hand before sending you on your way. This has all been a bit over the top actually. I wonder if they patched this quest."

"Hmm," Kurt left his brother to catch up and hurried after Mabel. She beat him to the house but waited with the door held wide, waving to him.

"Please come in Turk. I'll get my grandfather."

Greg barely made it in as she closed the door. Before sweeping out of the room she directed Kurt to a well worn stuffed chair. He looked around for a moment at the humble home. Everything seemed very simple but well cared for and routinely cleaned. Everything had its place. It was only a moment when Mabel returned with an elderly but fit man who walked upright but with a bit of a limp.

"Turk, I would like you to meet my grandfather, Edward Lennonbrook."

Kurt moved to rise from his chair but was waved down by the man. "I have no need for formalities young man. Stay seated and be comfortable. Mabel please bring us some refreshments."

The girl gave a small nod of her head before rushing off to the kitchen. Sounds of pouring water and clinking dishes soon wafted in as Edward began to speak. "So Turk is it? How did you come across my pocket watch?"

"Well there was an old dilapidated building and I found it there in the rubble."

"In the rubble you say?" Edward examined the watch. "It seems no worse for wear. It was just laying out like that?"

Kurt grew uneasy as the man's stare cut into him. He was fishing. Kurt just didn't know if he should take the bait.

"I'll take your silence as your answer. No, you see this particular watch was well hidden. It was left for someone to come along and find but only a particular kind of someone. Someone who could read the clues. Tell me Turk, are you that someone?"

"Dude this might not be a good idea, "Greg warned. "This is sounding like a trap. If this guy's with the temple and he catches you out having some darkspawn curse it could be game over."

Kurt thought about it. Greg had played more of the game than him so it might be best to listen. It didn't feel like that though. This felt like something else entirely. He decided to gamble on it. "Well actually sir, I did find such a clue. It wasn't so much a clue as it was directions on where to look."

"So it was," he said with a grin.

Mabel returned carrying a small wooden tray with a simple tea set and pile of cookies on it. Setting it between them she began to pour while the two sat quietly. Handing each a cup of tea with some shortbread cookies, Mabel smiled to herself until remembering. "Oh I'm sorry, I completely forgot your reward for the watch. Give me a moment, Turk." Once she left Edward began again.

"I try to keep my granddaughter out of all this so I'll be brief. If you could find the watch, I'm sure you've received a blessing from the Night Lord. Not the imposter who currently sits the throne but the true Lord of Night. Prophecy told of an awakening of his power ever since the usurper crawled out of the deep to seize control. I believe you can be the start of that awakening."

'Wait what?" Greg blurted.

"I'm sorry. I'm a bit confused. I don't know much about all of this."

"I wouldn't expect you to Turk. There are elements within the Order of Light who have worked very hard to bury this information. Many years ago the land existed in cycles of day and night. It was a world in harmony. There was balance. The peoples of the day coexisted peacefully with those of the night. Mind you this was long before I was born."

"So what happened?" Kurt asked, genuinely intrigued with the lore of the world for the first time.

"Who's to blame is up for debate. Some say the dwarves awoke something in the deep dark of the world. There are those in the Order of Light who would have you believe the Lord of Night went mad and seized control of the Temples of the Day plunging the world into darkness. Regardless what happened is the Lord of Night was cut from this plane while something took his name and claimed his power. It is believed that this creature fights even now to completely supplant the deities of this world to plunge it into an age of unending darkness."

"Sounds like bull shit to me," Greg blurted. "There already is no daytime in this game."

"Aren't we kinda in that situation now?"

"There is a difference between unending night and unending dark. Light is not the opposite of night. The people of the night still rely on moonlight and starlight for their survival. In fact if you asked them you'd find they prefer the day for sleeping. Most sleep by lantern light for this reason. You would not want a day that never ceased would you?"

"No," was all Kurt could manage.

"It's a lot to take on faith. I understand that. Perhaps if you were to see it for yourself you'd understand. While this watch is mine there is someone who can use it more than me. There is a man in the town of Black

Crystal that goes by the name 'Grins.' Seek him out and give him the watch. It might be you will see for yourself what has become of the world."

Will you accept the quest, "Time to Help II?"

YES

NO

"No way Bro. We've gone far enough down this rabbit hole."

"Greg it's the second part of the Mabel quest. I know this might not be the meta or what you're used to but I want to see this out. I mean the other option is run around killing time until we run the stuff you want to run." Kurt was getting annoyed at this point. He concentrated on the "YES."

Rising Kurt accepted an offered hand from Edward and shook. When he withdrew his hand he found himself holding the same pocket watch he'd meant to return. At this time Mabel came back carrying an old coin purse. With a quick embrace she gave it to Kurt.

"Thank you again, Turk. You will never know the service you've paid my family today."

You Have Acquired - Antique Pocket Watch
You Have Acquired - 25 Copper

"It was no trouble, Mabel. If you'll excuse me, I have some things I need to do."

Edward nodded and Mabel showed Kurt to the door. Exiting into the cool night air had a calming effect on Kurt. If the reward had been only the copper, Kurt could see it being a bit disappointing. There was something to this quest line though. As a single quest it would be one thing but as the first step in a series a small reward wasn't that out of the ordinary. At least in the games he played in the past it wasn't.

"When you reroll Greg we can do whatever quest line you want," Kurt said, turning to his brother. "You weren't going to do this quest in the first place so it shouldn't interfere with your plans."

"That's fine but if you can't do quests for the Order of Light, we can't do the main storyline and you're going to miss out on a ton of stuff you're going to need."

"If that's the case then I'll just reroll. I doubt that the developers would somehow lead me down a quest line where I can't participate in the bulk of the game. I just need you to chill so we can see this out."

"I don't know man," Greg said unconvinced.

"Look at it this way. It's content that you otherwise wouldn't even see. Maybe you'll prefer it to what you had in mind."

"We'll see. What else do you need to do in town?"

Kurt just shrugged. He was going to be a pain in the ass about this. "I need to get some healing and clear out my inventory a bit. Whatever order works."

"Well with that reputation getting healed at the temple is out. We're going to have to get a bit more creative. Players can still heal you but we can't exactly rely on that. I think we should pick up another knowledge skill. The medical skill isn't as fast as magical healing but we can use it to create salves and bandages. Magical healing only takes as long as the spell takes to cast but you have to make bandages and it takes time to apply them. Not the greatest in combat."

"I think that will work for what we need," Kurt agreed.

"Alright we gotta go to the city guard for this so don't do anything to let people know you're a darkspawn."

Kurt let that one go. Greg was taking this all a little too personally.

Hopefully it didn't screw up his plans. He was playing the game for Greg after all. His brother had been begging him all winter to start it up but in truth he hadn't played an MMO in years. It's not that the fully immersive game didn't interest him. He was just busy with other things. Maybe that's why he was so uptight about what they were doing. He'd keep it in mind.

Venturing back out into the city brought them back to the main gate. Not far from there within the city walls was a small series of plain yet sturdy buildings. One appeared to be for officers while another looked to be some sort of barracks. There was also a training yard and small stable here. The whole thing looked like it was for maybe a couple dozen guards at most. Amongst all of this was a small mostly open building next to the access stair for the wall. It resembled a barn to Kurt as much as anything else complete with large sliding doors. Within a number of people bustled between beds and tables tending to sick and wounded people, not just guards.

A nicely dressed man saw him standing in the doorway and approached. "Are you sick or injured?" He asked, looking him over critically.

"No. I'm here for medical training?" Kurt asked not quite sure how you broached the topic for taking on a medical skill.

"Is that a statement or a question?"

"I need training in First Aid."

"Good, we need the help. Come on in." The man walked back into the open building and led Kurt to a table. "My name is Doctor Darius Hourne and you are?"

"My name is Turk."

"We are a bit short staffed, Turk, so if you want training in First Aid you can learn on the job with me. The basics are not all that complicated but being trained is easier than trying to figure it out on your own. Do we have a deal?

Will you accept the quest, "Learn on the Job?"
YES
NO

Kurt concentrated on the "YES" option. As soon as he did he was put to work. Somehow he thought it would be different than actually working but he was wrong. Kurt began by running from bed to bed changing linens and bed pans for various patients. When this ended he began helping those same people clean up with a bowl of soap and water. Time seemed to drag on as he personally helped clean up all of the people. Thankfully outside of some interesting smells the game kept things covered and didn't make for any awkward situations. He was then passed off to a nurse where he was shown how to grind a few local herbs into a kind of paste to help fight infection. Another herb he passed out acted as a mild pain reliever when chewed. He wasn't sure how long he had been working but it was the first thing he would call useful.

"As tedious as this is for you Kurt, imagine having to watch it," Greg said when Kurt had commented on the training.

"Wasn't this your idea?"

"I didn't know the quest forced you to get a job."

Kurt could only shake his head as he finished his latest task. The doctor found him after that was completed and brought him over to a table with sheets rough-spun cloth. The next job was turning those into strips for bandages. It was tedious but again it was something he found useful. There was actually a right way to do it, he found after cutting a few too short to be usable. His final task involved following the doctor around and observing people as their bandages were changed. It reminded him a lot of holding a flashlight for his dad growing up. The difference here was the doctor explained what he was doing as he did it. When they were finally done the doctor wiped his brow and turned to Kurt.

"Did you get what you came for, Turk?" A prompt appeared.

Will you complete the quest, "Learn on the Job?"
YES
NO

"I did, doctor. Thank you." He concentrated on the "YES."

You Have Achieved - Novice First Aid - Level 1

Kurt was taken aback at the notification. With mining he had to grind the skill from Level 0 to Level 1. The quest while long had started him out at Level 1. Even so his skills icon was still flashing and he opened the screen.

Skills

- **Medical**
    Novice First Aid   Level 1 (500/1000)
    Novice Herbalism   Level 0 (25/500)
- **Mining**
    Novice Miner   Level 1 (500/1000)
    Novice Smelter   Level 0 (25/500)
- **Spells**
    Shadow Sight   Level 0 (25/500)

Seeing Herbalisim surprised him further but it made sense with the time they had devoted to the use of herbs. Comparing it to the work he did on the mining quest his progress was identical. Even more unexpectedly his Shadow Sight ability was listed as a skill under the spells heading. It only stood to reason that he would become more adept at using magical abilities by using them but he didn't think to check to see if his progress would be tracked here. There was still a lot he didn't know about this game. Before he could leave one of the nurses waved him down. He turned to her as she handed him something.

You Have Acquired - Rough-spun Bandages x5

"Thank you for the help today. If you ever decide you want a career change I'm sure the doctor would take you," the nurse said warmly as she lingered a moment.

"Thanks. I'll keep that in mind." Kurt wondered if that was a hint at further training available later or if it was just flavor text.

"Finally! Let's get your stuff sold so we can get to something interesting. I don't even care if it's the Mabel quest line. I can't watch any more skill progression tonight."

"So can I use these bandages now or do I need to wait until I have a fresh wound?"

"You should be able to use them," Greg said after thinking for a moment.

Kurt pulled a bandage from the stack he'd been given and began to apply it to his leg for lack of a better place. To his surprise the bandage dissolved as soon as he finished applying it. A quick look to his health bar so a small bump in the right direction. He repeated the process three more times and saw his health was mostly full. He examined the bar and was

111

pleased with what he saw.

Health: 95/100

"It's slower than magic I'm sure but I think it'll work," Kurt said, happy with the results.

"First Aid's not going to work for you in combat but it's what you got for now."

Kurt wasn't sure if that was a ringing endorsement but it worked for him. Moving back toward the city, Kurt felt a spring in his step as the aches and stiffness from their ordeal faded from his body. His fatigue dissipated and his head cleared. Kurt wasn't sure what healing would feel like but he wasn't expecting it to feel like this. He hadn't even realized some of the symptoms he was feeling.

"I see you're feeling it now," Greg chuckled. "Last time you were healed so soon after taking damage you really didn't have time for the weariness to set in. It's gradual so it's not a big problem but it keeps you from running around at low health for too long. Since there isn't a debuff or stat tied to it people didn't pick up on it right away in beta. A similar thing happens if you go too long without eating something. You won't gain healing from food but you saw the buff."

"Are there a lot of things like that?"

"Not really but the game changes a little bit with every patch. They're always trying to make it more realistic. In a lot of ways it's still a work in progress."

Moving back toward the main thoroughfare, they found themselves back in the market district before long. Kurt considered seeing what he could do at one of the many player run carts in the area. There were many of them and, since he was carrying crafting materials, he was pretty sure he

112

could find a buyer. He had an idea though. Soon Kurt found himself standing in front of WGD's guild store.

Upon entering he was greeted once again by the anime inspired NPC. A couple players shopped the nearby shelves looking at what appeared to be crafted weapons. Moving up to the counter Kurt got down to business.

"Hi my name is Turk. Earlier when I was here I spoke with Therin, he said I could bring materials here to sell. Is that still right?"

She made a show of looking at a ledger before responding. "Yes sir. I have you on our list. Would you like to sell to us or place the items on consignment?" She gave a sheepish giggle and blushed.

Kurt thought he would need to meet the guild leader who set this up some time then he thought better of it. "Okay, can you explain the difference between selling to WGD and selling on consignment?"

"Well Mr. Turk we give a going rate for any items sold directly to us within reason," the clerk began in a rehearsed tone. "WGD does not buy high end magical items without the seller speaking with a ranking member. Trade goods, low end potions and most materials, I can handle. Now more hard to find items can be sold on consignment. You can set a price or meet with a ranking member to set a price. The guild keeps a flat five percent of the sale price on anything sold in this way. What are you looking to sell today?"

"I just have some crafting materials." Kurt produced the hides and stone and the clerk looked them over. He guessed this was for effect too so he waited patiently..

"I can buy these outright. The stone pieces are forty copper each and I can do a silver each for the hides."

Kurt looked to his brother who only said, "You might be able to get a little more selling directly to someone looking for them but it's not a terrible price."

"Sounds good to me." The two shook on the deal and the clerk collected the items while producing a small coin purse.

You Have Lost - Block of Usable Stone x5

You Have Lost - Torn Gecko Hide x2

You Have Acquired - 4 Silver

The clerk bounced away a little too happily carrying the crafting goods and Kurt decided it was time to take their leave. It wasn't the amount he had started out with but it felt good to have a little walking around money again. He made it as far as the cobblestones in front of the shop before he stopped. "Any idea on how to get to Black Crystal?"

"Not exactly. I know it's on the other continent near the Darklands. I haven't been there though."

"Okay how do we get to the other continent?"

"We will need to take a ship from Corwood further upriver. We should make the trip eventually. It's a good one to visit for fast travel anyway."

"And how do we fast travel? Wait nevermind. We've already been at this for hours. It's getting late. This might be a good place to call it. Tomorrow's Sunday and we can get back at it after you reroll."

"No, wait. Hold up a sec," Greg stammered. "You know that there is a time difference in and out of game right?"

"Was it in the background I was supposed to read?"

"No."

"Then, no, I didn't know that."

"The ratio isn't exact but about one hour in real life is around ten hours in game."

"How is that even possible?"

"Dude they are projecting a video game into your brain and back out again but the part you take issue with is the fact that it's not in real time?"

"Well when you say it like that…"

"Right now I have like an eleven hour wait to reroll. That's real world time not game time. I was kinda hoping we could get a bit closer and then sleep away most of that deficit."

"I can go a bit longer but I don't know about committing that kind of time to this in one go. I mean why would they go for that kind of gap anyway?"

"Who knows? It rewards not dying," Greg said slightly annoyed. "Maybe because it gives the hardcore crowd long play sessions without the need for a ton of real life hours to commit to the game. It lets people immerse for long periods of time without needing to break character."

"I get it man," Kurt realized that his constant questions were wearing on his brother but this is what he had asked for in the first place. "I wasn't looking to offend you. We can play a bit longer. Where to?"

"If we're going to the port it's north out of town. If we follow the road we shouldn't run into much trouble from mobs."

"Lead the way."

Greg took off to the right and led them back to the main road through town. The village of Silent Grove had three gates, Kurt soon learned. He had been out of the Crafter's Gate and when he arrived he had entered through the South Gate. The last entrance to the city followed the main road used in the zone through the North Gate. In effect you never had to leave the road to enter the city. It made sense when you realized that most NPCs feared the things that hid in the dark places of the world.

Leaving through the North Gate, the road opened before them.

Trees had been cut back on either side for a good fifty yards give or take. Beyond that the woods were only sparsely populated. Occasionally someone running the opposite direction toward town would pass but without acknowledgement and always giving a wide berth. Once Silent Grove was out of sight a new zone notification scrolled in the bottom right.

Southland Trade Road (PVP Zone)

"Whoa we're going into a PVP Zone?"

"Most of the game is one," Greg said in a noncommittal tone.

Kurt stood in the middle of the road for a moment with his mouth open to say something. He thought for a moment. The idea of PVP coming up was the main reason his brother had gotten him into the game. It wasn't so much that he wanted to live that PVP life but Greg was eager to have him as back up. Honestly he hadn't given much thought as to what he wanted to get out of the game. When he did answer the best he could manage was, "Okay."

'You sure bro?" Greg asked, a little surprised.

"Yeah, it was bound to happen eventually."

"Most people aren't looking for trouble. It would be better if there were two of us but most people are more worried about losing their gear. Guys like the guild we ran into earlier are out there. If we see a group of guys out roaming like them we'll have to figure something out."

"Man that's not much of a plan. I'll try to stay alive until you reroll but I'm not making any promises."

The two walked on for a while. Bears, spiders and wolves all came within eyesight of the road but none came close enough to aggro onto Kurt. Their levels were relatively low with the highest being around level three. In a one on one situation it seemed like it would be manageable enough.

Players on the other hand had Kurt reaching for his dagger on more than one occasion. He eyed each warily as they passed but never really became comfortable until they were out of sight. No one was overtly unfriendly but at the same time everyone seemed as cautious as him. The people further from the road didn't seem to pay much attention to them as they went about their business farming whatever mobs roamed the area. From time to time people would move in and out of the woods in this manner.

They had been traveling for some time when something caught Kurt's attention just off the road maybe halfway to the tree line. It was some kind of plant that had a faint green glow around it. Kurt stopped examining it from the road. He attempted to concentrate on it but was just too far away. Turning to Greg he asked, "Do you see that glowing plant out there?"

"What color is it?"

"Green."

"I don't." He answered after appearing to look for a moment. "Did you pick up Herbalism at some point?"

"Yeah I got a little bit in it when I completed the First Aid quest."

"That makes sense, they go hand in hand. It's your call. We haven't seen anything too crazy out here."

"Let's check it out," Kurt said, eager to do something besides walking.

Kurt moved from the road with the wisp in tow. Outside of the occasional old tree stump the area was largely empty field. Ankle high grass concealed the occasional hare or other small critter but nothing seemed too threatening. A small thorny plant sat glowing amongst other weeds. Kurt concentrated on it to see the details.

Black Sparrow Thistle

Uses: Alchemy, Cooking and First Aid

Quality: Normal

Requirements: Novice Herbalism

"It looks like I can harvest it. How do I do that?"

"I'm not sure. I've never messed with herbalism."

"Have you done anything in this game besides combat?"

"I've done a lot of the main quest line. I'm just not that into crafting."

Kurt bent down to give harvesting the plant a try. He thought to just pick it at first but the green light shining from the plant moved as he went to grasp it. Thinking back to how mining worked he moved his hand over the plant and watched as the light reacted. He was about to make his attempt when he heard a low growl from somewhere inside the tree line. Springing to his feet, Kurt had his bow drawn and an arrow knocked. With his heart thumping in his ears, he activated his Shadow Sight. The world exploded into brilliant detail as the moonlight's illumination was amplified ten fold.

"Dude what do you see?" Greg asked on edge by Kurt's sudden use of his power.

Kurt ignored his brother. Just inside the treeline a wolf stalked in the shadows watching Kurt, looking for a moment to pounce. He tracked the creature as it made its way toward the clearing. It moved to the side preparing to attack from Kurt's flank. He didn't look directly at it. Instead Kurt tracked the creature from his peripheral vision inviting it to come forward. Checking its tag only gave him confidence.

Young Wolf | Level 1

The young wolf made its move. Darting from its hiding place, it came on at a nearly silent run. Kurt wheeled, drawing a bead with his bow. He didn't fire at first. He let himself calm as the beast closed the gap lining up his shot. With an exhale he released the string. The arrow flew taking the wolf just behind the shoulder sending it sprawling. It tried to stand and failed instead thrashing on the ground biting at the arrow it couldn't reach. Shouldering the bow Kurt moved in and drew his dagger.

It had been years since he hunted. His skills with a bow were coming back but even then he had never hunted anything that could in turn hunt him. There was a big difference between hunting deer and fighting for his life. One lesson that he never failed to learn was the most dangerous animal was the wounded one. Knowing he only had one shot to do this safely he waited. When the wolf thrashed away Kurt slid in on his knees. He drove down as hard as he could slamming the dagger into the wolf's throat. A final death throw threatened to wrench the dagger from his grasp but knowing his own well being was at stake he held tight. In an instant it was over.

You Have Slain - Young Wolf | Level 1

"Dude that was badass." Kurt's brother bounced around in front of him. "You could have probably taken a hit or two from him but you totally executed him."

"Whoa nice job, Turk!" Another voice called out from behind him. Kurt quickly dismissed his Shadow Sight. He hoped it wasn't too late. Clenching his dagger tight he stood and turned. Approaching were a pair of fighters. He nearly choked when he saw one wearing full plate from head to toe. Neither had weapons drawn and he quickly took notice of their tags and exhaled.

Bhae | The Premade | Level 6

Carmen | Queue Me Up Buttercup | Level 5

"Hey Bhae, you're the last person I expected to see out here," Kurt managed forcing his nerves down.

The two fighters made an odd looking pair with Carmen looking every bit the armored knight with an antlered greathelm. Across her chest in red paint were scrawled the words "Player Killer." Bhae by contrast wore a series of hides and animal furs. A round shield and well worn battle axe strapped to her back. Bhae took a moment then she realized just where she had seen him from before.

"Whoa you're the guy from the market right?" She pulled back the hood of her fur cloak to get a better look at him.

"Yeah thanks for the save back there."

"Hey Carmen, this is the guy I was telling you about saving."

"Cool," the plate wearing warrior managed to mumble clearly unimpressed. "She hasn't shut up about it since we left."

"Oh like I haven't heard your PVP stories before," Bhae barked, slugging her friend in the arm. "What did you do to piss those guys off anyway?" She asked, turning back to Kurt.

"Well I killed their buddy, who killed my brother here, when he tried to gank us outside of town." Kurt jerked a thumb toward the wisp who was oddly silent. "From there it was a case of mistaken identity."

"Sounds about right. Guys like that can't stand to lose so they call their guildies to fight their battles," Carmen added casually.

"Hey you looking to run a dungeon?" Bhae added excitedly.

'What?" Carmen blurted.

"Uh yes please," Greg added, finally waking up.

120

"Oh come on Carmen. It will save us having to body pull the whole thing."

"Well I'm a little short on arrows. I'm not sure how much use I''ll be..."

"I have some extra and I'm sure Carmen can part with some." A prompt filled his screen causing him to grimace inwardly.

You Have Been Invited to a Party by Bhae

    Accept   Decline

"Dude this is a good thing," Greg said, speaking rapidly. "They can carry you for a bit and you can get some loot. Watching you do skill training and walking around in town has gotten old. Going to Corwood is only going to be more walking followed by sitting on a boat. You need to take this opportunity."

"Alright, alright," he grumbled under his breath. Kurt concentrated on the "Accept." A pair of player icons were added to his top left with a pair of health bars. Bhae's portrait also had a frame which Kurt guessed made her party leader.

"The wisp is like a free party member," Bhae justified still trying to sell her friend on the idea. "The loot will still spread for three but he can mark targets for us and be an extra set of eyes."

"You went to all the trouble of saving him," Carmen said, still leery on the idea. "I just don't want you to get him killed or worse have him get one of use killed."

"We were about to two man this dungeon. I doubt adding someone will make it worse."

Kurt just shrugged while the two talked about him. Greg chattered excitedly but he wasn't really listening. He was sure it had something to do with dungeon loot or the fact that there were two girls gamers having Kurt and by extension Greg join their party. Leaning down Kurt looted the wolf corpse he had been standing over before moving back to his plant and looting that too.

You Have Acquired - Broken Wolf Claw
You Have Acquired - Slab of Wolf Meat
You Have Harvested - Black Sparrow Thistle

When he stood back up Bhae shoved a bundle of arrows into his hand. He was still a bit zoned out but now everyone was looking at him. Carmen put her head in her hand to cover whatever face she was making under the helm. Greg stopped moving altogether and just hung in front of his brother's face.

You Have Acquired - Hunting Arrows x15

"I'm sorry what?" Kurt asked sheepishly.

"I asked if that was enough to get started," smiled Bhae.

"Um sure. I guess."

"Have you pulled this dungeon before?" Carmen asked critically.

"I've only actually been playing for a couple hours. I'm not even sure what dungeon we're running."

"It's pretty standard stuff," Carmen explained. "There's a lost elven city with trees that we pick from and work our way through. The whole thing is a straight up dungeon crawl. We run one need, one greed on bosses. Loot your own kills on trash. We'll talk out anything that comes up that is questionable."

"It'll be fine," Bhae waved dismissively.

Moving into the treeline, the bright night sky quickly became obscured. Kurt didn't dare use his Shadow Sight fearing an adverse reaction from the rest of the party. Instead he kept his bow at the ready watching shadows as they passed as quietly as possible. Twice wolves attempted to attack the party but were easily dispatched by the two fighters. Kurt also had a handful of options to harvest more Black Sparrow Thistle and netted himself two more. As they ventured deeper in a trail emerged with the odd cobble half buried in the dirt. Carmen drew her greatsword and ignited it in brilliant white light. Darkness in the immediate area retreated and distinct features of a long abandoned settlement emerged. Fallen statues covered in moss and toppled walls jutted out at odd angles just inside the light. Kurt glanced down to his bottom right.

Lost City of Ullanore (PVP Zone)

Chapter 8

"So the dungeon is in a PVP zone? Seems like that would invite griefing," Kurt ventured to break the silence.

"Man you really are new to this aren't you?" Bhae jabbed. "We could get some trouble on the way in but I doubt it. The dungeon isn't instanced like old school games but there are mechanics or events that lock players in and out. The stakes are higher because there's no going back but you also get some safety from other players. The loot is worth it if you're willing to risk it."

"Gotcha," Kurt said, still keeping his head on a swivel looking for threats.

"You know bro the world of Darklands is supposed to be about half the size of earth when everything they have planned is finally rolled out," Greg added. "Even with the subscriber base of around fourteen million those people are spread out all over. The further you get from towns the less likely it is to run into someone. Getting ganked isn't really all that common."

"Thanks poindexter," Kurt jabbed.

"What?" Bhae screwed up her face as she shot Kurt a look.

"Not you Bhae. My brother had to add his explanation to yours."

"Oh okay," she chuckled.

"Dude really?" Greg protested.

"Look alive, we're here," Carmen announced. The forest gave way to an ancient city nestled into a wild overgrown valley. A rough road that appeared to be grown as much as built extended from the valley rim to the city below. Large petrified trees which were converted into homes and places of business replaced their more natural kin. Long standing monuments still towered over the nature that sought to retake them while vines and shrubs obscured the smaller ediffices that once populated gardens and public spaces alike.

Bhae led the way with Carmen just behind while Kurt continued to scan the area with his bow. Greg even took part as he circled the group acting as a kind of scout. Moving deeper into the city thick green vines with red thorns became more prominent. At first they started out thin like the width of a pencil. As they moved closer to their destination they gradually increased to the size of Kurt's wrist. Finally the group came to a tree building wrapped in vines as large as his leg. Outside the door stood a pair of man sized walking tulips. Kurt checked their tags.

Wereflora | Level 3
Wereflora | Level 3

"Save your arrows Turk, Carmen and I will each take one. Look out for any adds."

Kurt nodded while Bhae drew her axe and shield. Carmen charged her sword with energy and the two looked at each other. Simultaneously they each charged a target. Carmen took her's instantly with a heavy overhead strike that erupted in brilliant energy. Meanwhile Bhae entered with her shield driving the creature back into the wall. Two blistering strikes later and she stood over her own fallen foe. In a moment the night was quiet once again and the two looted their kills.

"You two ready for this?" Carmen asked, gesturing to the door.

Without answer Bhae entered followed by her friend. Kurt hurried after the pair not enjoying the thought of being left behind in the middle of nowhere. Once inside the entry quickly disappeared as a mass of vines completely enveloped it plunging them into darkness. On cue Carmen ignited her sword, lighting the way. The base of the tree was probably sixty feet in diameter. The room itself was devoid of anything noteworthy other than a spiral staircase that ran around the circumference up to the next floor. Two people could comfortably walk side by side so Bhae and Carmen did just that while Kurt once again stayed in the back.

The second floor was behind a nondescript door who's decorative details were worn away by age. When Bhae pushed to open the door it cracked slightly before jamming on something. She inspected it briefly for shrugging her shoulders. Without a word Carmen reared back and kicked the door resulting in a loud crack but little else. Bhae nodded and the two kicked at once, splintering the door. Using their momentum they pushed into the room. Kurt cringed inwardly at the sound. They had brought him in to pull but at this rate there would be little use for that.

Leveling his bow, Kurt crept over the ruined door and scanned the room. Bhae and Carmen were engaged with four creatures identical to the ones that guarded the tree's entry earlier. He dropped his bow and the arrow he had knocked immediately. There wasn't a safe shot. Instead Kurt charged drawing his dagger. With all of the creatures focused on the two fighters he saw his opening. The nearest plant had its back to him. Throwing an arm around the creature's neck he buried his dagger to the hilt in its back. Maintaining his grapple he repeated the process a number of times before a prompt appeared. He kicked the corpse to the ground and moved to flank another.

You Have Slain - Wereflora | Level 3

The kill opened Bhae up to concentrate on one target and Kurt

126

moved to help Carmen. The Wereflora saw him before he could move behind so he had to settle for a slashing attack spraying green ichor in a wide arch. It was all the opening Carmen needed to boot it against the wall before decapitating it. In another moment the fight was over. Kurt leaned down to loot his kill while Bhae and Carmen looted the other three. Kurt moved to recover his bow and the stray arrow.

You Have Acquired - 3 Silver and 13 Copper
You Have Acquired - Large Sharp Thorn

"So should I stick with the dagger or am I actually pulling things for us?" Kurt questioned with a smirk.

"It's up to you," Carmen laughed. "We probably won't need you to pull anything for at least a few floors. All of these trees are a little different but they follow the same kind of progression in difficulty."

"Can you harvest this, Turk?" Bhae asked, already moving around the room looking for any hidden loot.

"Um I can try but I just started Herbalism." Kurt moved to her side to inspect the plant.

"Go for it. Neither of us have it."

Redtip Stranglevine
Uses: Cooking and Poison
Quality: Fine
Requirements: Novice Herbalism

Kurt studied the plant carefully. At first he didn't notice the green light to guide him until he followed the vine back to what looked like a branching section. Kurt grasped it gingerly as the light guided him before snapping it off. Just like past failed attempts however the herb disintegrated in his hand as he failed to harvest.

"No worries Turk, Carmen shouted to him when she noticed the failed attempt from across the room. "There'll be more to try. That stuff is all over the place."

Kurt stood and surveyed the room for the first time. A large wall bisected the room cutting it in half. Moonlight illuminated the room from a series of windows partially covered by vines that wrapped around the outside of the tree. Larger double doors that sat closed to the party blocking their progress. Bhae moved to the door and pushed before turning around to shake her head. Carmen was readying to kick at the door when Kurt put a hand on her shoulder.

"Hold up a second. I know it worked last time but I'm a bit under leveled for this place. One bad pull and I'm done. Can we try this one a little more subtly?"

"What do you have in mind?" Carmen chuckled.

"Greg see if you can fly around the outside and see what we're up against."

"Okay, be right back," Greg said excitedly as he flew through the window.

"We can try that," Carmen nodded in approval. "It's not often we have someone to scout for us."

The three waited a few moments before Greg returned through the open window.

"The next room looks to be clear but there's a catch. Those double doors are barred with a giant vine. It's going to take a lot of work to get through it. There is no door at the top of the stairs so if you make a bunch of noise you'll pull the next floor." Greg flew across the room to another window as he continued. "It looks like you can go out this window and

128

scale some vines on the outside to bypass the barricade. It doesn't look too difficult really. It's probably the intended path."

Kurt turned to the others. They stared at him expectantly and he remembered that they couldn't hear his brother. He relayed the information to them and they all went to the window to have a look. It was like his brother said. The large vine blocking the door on the other side of the wall also served as a bit of a foot bridge along the outside of the tree. Smaller vines also snaked around the tree which could serve as hand holds. A breach in the trunk where the vine entered left enough room to follow it back inside. Shrugging his shoulders, Kurt put his dagger back on his belt and climbed out.

Stepping outside the tree was intimidating but not as bad as it could have been. Looking down Kurt guessed he was about two stories up. The night was clear and calm aiding his confidence as he moved along the walkway. He had moved maybe ten feet out when he saw where the vine broke through the outer wall and entered. Turning his head back he saw that the others had joined him.

"I can see the hole up ahead," Kurt told them, doing his best to be heard without shouting. "It's not really that far. I'm maybe halfway there."

Bhae who was nearest to him nodded but was not nearly as comfortable with the height. Kurt thought he should say something but then thought better of it. Instead he went back to concentrating on the task at hand. Sticking close to the tree he made slow but steady progress. Sliding more than stepping, he inched his way around concentrating on the hand holds before moving his feet. Before he realized it, the wall gave way into a gap large enough to squeeze through. Greg flew in ahead of Kurt and did a quick circuit of the room. It was like he had described. Once inside Kurt waited offering a hand to Bhae and Carmen helping them through the hole.

"Let's not do that again," panted Bhae.

"Oh I don't know. Your boy has already made this run more exciting than the past few we've done," Carmen smirked.

Bhae shot her a withering glare and Carmen only chuckled. Kurt drew his bow, nocking an arrow. He watched the stairs cautiously. If the trap was alerting the next floor they might not have avoided springing the trap entirely. Even worse there was a possibility that they were in a worse situation with no easy fall back point.

"We still taking the careful approach?" Kurt questioned. "There's a good chance we're not out of the woods yet."

"We can hold the steps if it looks like there is a way to pull the next room," Bhae stated eager to change the subject. "It might be we have to fight the next room all at once regardless but we can hinder their numbers from the stairs."

"We'll go about halfway up and hug the wall," Carmen added. "You and your brother can sneak up and check it out. Let us know if you're going to pull then haul ass down and get behind us."

"Sounds like a plan," Greg chimed in, feeling a little left out without any combat capabilities. "I'd really like something to do."

The players all moved into position and Kurt crept toward the landing above leading to the next floor. Greg moved to the door and stopped. He waited as Kurt made his way up at a crawl. Pulling himself up into a crouch he angled so he could see in the door. A quick head count showed six targets moving around the room aimlessly. A couple of which were of a new type. He looked at their tags.

Wereflora | Level 3

Wereflora | Level 3

Wereflora | Level 4

Wereflora | Level 4

Florahound | Level 2

"Okay, what's the play Greg?" Kurt whispered to his brother.

"It's doable. I think you could pull this and get a single maybe a double with the way they are moving around. If you botch the shot you could end up getting the whole room."

"Will they see you if you fly in there?"

"They might but they also don't seem too smart. You probably have even odds on it."

"Only one way to find out. Let's see if you can fly around and mark a good target. If it's like other games your aggro shouldn't spread to us automatically so if they come after you fly out the window or something."

"Well if I do aggro they can't hurt me."

"Honestly that might be even better," Kurt thought aloud. "I could just peel one off of you then."

"True. I'm ready to try it if you are."

"Go for it." Kurt turned to the others and made a finger gun sign with his hand. It might not be standard operating procedure in this game but they got the idea. Greg flew into the room and zipped for one of the patrolling targets strafing it to test its reaction. It gave none. Kurt allowed a grin and readied his bow. He waited for his brother to settle on a target as the mobs moved about the room. Eventually one of the level fours moved away from the group and Greg settled on it.

"You're all clear," Greg shouted.

Kurt winced inwardly at the sound before remembering that he's the only one that heard. Taking aim he steadied his breath and let his shot fly. As soon as it left he knew it was going wide. With a grimace he backpedaled from the landing toward the steps as quickly and silently as possible. Before he turned he saw the arrow deflect off of the side of his target before clattering against the wall. Stepping down to the steps, he turned and ran. Bhae and Carmen grinned as he passed moving in lock step to close off the stairs.

Behind his tanks Kurt allowed himself to turn and see the results of his pull. To his surprise only one mob trundled down the stairs toward a waiting Bhae and Carmen. Heart pounding he drew his bow and watched the door for any additional mobs. No adds came, however, as the wereflora crashed into Bhae, who took the impact on her shield giving only a single step. Carmen followed on cue stabbing deep into the creature's side with her greatsword pinning it in place. The two took a couple minor shots but the fight was quickly over as Bhae repeatedly rained down blows with her battleaxe splintering her foe. Kurt stood dumbfounded.

"You ready for another?" Bhae asked, reaching down to loot the kill.

"Yeah. No problem," he answered, shaking his head.

Kurt crept back up to the landing and Greg flew back in to find a target. The five remaining mobs milled about the room. There wasn't a clear cut pull to get a single. Greg settled on one of the level threes next to a hound and Kurt signaled back with two fingers. Getting the thumbs up, he took aim. His shot found the mark this time striking the wereflora in its center of mass. It rocked back, stunned, before starting toward the door. To Kurt's dismay the hound had no hesitation. He turned to run but the hound was on him in an instant.

Armed with only his bow, he tried to bring it to bear only to eat the hound's pounce. The two tangled and rolled to the landing's edge. Kurt's bow fell free and tumbled to the ground below. He glanced to his health and noticed the attack had taken a small chunk but not anything too worrisome. Forcing his forearm into what he guessed passed for the creature's throat he held it back while a thorny maw snapped at his face. Razor sharp thorns dripped green spittle as the hound snapped just inches from him. Sneaking a glance at the coming wereflora, Kurt made the only decision he had readily available.

Holding tight Kurt thrust over with his hips and rolled. The next thing he knew they were in free fall. The florahound tried to kick free but Kurt held fast keeping the creature beneath him. In the next moment they landed and were jarred apart. Kurt's health bar dipped and he concentrated on it.

Health: 62/100

"You okay Turk?" Bhae called.

"I'm fine. You got incoming!"

Bhae and Carmen turned and set themselves as the wereflora moved down the steps. Kurt couldn't concern himself with them as he drew his dagger. The florahound looked to be in worse shape than him after the fall and Kurt meant to keep it that way. Charging in on the dazed creature he booted it in the head with all his strength. The plant canine hybrid flipped back onto its side. Pressing the advantage he slid into the beast and drove his dagger into its underbelly. He used his free hand to pin the hound while he sawed downward against the tender underside. He took a few more minor cuts but soon the fight was over.

You Have Slain - Florahound | Level 2

Kurt glanced at his health again and to his surprise another message scrolled on his bottom right as well.

"Looks like this one's yours too, Turk," Carmen called down from the stairs.

"Huh, how's that?" He asked, still a bit dazed.

"The game decides based on damage split and other factors who gets to loot kills when in a group," Bhae explained. "Your shot on the pull probably did most of the damage because it dropped easily once it got to us."

Kurt gathered his bow which looked no worse for wear. He also found and failed to harvest another Redtip Stranglevine before moving over to loot the two corpses. Bhae and Carmen took the opportunity to come down and take a breather as well. Carmen tossed up a group heal that topped everyone off as they sat at the base of the steps.

You Have Acquired - 2 Silver and 85 Copper

You Have Acquired - Large Sharp Thorn

You Have Acquired - 1 Silver and 6 Copper

You Have Acquired - Black Sparrow Thistle

You Have Acquired - Roughspun Cloth

"So how many are left?" Carmen asked.

"Just three left," Kurt said, rubbing his face. He wasn't sure he would ever get used to the intensity of the fights here. "There's a hound and two others."

"Sounds doable. What do you think Bhae?"

"We'd have more room to work off the stairs. The last pull didn't quite work out for Turk," her grin barely visible beneath her helm.

Greg laughed but thankfully only Kurt would hear it so he ignored his brother. "I'm fine with just pushing the room now. You two can hold your own one on one. I think if I take one of the wereflora I can stick and move. I'd rather not try my luck with the hound."

"Sounds good," Carmen decided. "You take the lower level one if there's a difference. Just kite it if you have to. Whoever finishes first will move on to your target."

"Hey Greg, stick to my target just in case something happens," Kurt whispered to his brother.

"Yeah sure. What you thinking?"

"Nothing in particular," Kurt shrugged. "I've just been under leveled the whole way. Better safe than sorry."

"No problem. Don't sweat the level thing," Greg encouraged him. "It's not as big of a deal as you think. You'll probably be level one for quite a while. Getting triumphs tends to take a while."

The group ascended the stairs without any attempt at stealth. Looking to Carmen, Kurt could tell by the way she carried herself that this was much more in line with how she played. After the first few steps the two fighters increased to a light jog in lock step. Carmen's boot falls announced their approach as Greg flew into the room to find his brother's wereflora. It probably wasn't the time to try a new tactic but Kurt couldn't help himself as he pulled the throwing knife from his belt.

"Awww yeah!" Carmen bellowed, hitting the room at a full sprint just ahead of Bhae.

Banging her shield with her axe Bhae split off just behind her seeking out the level four wereflora. Greg had found Kurt's target for him. As the battle erupted he let his throwing knife fly end over end smacking the creature with the flat of the blade. He would have to work on that, he realized, pulling his dagger from his belt. Charging forward Kurt launched himself into the air hitting the creature center of mass with a hard kick knocking it back. Chancing a look to Bhae he was happy to see a nod of approval.

When Kurt stole a glance at Carmen, he watched in awe as she drove her sword down the hound's gullet. Impaled to the hilt the creature tried to squirm backwards off of the blade when Carmen pulled the trigger on her sword ability or spell or whatever it was. A jet of yellow energy exploded from the backside of the creature rending it in two. Carmen took a boot to the creature's burnt husk and wrenched her blade free.

Kurt knew he had work to do. Turning his attention back his target, he could see that it had now recovered from his opening salvo. He stepped to the side as a thick vine crashed down where he had been standing a moment ago. Luckily speed was on his side as he slashed out at the appendage on its way by. Lashing out with his free arm, Kurt drove an elbow into the back of the monster's head taking advantage of the creature's own momentum. It seemed to do little damage but he had created enough space for a deep slash across its back. Kurt had taken his eye off the other vine arm for a split second and it nearly cost him. Bending at an impossible angle for a human the limb flailed backwards as Kurt instinctively brought his arms up in a block catching the brunt of the attack on his forearms. Points of health ticked off of his bar as Kurt was sent skidding backwards on his heels for a few feet.

It was all the opening Carmen needed as she brought her blade around in a sweeping strike, severing the extended appendage. Not to have his kill stolen Kurt drove in on the creature raising his left arm to block a possible blow while driving his dagger into the monster's neck. To his relief a retaliatory strike never came as the plant creature slumped over inert. A quick glance to Bhae told him that his was the last target to fall.

You Have Slain - Wereflora | Level 3

"Now come on Bhae, Carmen taunted. "You gotta admit that was much more satisfying."

"Girl had we tried that room like that, Turk wouldn't have made it and we both would need some healing. Ain't gonna hurt you to chill and think stuff out a bit."

"Whatever you say," Carmen chuckled looking at Kurt. "I'll remember your new lease on life next time you want to run duos. That is unless I'm out of a job."

"You're such a bitch sometimes," Bhae huffed, turning to look over the room.

Kurt decided this was a good time to mind his own business. He took a moment to find his throwing knife and he picked up his loot. After a moment the two fighters did the same.

You Have Acquired - 3 Silver and 4 Copper

Searching around the room Kurt found that there were two separate plants he could harvest. The first attempt was met with failure but to his satisfaction the second succeeded.

You Have Acquired - Redtip Stranglevine

"I told you this was going to be your type of game, bro. You're a natural," Greg said excitedly, finally turning his attention back to Kurt.

"I don't know about all that but this game is something else," Kurt admitted.

"Whatever dude. I don't know who you're trying to fool. This is why I got you in on this. Next you'll try and tell me you don't have those two on the hook."

"I think you watch a little too much TV, Greg."

"Hey what are you two talking about?" Carmen chided.

"Just about how my brother's crazy, Kurt answered, not exactly considering it a lie. "You ready to move on?"

"Waiting on you lowbie," she prodded.

Bhae punched Carmen but she didn't seem to notice. The vines had grown thicker on the walls of this room and another set of stairs took them higher up the tree. A mass of vines forced the door into a permanently open position. Moving to the landing revealed a room even more overgrown than the last. Moonlight struggled to peak through windows nearly completely occluded with fauna. Thick vines lay across the floor at random intervals threatening to trip up anyone foolish enough to enter carelessly. In the room center was a creature made entirely of writhing vines acting in concert. The beast was easily twice the size of anything they had encountered so far.

Enraged Thorn Hulk (Special) | Level 5

"Ooh, miniboss," Bhae cooed.

"Yeah that's more like it," Carmen agreed. "It's time to get some real loot."

"I don't suppose you two have a plan of attack," Kurt asked, already knowing the answer.

Carmen only shrugged, igniting her blade with brilliant white light. Bhae banged her axe against her shield slowly at first then increasing in volume and pace. Greg flew into the room toward the mini boss followed by Carmen and Bhae. Drawing his trusty dagger, Kurt decided to circle instead of rushing into the fray. He was glad he did. As the two fighters closed, the thorn hulk brought up a pair of limbs composed of twisted vines. Each appendage was easily as big around as any of the players. In unison Bhae and Carmen blocked and were driven down to a knee stopping their assault cold. Now that the thorn hulk was engaged small finger like vines sprouted from the floor straining to grasp at each of the players. With the fighters being forced down they became more susceptible to this aspect of the fight as vines stretched for arms and waists.

Warmth flowed down Kurt's arm and he continued to strafe around the room. Vines snaked around his ankles but slipped away as he moved angling for the back of the boss. The beast failed to notice him as it rained heavy blows on the defending fighters. Thinking for a moment Kurt decided to focus on Carmen and Bhae as if they were items or mobs. He was not disappointed

| Bhae | Health: 94% | Mana: 100% |
| Carmen | Health: 81% | Mana: 83% |

Once in position Greg brought his dagger up and something new happened. Faintly at first a bit of orange light ebbed in and out on the monster's back. It was dim and barely noticeable but in the low light of the room he could now see it. He focused on the area and saw a pattern. The light was a partial circle growing smaller and larger. With the way the game had used light to guide him in his knowledge skills he guessed it was some kind of target. He jammed his blade into the thorn hulk's back. A notification scrolled.

You Have Achieved - Novice Tactics - Level 0

He hadn't been notified for gaining a Level 0 skill before but he had not discovered one outside of a quest. The mini boss reminded him it wasn't really the time to mull over it when a vine shot out launching him across the room taking a chunk of his health. The strike did the trick though as the other party members took advantage of his momentary distraction. Bhae was able to center up the creature and take his full attention alternating shield bashes and flurries of axe strikes. She took her own hits but now her fight was on more favorable terms.

Meanwhile Carmen charged up her greatsword ducking in and out of melee range dropping chunk shots with her empowered strikes. Kurt shook off the shock of the hit and reentered the fight. A thick appendage whipped out but Kurt rolled to the side. Knowing another attack was coming he darted forward for a low slash at the monster's legs. The hit was shallow and he was forced to dodge to the side to move out of range. The ensuing strike cracked the floor sending small fissures out in all directions but did no damage. Carmen followed Kurt's attack attempting to cleave through the extended arm. The attack was effective but failed in its intent. Both of the thorn hulk's arms unraveled abruptly.

"Shit get back!" Bhae screamed. "It's going to…"

Abruptly the unraveling vines pinwheeled lashing out in all directions. Bhae and Carmen took the brunt of the punishment while Kurt only took a glancing blow. The force was immense though throwing the players to all sides of the room. Once the space had been cleared, Kurt watched in horror as the monster rooted all of his vines into the ground and glowing green energy seeped upward into its body. Seeing a large chunk of his own health gone Kurt checked for an exact number.

Health: 26/100

It wasn't good. Bhae was the first to her feet charging in with a

140

shield slam. The attack seemed to interrupt the boss's regeneration. Carmen did not waste a moment charging her sword and dashing forward for a big attack. Sweeping her blade before she reached the target sent an arch of energy ahead buffeting the rooted vines. Her follow up sweep severed several of them. Meanwhile Bhae resumed her axe flurry while peppering in shield slams to interrupt what healing she could. The combinations looked like what he would expect out of a dual wielding pvper rather than a traditional tank.

"He's low, let's get this!" shouted Bhae.

Low on health himself, Kurt was hesitant to rejoin the fray but the opening was there. Bhae had the boss turned away from him. Letting out an exasperated breath, he ran forward pulling out both of his blades. Warmth seeped down his arm again as vines reached up to grab him. Within a few feet the orange light dimly showed guiding his strike. He thrust his dagger into the hilt. Immediately he followed up with the throwing knife right beside it. The thorn hulk spun flinging Kurt free, disarming him. He braced for the coming strike when Bhae dropped her shield switching to a two handed grip on her battle axe. With a single strike she severed the monster's leg dropping it onto its side. Her follow up beheaded the creature lodging her axe into the floor.

You Have Slain - Enraged Thorn Hulk (Special) | Level 5

A new prompt filled Kurt's screen and a smile crept across his face.

Roll For Loot (Need) - ??? Short Sword
    Roll   Pass

"Pass," Carmen said dismissively.

141

"Pass," Bhae answered.

"You gotta need that shit bro!" Greg squealed in an excited voice. He bounced around the room like a five year old who had just chugged a Mountain Dew.

"Dude take it easy." Kurt focused on the "Need" command.

You Have Acquired - ??? Short Sword
You Have Acquired - 6 Silver and 18 Copper
You Have Acquired - Large Sharp Thorn x4
You Have Acquired - Black Sparrow Thistle x2

"Grats Turk," Carmen said.

"Yeah grats," Bhae smiled. "It should be an upgrade. Hopefully it works for your build."

Kurt tried to move the sword to his belt but whenever he tried it simply moved back into his inventory. Greg saw his confusion.

"You're not going to be able to use it until you get it identified," Greg informed him.

He stopped trying to put on his belt and deflated a bit. He would need to find another place to get identified and he would need to raise some more funds. A wave of refreshing energy washed over him and his health refilled most of the way. After a moment Carmen cast another spell filling his health the rest of the way before sitting on the ground.

"I'm going to need a couple minutes," Carmen explained. "My mana is about tapped."

"Either of you have the identify spell?" Kurt asked as he joined the other two on the ground.

"Nope. I only have a couple attacks and the group heal," Carmen shrugged before taking a chance to poke at her friend. "Bhae doesn't have

142

any spell abilities because she's too good for running story."

"I've lost enough characters on the main storyline," she explained. "I'd rather stick to PVP and not start over after months of work. Besides on my last reroll I got an affinity that makes running it pointless."

"The spell is kinda rare," Greg explained. "A lot of spells and abilities come from choices in the main storyline but other stuff comes from drops. Most of the rare or really useful spells are like that. There are NPCs that can identify stuff if you have enough reputation with their faction."

"So how far into this dungeon are we?" Kurt asked, changing the subject.

"Well the miniboss is halfway. It's hard to say what exactly we'll run into because all of the tree dungeons in Ullanore are randomly generated. There is a whole city of them but each one can only be run once. It's kinda in line with DO's evolving world philosophy. You'll see what I mean once we clear this one," Bhae added.

"We haven't gotten a great layout so far," Carmen complained. "It's been pretty linear without any chests or decent drops. The boss will have some gear but typically these are a little more lucrative than what you're seeing."

"We still have half the dungeon left," Bhae added. "I'm not ready to write it off just yet."

The two bickered back and forth as Kurt got up and walked the room. He hadn't noticed it during the fight but there were a lot of harvestable materials here. Once Greg noticed what he was doing he began a search as well in the low light. He failed a number of times but when the room was cleared he had a handful of herbs to add to his supply.

You Have Acquired - Black Sparrow Thistle x3

You Have Acquired - Redtip Stranglevine
You Have Acquired - Walking Grass x4

The walking grass was new and he'd failed a number of times trying to harvest it. It's mechanic in the fight was straight forward enough as it helped slow player movement. He inspected it to get a better idea of what it was about.

Walking Grass

Uses: Alchemy

Quality: Subpar

Requirements: Novice Herbalism

Kurt shrugged. Maybe once he improved his herbalism he could get more information on what he was harvesting. Either way he'd hoped they would sell. With his work done the two fighters rose to their feet and checked their gear before proceeding.

"So is the only way to get mana back to rest?" Kurt asked not really having experience with casting yet.

"Nah. You can eat food to speed up the process or use potions," Carmen explained. "I have some mana regen gear so I don't waste slots on food. No need to burn potions outside of combat."

"Sounds like pretty standard MMO stuff," Kurt ventured.

"Yeah it's not all that different from the non immersive games," Carmen agreed.

The group pushed up another flight of stairs to a doorway covered in thick thorny vines. Bhae made short work of the obstacle with her axe cutting a path to the next room. Stepping into the room Carmen was met by a cloud of yellow dust that ballooned out onto the landing. Kurt slipped

144

back down a few steps to avoid the area of the attack. Bhae must have had the same idea as she nearly ran into him falling back.

"What was that?" Kurt shouted.

"Spore pod," Bhae said through gritted teeth. " A couple different mobs launch them."

"What about Carmen?" he asked.

"She's probably fine. I'm not sure what kind of effects that cloud has but we need to push the door. Once we regroup we'll be able to see what we're dealing with."

"Let's go," Kurt said, shaking his head in agreement.

Bhae led the way, shield up in front of her. Another pod launched immediately which she batted away with her shield before it exploded. Carmen was not far ahead surrounded by spider like plants that seemed content to try and wear her down before committing to a direct attack. Kurt pushed in behind her and took a quick assessment.

Flora Pollenator | Level 5
Flora Pollenator | Level 5
Flora Pollenator | Level 5

There were only three of them but they were all the same level as Carmen. A quick glance told him she had already lost over a quarter of her health. Bhae sprang into action engaging the closest one severing a limb in the process. It took a moment but Kurt switched back to his bow. With the fighters taking damage like they were, he knew standing in melee was a lost cause. He concentrated on Bhae's target, firing off two arrows in quick succession. The first sailed wide shattering on the wall across the room but the second stuck in the plant's bulbous abdomen.

One of Carmen's targets launched another spore pod in Kurt and

Bhae's direction. Unceremoniously Kurt threw himself to the side to avoid the explosion. Bhae was not so lucky. The initial burst hit her for about ten percent of her health but standing in the cloud was also steadily ticking at her hit points. Unlike the previous mobs these appeared to be using tactics. Everytime Bhae tried to exit the zone, the spider she was fighting did something to redirect her back in. He fired two more arrows in the hopes of creating some sort of opening for her. Thankfully this time both shots found the mark.

Kurt had been too focused on Bhae's target. He didn't notice the pod until it landed. The blast flung him onto his back knocking the wind from him. Involuntarily he inhaled and immediately started coughing. It didn't hurt per say but he was definitely uncomfortable. A look to his health bar told him why.

Health: 47/100

The red of his health still ticked away in chunks as he lay there. A hand firmly grabbed his collar and pulled him back out of the yellow cloud. Still seated he looked on as Bhae joined Carmen's fight. Both of her targets were still up but had taken significant damage. Once the numbers were even the two women made quick work of the remaining mobs. Kurt couldn't do much but sit dumbfounded for the moment. He wasn't injured or in pain but he was just stunned.

"Hey you okay, Turk?" Bhae called over to him. "You took a big shot there."

"Yeah I think so. My head is a little foggy still. Wasn't really expecting that."

"That's the stun effect," Carmen explained. "Those spore pods are nasty. At your level resisting the stun isn't going to happen so you get stuck in the dot. It might not one shot you but it'll leave you in a bad way." Carmen refilled the group's health with a couple quick spells casts. "Looks like we get more adventures in sitting everyone."

"Yo Kurt check this out," Greg called. "There's something covered by the vines. I don't want to get anyone's hopes up but it's probably a chest."

Kurt walked over to the spot where Greg hovered. He was right there was an oddly shaped pile of vines growing over something. Drawing his dagger, Kurt lifted the first vine he could find with some slack and cut it free. Continuing to cut vines away one by one, he was soon joined by Bhae.

"Find something?" she asked curiously.

"I'm not sure," he replied. "Greg thought there might be a chest under here so I thought I'd check it out while Carmen regened."

Bhae lifted pieces up so Kurt could cut them more easily. Removing more vines revealed the top of an old iron bound chest. Carmen joined them and soon they had cleared enough to try it. To everyone's disappointment the lid was locked.

"You wouldn't happen to have lockpicking would you, Turk?" Carmen asked.

"Nope," Kurt shrugged.

"Either of you come across any keys?" Carmen continued unperturbed.

"No," Bhae and Kurt answered in unison.

"Damn. Looks like we'll have to break it," Carmen grumbled.

"You know we'll lose half the loot doing that Carmen," Bhae said, equally upset.

"We really don't have another option. You want to do it or should I?"

"I'll try it," Bhae sighed.

147

Kurt stepped back as Bhae drew her axe in two hands. The chest's lock was inset into its front so there was no way to simply knock it off the chest. She brought the weapon down on the corner of the lid with a loud crack. Carmen winced at the noise and looked at a sheepish Bhae. Reluctantly she struck the chest again and it disintegrated before them. There was a moment of apprehension and a prompt appeared on everyone's screen.

Roll For Loot (Need) - ??? Gauntlets
       Pass

The "Need" option was missing from his prompt but that made sense considering the way Carmen explained things before they entered. He concentrated on the "Pass" option and looked to the others.

"Pass," Bhae said.

"You know I'm going to roll the dice on this one," Carmen said thoughtfully. "I've been looking for a glove upgrade for a while."

"I passed," Kurt added.

Carmen nearly jumped with excitement as the piece of gear entered her inventory. Once the moment passed Bhae went back through the remains of the chest.

"Looks like we have some broken glass and something that was made out of metal. None of that is lootable. There is some money and some roughspun. Mind if I give the cloth to Turk?"

"Nah I'm not using it," Carmen said absently.

"Sounds good," she replied, handing the others each a small cloth sack.

You Have Acquired - 4 Silver and 22 Copper

Having found a secret chest the group combed over the rest of the room searching for anything of value. Vegetation covered nearly every surface but there was nothing Kurt could attempt to harvest. The room layouts were all pretty similar Kurt had noticed. Except for the one room they had to bypass along the outside of the tree, each floor had only a large single room and a set of stairs leading up. Plant growth had long since overtaken any distinguishing features that would have given a clue as to what they had been used for previously. Once the others decided the room was equally picked over they looked to move on.

The stairs leading up were a bit more treacherous with the increased plant growth. Carmen and Bhae seemed undaunted by this fact. Kurt on the other hand drew his bow and picked his way through the obstacle more carefully. It was for this reason that he was still a handful of steps from the landing when Carmen kicked in the door.

"Didn't they bring you along to pull?" Greg asked in an attempt to be funny.

"Hell if I know Greg," he rasped, sprinting for the top of the stairs. Carmen and Bhae were already through the door when Kurt reached the landing. The scene was chaotic as Bhae and Carmen tried to hack their way through a large pack of florahounds.

Florahound | Level 3

Florahound | Level 3

Florahound | Level 3

Florahound | Level 3

Florahound | Level 3

Florahound | Level 3

They were only level three but Kurt blanched as he counted up eight of them. Even worse they seemed to be making coordinated attacks darting in and out of the fighter's range. Any one of the monsters wouldn't have been an issue but their speed combined with their numbers threatened to wear down the two women if Kurt didn't act. He had an arrow ready but getting a clean shot was proving difficult.

"Hey Bhae can you get me a shot?" Kurt called out.

"Yeah just be ready!" the warrior answered, already attempting to turn her target.

Florahounds darted in and out at Bhae while she waited for an opportunity. It wasn't long before it came. One of the hounds leaped while she ducked low. In one fluid movement she thrust her shield under the monster and used its momentum to hoist it into the air. Raising the creature overhead she opened it up for Kurt. It was all the signal he needed.

Releasing his first shot Kurt didn't even wait for it to land before drawing a second arrow. Bhae turned slightly, presenting more of the creature to Kurt as a target. His second shot found the mark while he pulled a third arrow. When one of the other mobs lunged in Bhae slammed the wounded creature down onto the would be attacker. The two thrashed in a tangle at Bhae's feet and threatened to knock her down. Kurt fired his third arrow into the melee hitting one of them.

Carmen had taken a few hits from the four she was currently facing down. All of them were injured to some degree thanks to a series of powered and unpowered sweeping strikes. Her long greatsword often found more than one foe on a single attack but the rapid succession of attacks was taking its toll. She looked over to see Bhae drive her axe down through the head of one of the hounds while Kurt put arrows into two that were fighting each other. Not to be out done Carmen found a target that appeared to be struggling and pressed the attack.

Kurt drew and fired another arrow. Carmen savagely hacked at her wounded foe before letting out a primal scream. As her quarry fell she was swarmed under by the other three hounds. He almost didn't notice the notification in the confusion.

You Have Slain - Florahound | Level 3

Kurt wanted to shout to her but had problems of his own as he instinctively rolled backwards to avoid the leaping mob. Having killed one of the fighting pair, Kurt must have been the next one on this hound's aggro list. He swung feebly with his bow as he tried to create some space and find time to think. In frustration he kicked the flora hound in the side and was rewarded with a clamping bite on his calf. Abruptly his leg was pulled out from under him and Kurt found himself staring up at a menacing creature getting ready to stand on his chest.

The fight was turning south and Bhae knew it. Both of her teammates were down and wouldn't last much longer unless she acted now. Launching into a combo of axe and shield strikes. She walked the hound back to create space chipping away at its health. It only took a moment for her opportunity to emerge as it lunged at her desperately. Allowing the creature's momentum to carry it by her she swung down hard with her axe severing its head. Raising her shield she wasted no more time and broke into a sprint.

Kurt was freed abruptly as Bhae strafed the florahound that had him pinned. Her shield bash did minimal damage as she delivered only a glancing blow on her way by but it was enough to free him. Dropping his bow Kurt pulled his dagger free and rolled. The monster landed heavily beside him and Kurt slashed outward catching its flank. Rearing up in pain the hound attempted to pounce again. Kurt was ready this time drawing his throwing knife from his belt and driving it through the creature's back paw into the ground. In the confusion the monster turned to try and free itself. Kurt didn't even need to see the orange glow on the side of its neck to know it was a weak point.

You Have Slain - Florahound | *Level 3*

Carmen's armor was protecting her from the worst of the attacks as she tried to free herself from the three trash mobs. With her hit points being chipped away, she tried to bring her sword to bear with little effect. Two of the three hounds snapped at her face while the third chewed on her grieves. Dropping the weapon she reached out with both hands grabbing a hound in each by the throat. She squeezed for all she was worth letting loose a gutteral snarl as she pulled them in. To her surprise the weight on her legs was ripped away. Carmen tried to use her legs to leverage herself and up end the two remaining hounds. With a metallic crash she was forced back down onto her back by the mobs combined weight and something else.

Kurt fell onto one of the florahounds that Carmen had grappled. With the target otherwise occupied he was more than happy to mount its back and stab wildly with both hands. Some cuts were only shallow while others sank deep biting into vital parts of the monster. The mob thrashed wildly once he had its attention but Kurt clamped down hard with his knees. He felt the air pushed out of his lungs as the florahound rolled to dislodge him. Driving his throwing knife in he used it as a hand hold while sawing a large gash with his dagger. As quickly as it began the fight was over.

You Have Slain - Florahound | Level 3

Forcing the corpse off of him Kurt emerged just in time to see Carmen rend the last hound in two. Both of the fighter's looked like they'd been put through the ringer. Carmen's plate was covered with blood and green ichor while Bhae's hides were dark and matted. Both just sat for a moment breathing heavily. Kurt decided to just walk around the room for a moment and loot his kills.

You Have Acquired - 2 Silver and 2 Copper
You Have Acquired - Large Sharp Thorn
You Have Acquired - 1 Silver and 37 Copper
You Have Acquired - Large Sharp Thorn
You Have Acquired - Black Sparrow Thistle
You Have Acquired - 1 Silver and 62 Copper
You Have Acquired - Roughspun Cloth

A wash of healing swept over him sending a small amount of exhilaration to race down his spine. Bhae was finishing looting while Carmen sat back on the floor. She was apparently looking at some menu as she stared into space. After a moment she snapped back into focus on the rest of the group.

"I'm tapped on mana. I had to use quite a bit there so we're going to need to take a time out before the boss room."

"That's fine," Bhae added. "I need to go through some of this stuff anyway."

Kurt took the opportunity to bring up his inventory and he quickly

153

dismissed it as his entire character sheet covered his view. Last time he had opened it there was a lot less to it. Now looking at it blocked his view of everything around him.

"Hey is there a way to make your inventory not cover your entire view?" Kurt asked the others.

"What setup are you using?" Bhae asked.

"Combined view."

"Eww gross," Carmen chimed in.

"Come on now wait a second," Greg whined.

"What's wrong with Combined View?" Kurt asked, honestly curious.

"Well it's kinda a beginner's option," Bhae explained. "It just throws all your information out there at you and it gets really cluttered. DO is really intuitive. You should tell it to enable custom view. Giving mental commands with this will let you just pull up the things you want to look at."

"Yeah I got rid of the icons altogether," Carmen added.

"I've never even heard of that," Greg said dumbfounded.

"Enable Custom View," Kurt commanded. Immediately he heard a chime and received confirmation of his action. "Okay now what?"

"Now just give a mental command for what you want to see," Bhae instructed.

Kurt thought about his inventory for a moment and a listing came up.

Starter Backpack (12/20)
Wallet

    0 (G)   33 (S) 84 (C)

Dwarven Dowsing Rod

Portable Copper Mining Pick

Roughspun Cloth x5

Rough-spun Bandages

Broken Wolf Claw

Slab of Wolf Meat

Black Sparrow Thistle x10

Large Sharp Thorn x8

Antique Pocket Watch

Redtip Stranglevine x2

??? Short Sword

Walking Grass x4

"Okay that worked. It's much more manageable just looking at my inventory."

"That's only the start, Carmen explained. "You can also do things like increase window and text size. Transparency is also an option and on things like your inventory and quest log. You can also reorder pretty much any of the menus."

Kurt played with the options a bit making the window and text more transparent with a thought. His main curiosity was how much money he'd earned so far which was coming right along. Playing with the UI options was definitely going to be a priority in the future. He dismissed the menu after a couple minutes of examining the items he'd acquired. He could have fallen down a deep hole with his new way of interacting with the game. The sounds of Bhae and Carmen rising up jarred him back to the fact they were still in a dungeon.

"Alright, people boss is up next.," Carmen announced, rubbing her hands together eagerly.

"I thought the dungeon was random." Kurt looked for some kind of sign but saw nothing different from the previous rooms they had explored to this point.

"The tree dungeons in Ullanore are randomized but they are predictable," Bhae explained. "You get a miniboss halfway up. The length of the dungeons varies but once you get that you know how far you have to go."

"Makes sense," Kurt admitted.

'So yeah make sure you have your gear ready," Bhae instructed, "You'll probably want to start out at range until we see what we're dealing with."

Readying their weapons the group ascended the final set of stairs. Very little of the original tree was visible at this point. Every surface was covered by invasive vines and plant growth. Moonlight struggled to seep in through the few remaining windows that were uncovered. Once they reached the halfway point up to the final floor, the darkness had forced Carmen to light her sword. Writhing vines hung from above impeding their path but Bhae took to hacking through them with her axe cutting a path that forced them into a single file. They reached the landing and a doorway into a pitch black room.

"Greg go have a look around," Kurt said, pointing into the darkness.

Carmen nodded to Kurt as the wisp flew in and made a pass around the room. What little light he gave off showed very little but the group saw nothing in the way of movement. Greg circled back and took another route around the room. The three players searched again but nothing seemed to be moving amongst the overgrowth common to the dungeon. With his circuit complete Greg joined the others on the landing.

"I didn't really see anything in there, the wisp admitted. "Lots of vines but that's about it."

"Yeah man that's about what we saw from out here," Kurt frowned.

"You run anything like this out here Carmen?" Bhae asked, trying to peer into the seemingly empty room.

"No, I haven't had a boss room like this yet, she answered a little frustrated. "Looks like it's supposed to be a blind fight of some kind. Maybe an invisible boss?"

"Doesn't really fit with the theme," Bhae speculated.

"Maybe a boss that teleports in somehow?" Kurt ventured.

"Could be. I don't think we're going to get a chance to scout it," Bhae added. "We're just going to have to roll with this one."

"Sounds good. Turk, get that bow ready," Carmen said taking charge. "You should probably hang near the door until we have a solid target. Can your brother mark targets?"

"Yeah I got it," Greg answered easily.

"He says he's got it," Kurt repeated to the group.

"Alright. Follow my lead," Carmen directed.

Carmen moved quickly to the center of the boss room taking up a defensive stance. Holding her blade out in front of her she did her best to illuminate what she could. Bhae moved in quickly behind her, surveying the room for possible threats. As Kurt stepped in he noticed something move behind him. Spinning back toward the door he groaned as vines grew in to block their escape. Greg flew in circles around the room steadily climbing until he stopped abruptly.

"Yo Kurt the boss isn't in the room. It is the room," he shouted as he floated next to a large bulbous shape hanging from the ceiling.

"Everyone look up!" Kurt shouted just in time to see the large shape open to reveal two rows of teeth. Slowly the van sized creature lowered itself down to about ten feet above the party in the center of the room. With the light from Carmen's blade giving them a better look at the monster, Kurt read its tag.

"Turk, open up on it!" Carmen shouted as she leapt upward trying to make solid contact with her sword. Bhae followed suit as the pair of fighters managed only glancing blows. Greg began flying a path around the face of the creature illuminating it further. It was all he needed as he fired off three arrows in succession. Each found the mark but it was no difficult feat. While they each sunk in they appeared to do minimal damage and did not even draw the boss' attention.

There was a moment when the group wondered if they were missing something when thorny vines sprang up from the ground all around them. Kurt stumbled forward as pressure erupted up and down his back from a lash while a small chunk of health disappeared from his bar. As alarming as that was Kurt couldn't help but panic as both Carmen and Bhae were cut off from him by at least another dozen vines that thrashed about the room chaotically.

Attentions turned to the more immediate threat, Kurt realized Carmen and Bhae would not be helping with the main boss for a while. Sliding into a relatively open area, he fired off back to back shots into the main creature again. Knowing he was running low on arrows he concentrated on the fact and a counter appeared in his peripheral vision. The UI really was intuitive, he thought, as he noticed he only had twelve arrows remaining. Vines snaked their way to his location and he was on the move again.

Bhae did her best to cover Carmen's back while she used her greatsword to cleave through multiple vines at once. She would create enough space to take a shot at the boss high over head only to get forced into clearing more vines. While the vines did not have enough hit points to stay up for long their sheer numbers did enough to keep Bhae and Carmen from joining the fight in earnest.

Moving to another open area Kurt hit with two more shots. As he watched his ammo dwindle to ten he noticed that along the outside of the room the vines seemed to be slower and fewer in number. It was almost as if defending against ranged attacks was an afterthought. He moved again around the outside of the room making little effort to disguise his intent before stopping to fire off another two arrows. He was down to eight remaining with the two hits. Something wasn't right about it though. This was too easy.

The two fighters traded roles with Carmen clearing space using her long sweeping strikes. Bhae put away her shield favoring the two handed grip on her axe. When openings allowed, she attacked the creature's main body and head dealing what damage she could. With the creature hanging so high overhead none of the damage being done was very substantial. At this rate they would slowly wipe, she knew. Holding her axe in two hands Bhae hurled the weapon with all her might at the most damaged section she could find.

The stranglevine monstrosity shook violently rocking the entire room. Kurt fell to a knee and was struck from behind knocking him prone. The sound of clattering metal echoed from around the room while cracking wood and guttural howls added to a din that threatened to drown out the party. Pressure between his shoulder blades told him he'd taken a wound. Kurt looked to his health bar to see just what kind of damage he was looking at.

Health: 72/100

"Greg get us a look around the room!" Carmen commanded still fighting vines in the center of the room. The wisp did a quick sweep of the room and to everyone's dread they now saw the number of vines in the room had doubled. Now instead of vines just sprouting from the floor vines were detaching from the walls firing off at different angles to bludgeon the players. With a larger group this probably kept ranged players from getting too comfortable on the outside. As Greg flew by something glinted amongst the vines.

"Hey I think we've got something over here," Kurt shouted dodging amongst the swinging vines. Carmen and Bhae began clearing a path toward him as he searched the undergrowth. Seeing the group moving to a single location, Greg hovered above Kurt. With the light it didn't take long for him to find what had caught his eye.

Elven Long Spear

Damage: 6-12

Quality: Fine

Requirements: Instance Item

"Hey Bhae, head's up," Kurt shouted, tossing her the spear haft first. "Looks like we have a fight mechanic."

"Aww yeah," Bhae grinned, testing the spear's weight.

"Greg see if you can find anymore, Kurt yelled hopefully. "I think I heard more fall when the phase changed."

"Look out!" Carmen yelled cleaving through a vine that was meant for Kurt. " Stay close until we can get you a weapon."

The group followed after Greg while Carmen cut a path. Before long he was hovering over another item. It wasn't quite the same and Kurt inspected it.

Elven Steel Javelin

Damage: 4-9

Quality: Fine

Requirements: Instance Item

Kurt picked it up as they made their way around the room. Bhae's spear wasn't overly effective against the vines but combined with her shield they did well enough keeping them at bay. Carmen continued to cleave them down with relative ease alternating powered strikes with regular ones. Bhae and Kurt split another five javelins amongst themselves. Carmen's greatsword was easily the most lethal weapon they had in this fight so she declined to switch it out. Kurt found another longspear for himself as well.

"I'll keep the vines down," Carmen organized them moving back to the center of the room. "You two alternate spear attacks. Greg head up there and give them something to hit!"

"You got first attack, Bhae!" Kurt swung the spear in a long arc pushing back vines opposite Carmen. Bhae drove her spear up into the monstrosity's bulbous head letting loose a spray of green fluid dousing the party. Carmen rotated to Kurt's side to bring down the vines he'd been keeping at bay. Kurt rotated to Bhae's position and began his attacks on the main boss while Bhae picked up the vines filling in where Carmen thinned the vines. They kept the rotation going for a couple rounds dealing significant damage. Before long the boss thrashed wildly before pulling itself upward toward the ceiling. The room shook again as the creature evaded the group.

"Looks like a phase change," Bhae announced bringing up her spear to fend off the whipping vines. The three players faced outward from each other rotating and bringing the vines down to clear a path. Bhae and Carmen were knocked to the ground by two large vines extending down from the main body. Each was nearly as big around as the players and acted as a kind of arm for the creature. Violently the monstrosity swatted downward shaking the floor with each impact rending large furrows with its attached thorns.

Attacking the main body was nearly impossible now that it had moved out of range. Ranged attacks were even difficult to set up with the constant attacks coming from all sides. Carmen went back to work clearing the regular vines while Bhae did her best to help with the spear. The battle was turning into a stalemate they would ultimately lose if they didn't think of something. One of the larger appendages came down toward Kurt while he narrowly stepped away. When it slammed into the floor it hung there for a second before ascending again. It gave him an idea.

"Greg call those out to me! Carmen on my target when I signal," Kurt ordered taking charge of the fight.

The encounter continued with the group keeping the room's center clear. Kurt bided his time waiting for another big strike from above. It wasn't long before his brother called out.

"One behind, bro!"

Kurt spun away as the strike came cracking the timber floor. Without hesitation Kurt speared the limb with a two handed strike burying the spearhead as deeply as possible.

"Now Carmen!" Kurt screamed, getting the warrior's attention.

Seeing what Kurt had planned, Carmen unloaded with a powered strike cleaving a chunk from the vine. Wrenching upward the monstrosity's appendage came free nearly pulling the longspear from Kurt's hand. It whipped around clumsily trying to catch one of the players but was easily avoided.

"One on Bhae!" Greg called.

"Bhae look out!" Kurt echoed.

Bhae turned and speared her target in the same manner Kurt just had and Carmen followed suit delivering another powered strike slicing more from the other limb. Greg called out again and the limb came down on Kurt's right. He speared his target again but Carmen couldn't make the rotation. As the vine retracted Kurt was lifted from the ground and thrown fifteen feet in the air before he was able to pull his spear free. Landing hard outside their center circle the surrounding vines fell upon Kurt immediately taking chunks from his health. Having missed the rotation on Kurt's side, he watched Carmen return to Bhae's side for the next vine attack. Bhae stabbed and Carmen sliced shearing the appendage in two.

"Carmen, get to Turk!" Bhae called, turning to his side of the circle.

"On it," Carmen answered, already moving at a run.

Kurt took another hit as he struggled to his feet. Points of pressure radiated throughout his body telling him he'd taken more than a few wounds. Carmen was cutting her way toward him but he had clear the immediate area. Striking out with his spear like a quarterstaff he beat at the encroaching plants. Those that snaked for him on the ground he stomped on while doing his best just to move toward Carmen. She was only a few feet away when the appendage struck while Bhae turned and speared it.

"Get to Bhae now!" Kurt shouted.

Carmen turned and ran back toward the speared vine. Bhae was being lifted from the ground when Carmen unleashed a slash of energy from her sword bisecting the vine just over her head. Green fluid sprayed over the immediate area and the room began to shake again. Following suit Kurt charged through the last few feet of vines taking hits on his way by. His health bar flashed red and he brought up more detail.

Health: 13/100

"Got any more of those heals, Carmen?"

"Hang on Turk," she pleaded. "My Mana is tapped right now."

"Cover me then," he shouted searching for a semi clear area.

Kurt bent down and got into his pack. He only had one bandage ready so he had to make it count. The two maimed appendages flailed overhead as the room shook again. Kurt applied the bandage while Carmen and Bhae cleared the circle around him. Wrapping the wounds seemed to take an eternity while every vine in the room came to life at once. He looked at his health bar one last time just as he finished the process.

Health: 29/100

The stranglevine monstrosity lurched down enveloping Carmen before returning to its place above them. In an instant without the light of her blade the room was returned to complete darkness outside of Greg flying high overhead. Kurt looked to her portrait on the party interface only to see her information greyed out.

"Greg get down here so Bhae can see what she's swinging at!" Kurt screamed. "We gotta drop this thing now."

"Damn it," she returned swinging wildly. "How are we going to finish this thing?"

"Bhae don't freak out about what I do next."

"What?" she yelled, obviously confused.

Greg had just arrived giving Bhae enough light to hit the vines immediately in front of her. Wasting now more time Kurt activated his shadow sight casting the world into brilliant but muted detail. The monochromatic purple hue gave the monstrosity a sinister look but at least he could target the creature now. It's bulbous jaws churned from side to side occupied with its first kill. Dropping the longspear, Kurt opted for one

164

of the javelins from his bag and let it fly. The effect was immediate on impact as the boss swung from side to side and made his way toward Kurt. Without thinking he launched another one driving it even further into the beast causing it to retreat.

"What the hell are those glowing eyes?" Bhae shouted.

"Don't worry it's just a power I picked up. Toss your javelins on the ground quick!"

Confused, Bhae obliged taking a hit in the process. Kurt threw the last from his bag only to see it glance harmlessly off while the monster bobbed from side to side. Picking up his longspear Kurt crouched and prepared for the next coming strike. On cue the monstrosity dove in on him. Thrusting upward drove the longspear deep into the creature's flesh. Having learned his lesson Kurt released his grip on the weapon as the boss jerked upwards retreating into the darkness.

"Keep it up Bhae," Kurt encouraged moving over to the javelins she'd dropped for him. "I just need a little more time to hit this thing."

"When this is over we need to talk about what you got going on there," Bhae chided looking a little more confident.

"Sure just as soon as you explain why you aren't lighting this thing up with some magic like everyone else in this game."

"Let's make it through this fight first," Bhae laughed as she knocked back more vines.

Kurt picked up a javelin and made another attack. Reeling in pain the boss slammed into the side of the room throwing Kurt to the ground. Listing heavily from the impact the stranglevine monstrosity struggled to reach the players in the center of the room. A point on the creature's side pulsed and bubbled glowing faintly. Kurt dismissed his shadow sight as the point grew larger and brighter before erupting into a beam of light that lanced upward at an angle.

The monstrosity's corpse crashed to the floor a dozen feet away as the vines in the room collapsed inert at once. A glowing light emerged from the hole as a figure put on her helm just before her face came into view. A familiar silhouette stepped away from the gore holding her sword high illuminating the once dark room. Kurt concentrated on the party interface for confirmation anyway.

Bhae   Health: 28%   Mana: 100%

Carmen   Health: 17%   Mana: 4%

"I thought you died when your profile greyed out," Kurt blurted.

"Yeah it means that sometimes," Carmen explained. "When that thing tried to eat me I counted as out of range I think. You two were greyed out for me too."

Carmen reached down and activated the looting process. Immediately Kurt's vision was assaulted by prompts.

Roll For Loot (Need) - ??? Glaive

       Pass

Roll For Loot (Need) - ??? Headband

       Pass

Roll For Loot (Need) - Hearty Stranglevine

       Pass

Chapter 9

It got Kurt right in the feels to have to mentally click the pass button three times in a row. He could tell Bhae was considering things as she stared off into the distance. Carmen waited patiently being in the same boat as Kurt. They wouldn't know what their mundane share of the loot was until the higher priority items were distributed if it was anything like the miniboss had been earlier. Once she had made her decision a new prompt appeared.

Roll For Loot (Greed) - ??? Headband

    Roll   Pass

Kurt still did not have a head slot item so the choice was simple. He concentrated on the "Roll" option. A pair of ethereal dice materialized in front of him glowing a faint blue. Looking to the others he saw them all reach out and take them out of the air. Bhae and Carmen threw their dice forward almost in unison as Kurt scrambled to follow suit. Watching his own roll across the floor he thought they looked a bit generic compared to Carmen's glowing yellow dice and Bhae black steel dice. It was probably a cosmetic he could look into later. Another prompt appeared.

??? Headband - Roll Results

Bhae - 73%   Carmen - 26%   Turk - 4%

He wasn't necessarily sure if he needed to roll low or high on the dice but when Bhae pumped her fist he was pretty sure he lost the roll.

Roll For Loot (Greed) - Hearty Stranglevine

      Roll   Pass

Seeing the next prompt Kurt decided to roll again since it was an herb. If nothing else he might be able to sell it which was the whole point of a greed roll. Carmen looked to him as the dice materialized again with something similar in mind. They both let their dice throws fly.

Hearty Stranglevine - Roll Results

Carmen - 44%   Turk - 59%

You Have Acquired - Hearty Stranglevine

You Have Acquired - 24 Silver and 68 Copper

You Have Acquired - Redtip Stranglevine x6

You Have Acquired - Black Sparrow Thistle x2

Kurt's heart skipped a beat. He'd missed out on both pieces of unidentified gear but the silver was more than enough. Getting enough money for another identification spell had seemed like an impossible feat before the dungeon. There was no telling if the short sword would be worth using but even if it wasn't he should be able to sell it and make his money back. That on top of all the herbs he'd collected, Kurt thought he should have enough to start filling out some of his empty equipment slots. Maybe he could even look into an upgrade or two.

"Hey let's head up top and finish this one out," Bhae said, bringing him back to reality.

"What's up top?"

"There's a little place you can set up a camp," Carmen explained. "I can get some mana back and get us healed up. There's also a little thing that happens when you finish one of these dungeons."

Bhae led the way up one last flight of stairs. The landing above was covered by vines and overgrowth much like the rest of the dungeon. When they approached however the plants withered and fell away revealing a balcony extending out into the highest branches of the tree. Above them the clear night sky shown with starlight casting everything in a soft white glow. The railing at the balcony's edge appeared to be some sort of white stone that appeared to be grown and shaped from the tree itself rather than constructed. A small sitting area with a brazier and low benches sat center most in the space overlooking the city itself.

"Come on over and have a seat," Bhae said, waving him over to where Carmen was already lighting a fire.

"That was a pretty sweet dungeon," Greg beamed. "I didn't even know this place was out here. We'll have to come back and run one when I reroll."

"Sure but let's make sure we have a full group," Kurt agreed, already thinking about the next run. "That was a little close for me."

"We were fine," Carmen interrupted. "You didn't die did you?"

"No but I mean we barely got through it," Kurt protested weakly.

"But did you die?" Carmen teased. "What does your brother have to say about our run anyway? It's not really fair only getting one side of the conversation when you two are whispering to each other."

"He was just saying he hadn't run this one before and wants to come back."

"Well we haven't run that one before either, honestly," Bhae chimed in. "We won't be able to run that one again either. Once you complete a tree that one is done. There's a whole forest of them but each one is

169

different."

Colorful motes of light descended from the highest leaves while others flowed up and over the balcony. Waves of multicolored light flowed out from them and into the tree itself reviving it. The intrusive vines and plant life shriveled and dried sloughing off into the darkness below under the same illumination.

"What are those?" Kurt asked.

"I'm not sure," Bhae said while Carmen stoked the flame in the brazier. "They don't quite look like your brother the wisp. Maybe fairies or pixies?"

"Maybe you should help them out with that, Greg," Kurt laughed, sitting down next to the fire.

"Oh you're a funny guy, bro."

"If you have any food you can cook it on this," Carmen suggested as she pulled out some sort of uncooked bird setting it directly on the grating. "It'll be a few minutes before I have enough mana to get everyone back to full."

Remembering he had the wolf meat in his inventory, Kurt pulled it out and tossed it on the makeshift grill. He watched as Carmen sprinkled something on her meat. Turning to Bhae he noticed she was preparing something even more complicated for her meal.

"First time cooking?" Carmen asked.

"Yeah I haven't been to a trainer or anything," Kurt admitted. "I've cooked a bit in real life though."

"Put some of this on there," she said, handing him a small packet. "A lot of skills don't require a trainer. They just require you to get started."

You Have Acquired - Savory Spices

Kurt sprinkled the contents of the packet on the slab of wolf meat. He hadn't realized how hungry he was until the meat started cooking but now that he added the spices his mouth was absolutely watering. Bhae placed some kind of large banana stuffed and sealed back in its peel on the brazier. Carmen rolled her eyes when she saw it but Kurt really didn't know what to think. It smelled sweet but he wasn't sure what it was.

"Maybe I should let Chef Bhae tell you about cooking. She's the one out here flexing."

"Whatever Carmen. Using more than two ingredients hardly counts as flexing. If I were to flex on you, we'd have raid buffs for three hours. This is just having some taste."

Carmen just sat back and laughed while Bhae stuck out her tongue. Kurt pulled out his dagger and flipped the meat over. All in all it didn't look too bad to him. Carmen did the same and pointedly nodded in approval. After another couple minutes the meat looked done and he used his dagger to pull it up from the heat. The food disappeared and he saw two notifications scroll.

You Have Acquired - Savory Wolf Steak
You Have Discovered the Recipe - Savory Wolf Steak

"It's in your inventory," Carmen said absently. "Not sure if it's a bug or what but it happens sometimes."

"Thanks," Kurt said, pulling the steak from his inventory to inspect it before he ate.

Savory Wolf Steak

Use: Gives +5% Stamina Gain for 1 Hour

Quality: Normal

Requirements: None

"You know how food works in this game right?" Bhae asked.

"I know a little. Greg and I ate in town earlier."

"Okay so you know it won't heal you like in other games," Carmen chimed in.

"Yeah."

"It's a good skill to have anyway to get buffs and most food will take care of hunger. You should have the skill now," Bhae said.

Kurt pulled up his skill sheet to check.

Skills

- **Medical**

Novice First Aid	Level 1 (525/1000)
Novice Herbalism	Level 0 (115/500)

- **Mining**

Novice Miner	Level 1 (500/1000)
Novice Smelter	Level 0 (25/500)

- **Spells**

Shadow Sight	Level 0 (50/500)

- **Survival**

Novice Cooking	Level 0 (15/500)
Novice Tactics	Level 0 (25/500)

"Yeah I have it now," Kurt said mulling over his progress.

"Well you can increase it by discovering new recipes or training recipe cards. Even just cooking food on level will increase it. You might want to put some time into it because some food requires a certain skill

172

level to eat," Bhae informed him.

"Which makes absolutely no sense," Carmen chimed in again concentrating on her own food..

"Maybe in real life but this is a game. They have to put something in cooking to incentivize it otherwise only a couple would take the time to do it," Bhae retorted.

"Whatever it's still dumb," Carmen shrugged.

"Ignore her. She hasn't put the time into the skill," Bhae sighed.

"You know I would have thought being in a party with a bunch of girls would be more... interesting," Greg whined.

"Yeah I could see you thinking that," Kurt smirked.

"Thinking what?" Carmen asked, raising an eyebrow.

"He thinks he should be the center of attention and doesn't like that he can't get in on the conversation," Kurt covered.

"Dude..." Greg groaned.

"Ouch," Carmen laughed.

"Well he can run with us next time," Bhae said thoughtfully.

"Next time?" Kurt answered.

"Really? So this is going to be a regular thing huh?" Carmen needled.

"Yes!" Greg cheered.

"Why not? You don't seem like a jerk, like most of the guys we run into in here," Bhae added thinking aloud. "Your guild is rarely on Carmen and mine doesn't do anything but PVP. Besides you still owe me for the save and for the cart in the market. I barely broke even."

"Because it is so hard to make money in this game," Carmen chirped sarcastically.

"Let's make it official," Bhae said as a prompt appeared in front of Kurt.

Bhae | The Premade | Level 6 has sent you a Friend Request

       Accept   Decline

"Well I suppose I can get on board with running some stuff," Kurt said, concentrating on the "Accept" option.

"I'll friend you too I guess," Carmen said before sending him a request.

Carmen | Queue Me Up Buttercup | Level 5 has sent you a Friend Request

       Accept   Decline

"Are you sure you two aren't related?" Kurt laughed as he accepted her request as well.

Bhae snorted which Kurt hadn't expected. Everyone was instantly silent and that really got them all laughing. They sat around the fire finishing their meal all the while enjoying the light show as the pixies, or whatever they were, brought the ancient tree back to life. Looking out over the city Kurt noticed for the first time that not all of the trees were the same as he first thought. When they first entered the abandoned city all of the trees looked overgrown and petrified. Here and there others had been brought back to life in the same manner as the one they were sitting in. He wondered just how many other parties had enjoyed the same kind of fire and comradery that he'd stumbled onto. He couldn't mull over it for long as the girls soon brought him back into their banter and jokes at each other's expense.

When their revelry was finally done and Carmen had long since refilled everyone's health, it was time to depart. Despite everything Kurt had seen in the game, he wondered if the impromptu cookout wasn't the best part. The group wandered back down through the tree which was even now healing itself and rejecting the invasive plant growth. Visible now were signs of previous inhabitants. An abandoned toy, discarded furniture and long faded portrait emerged from the rubble now that the thorny vines retreated. Leaving the now open front of the once dungeon, the players headed back toward the road out of the valley.

"So what's the deal with your eyes?" Bhae asked conversationally.

"Ah shit," Greg groaned.

"Huh?" Carmen asked, looking confused.

"Well while you were dead or at least when we thought you were dead, we were stuck in the dark," Bhae explained. "I forgot about it until just now with the looting and all. It was a cool trick though."

"Girl you still aren't making sense," Carmen said, obviously confused.

"Turk was able to make his eyes glow purple and see in the dark. He did most of the DPS until you got back. I told you I wanted to hear what that was all about."

"Well it's an affinity I have is all," Kurt said sheepishly while the two warriors looked on expectantly. "What's the deal with you not using some magic in that run?"

"She should have some light powers by level six," Greg informed him.

"I would have thought at level six you would have some glowy badass powers," he continued."

"It's an affinity I started with when I rolled this character," Bhae explained. "I don't get access to light magic and magic is less effective on me. Now spill it. What's the deal? I haven't seen anything like that in game."

"Well like I said it's an affinity," Kurt shrugged. "It was given to me when I spared this little furry guy."

"Rosharn guy," Greg added.

"Rosharn guy," Kurt said, staring at the wisp. "Anyway I had him dead to rights and he was begging to be spared because he was an innocent. I believed him and he said he'd give me a boon. So he touched my head and now I have this ability called shadow sight."

"Dude aren't those things evil?" Carmen asked. "Like fiends of the Dark Lord?"

"Thank you," Greg interjected. "Exactly what I've been telling you bro."

"I'm not so sure," Kurt went on. "Getting the power led me down a quest line where it seems to question some of the stuff The Order of Light has been saying. I mean has anyone even been attacked by the Rosharn?"

"You're the first person I know that's even seen one," Bhae answered thoughtfully. "There are quests to search their hideouts or raid their camps but I think you fight everything but them."

"So you think everyone in game has the wrong opinion on these guys and the Dark Lord?" Carmen asked skeptically. "I mean you just happened to crack the code on your first day?"

"This girl's making a lot of sense, bro," Greg added eagerly.

"Yeah I guess it sounds crazy but why would they put a power and a questline in the game if it wasn't meant to be used by players? It seems like there is something deeper here than the light side are the good guys and the dark side are the bad guys," Kurt said.

"Well you don't seem evil," Bhae prodded. "I suppose we can wait to kill you until we have some evidence."

"Yeah I won't kill you yet," Carmen said matter of factly.

"You're messing with me right?" Kurt asked a little unsure about his decision to tell them about his affinity.

"Right," Carmen winked from behind her helmet.

"Yep," Bhae agreed.

On the long walk back to the road, things were uneventful for the most part. Kurt told Bhae and Carmen about flaming out in the state wrestling tournament and how his brother cajoled him into trying the game now that the season was over. He even relayed some bits about his brother's obsession with online games without getting too personal at his request. Carmen talked about living with her old school grandmother who didn't understand her desire to hole up in her room all day. Bhae added her own bits of real life with her struggles living away from home for the first time while attending university. From the sound of it they were all about the same age with Greg being the youngest. Without going into too many details it was good to meet some new people.

Southland Trade Road (PVP Zone)

They emerged from the forest in a spot that appeared to be similar to where they had left the main road. With Carmen and Bhae turning back toward Silent Grove, they said their goodbyes as Kurt resumed the walk toward the port city of Corwood. The open sky combined with the lightly trafficked road made for a peaceful walk on a quiet night. Kurt just took a moment to take it all in, from the sounds of nature to the scent of the clean air. Being away from civilization had always had a way of centering him in real life.

"Bro I don't know how you're out here picking up girls like that," Greg said.

"If by picking up girls you mean joining a party in a videogame with two people who may or may not be women? It's called talking to them like people and not being a huge creeper," Kurt remarked snidely.

177

"Don't be like that," Greg whined.

"Be like what?" Kurt asked softening his tone with his brother.

"You know what I mean. Besides you can't gender swap. When you roll a character it assigns whatever gender you see yourself as."

"I'm sure the main reason I got friend requests from them is I wasn't fawning over them or insulting them just because they happen to be women," Kurt said. "That's the secret right there. Don't be a douche."

"Dude, come one," Greg said a little hurt.

"I'm not saying you specifically. All I'm saying is they are here for the same reason you are. They're playing a game to escape and have fun. They're not here looking for a boyfriend. It's not like streamers out there flirting with you to get you to empty your pockets while they muddle through a game."

"I don't even watch anyone like that," Greg protested.

"But you know what I mean," Kurt went on. "You know which streamers are real gamers and which ones who are just showing their tits off."

"You know outside of here it's a little difficult for me," Greg said still a little defensive.

"Greg, I'm not even talking about that. All I'm saying is be a decent person in here and don't make it a big thing. Bhae and Carmen are just people playing the game, having a good time. If you remember that you'll be fine. This game is your world. Have a good time and don't make it into a thing."

The two walked in silence for a while. Kurt knew distances were realistic in Darklands but it never took so long to get from place to place in the MMOs he'd played in the past. Maybe that's why a starting town like Silent Grove was still a bit of a hub for players even though they had a few levels under their belt. Lots of people never left the town they grew up in.

Maybe that was the videogame equivalent.

"Are we going to get mounts or some kind of fast travel at some point?" Kurt asked, eager to lighten the mood.

"You're going to need more money to buy a mount," Greg replied happy to show off more of his in game knowledge. "Either that or you need to loot one somewhere. You ever ride a horse?"

"No. I take it that it's something that depends on what I actually know how to do."

"Yeah bro," Greg chuckled. "If it wasn't then the ganking would be crazy. They make them friendly for the most part so riding isn't hard to pick up but if they didn't make it somewhat realistic every passing rider would be one shotting people. It was something they worked out in beta. Riding a mount started out like just a speed buff at first with the horse just doing whatever you wanted. There were huge balance issues. So they just made it progressively harder until it stopped being an advantage just hopping on a mount."

"So mounts are a waste of time then?" Kurt asked.

"If you know what you're doing then mounted combat is awesome," Greg answered. "Until you learn how to ride, you're most likely going to fall off and hurt yourself. They are still a really reliable way to get around once you get a few hundred gold."

"Yeah that's not really an option right now," Kurt said shaking his head. "Anything else we can do about the walking?"

"Well we'll take a ship for the longest part of this run. So that'll be a kind of fast travel. We'll make it to the southern continent in no time instead of what would take weeks in real life. Rumor is that might be temporary though. The devs are going to try and move to be more realistic across the board."

"So that's it?" Kurt asked, disappointed that so much of their game time would be taken up by traveling. "Any other way to go from city to city?"

"There are portals that can take you to places you've been before but there's always a price," Greg said after thinking about it for a moment.

"Like what?" he asked.

"Sometimes you lose health, sometimes money, or they cap your max mana for a while. It's good if you need to get somewhere but it can be risky."

"Sounds like it," Kurt admitted.

"Yeah and they typically aren't in the best areas," Greg went on. "They're kinda like witches and warlocks a lot of times. They are supposed to be like fringe members of society."

"Yeah I'm not sure about all that," Kurt said.

The two continued walking. Occasionally someone would pass them going the opposite way making for a tense moment but nothing came of it. Before long Kurt had even seen his first mount as a level ten player on a brown horse overtook them headed in the direction of Corwood. Kurt made sure he was well off the road to avoid being run down but like the other people he'd encountered the player had no interest in starting something. In time the road turned close enough to the Slipwater Rush to really hear it moving in the distance adding to the tranquil night sounds.

The hours went by and on more than one occasion he'd thought about logging off and picking it up another time. Even though Greg assured him time was moving much slower out of game, he was definitely feeling the marathon session mentally. Once Kurt had finally decided to broach the subject with his brother, he noticed something in the distance. It looked like light reflecting off of the horizon.

"Is that it up ahead?" Kurt asked.

"Yeah we should be about there," Greg thought aloud as he flew upward to get a better view. "It's the next town we were going to run into anyway."

Kurt let out a heavy breath and picked up his pace. The terrain rolled gently here and as they crested the next hill, the city and river both came into full view past the trees that had been cleared away from its borders. Corwood stood in stark contrast to the village of Silent Grove. Where the village was protected by rough timber palisade, Corwood featured a legitimate stone wall that enclosed the city on the three sides bordered by land. On the river side long piers extended at regular intervals from a steep seawall that retained the Slipwater Rush. A number of large ships sat moored to the piers while smaller river vessels moved to and from the city. Beyond the walls large multistory buildings built from cut stone with shingled roofs stood in stark contrast to the log homes and thatched roofs, he'd seen frequently in Silent Grove. Even from here the sprawling city stood a good distance away.

"Wow. I wasn't expecting all that," Kurt said as he stopped to take in his surroundings.

"Yeah it's a lot the first time out here," Greg added. "You start in Silent Grove with a few hundred people and then when you get to Corwood you are in a place with a few thousand."

"It's just huge for a game ya know?"

"Most city hubs in old games are the size of Silent Grove so when you get to your first city in DO it's really cool. You'll be able to get anything here." Greg said excitedly moving forward.

"Well there isn't much that I'd want right now," Kurt said, reminding himself as much as Greg about why they were here. "The main thing is getting this sword identified. So if we could get a spell so I can do that or find a guy to do it."

"You can't afford the spell if we find it but I'm sure we can find someone to figure out what's going on with the sword," Greg said.

Approaching the city Kurt was taken aback yet again at the sheer size and scope of what lay before him. Players and NPCs entered and exited the main gate joining up with a number of smaller roads that connected to the Southland Trade Road. The last mile of their journey saw much more traffic than their entire journey north. Players on foot and mounted joined the road as well caravans of NPC traders, farmers and soldiers. While the game had seemed populated before just coming to the edge of the city had already made it feel like a much more real place.

Port City of Corwood (PVP Zone)

Passing under the outer wall, Kurt couldn't help but look up at the barbican guarding the entrance. A pair of towers housed a number of soldiers with crossbows standing at the ready while murder holes sat silently waiting to cast any number of vile things down on an invading horde. The whole thing felt intimidating despite knowing they weren't using it at the moment. Once they emerged into the city, Kurt was overwhelmed by a level of activity he had yet to see in DO.

"Alright Greg this is your show. Lead the way," Kurt said.

Kurt followed the wisp deeper into the city in the same way he had his first time in Silent Grove. Before long they were into a much larger marketplace complete with a number of stand alone shops. While street vendors still existed, Corwood's trade district seemed like a much more organized thing. People came from smaller villages to sell their wares in carts and wagons but they were dwarfed by the number of permanent structures complete with hanging wooden signs describing their business. Specialized shops existed for things like flowers or cheese while numerous options existed for more common trades like leatherworking or restaurants.

"So what are you looking for first, bro?" Greg asked, buzzing up and down the street. "We can go figure out that sword or we can see what we can get for the herbs."

"Let's see what we can get for the herbs first," Kurt decided after thinking for a moment. "If I can scrape together enough for something upgrade wise it might be worth it."

The two moved up and down the street for a while checking in various stalls and stores talking to cooks, vendors, alchemists and anyone who might be interested. The broken wolf claw he'd collected was junk, they soon learned. An NPC vendor gave Kurt five copper and he was happy to be rid of it. The same vendor took the large sharp thorns for seven copper each which seemed like the same story everywhere. Having spent the better part of an hour talking to people, Kurt was ready to be done shopping around.

"It seems like this stuff is going for pretty much the same price everywhere. Wouldn't it be easier if the game just had an auction house like every other game?" Kurt asked, already annoyed with the time they'd spent looking for the best price.

"Yeah I'm sure it would be but they are really trying for the whole player run economy thing. They want people owning food carts and shops. I heard eventually they plan on removing as many NPC vendors as possible."

"It's a cool idea I guess," Kurt said. "Let's just pick a place and sell this stuff."

Giving it some thought they decided the best place was an herb vendor they had talked to earlier. After a couple minutes of walking they entered the front of a building that appeared to be a store on the main floor while serving as a residence on the second. Every available space had well manicured herb boxes, hanging plants and flower beds. A wooden sign read

Herb by Herb. A spicy floral scent assaulted Kurt's senses as he opened the door. Behind a rickety table a skinny middle aged man pruned a number of small plants. At Kurt's approach he looked over his glasses with a look of apprehension and curiosity.

"How may I help you?" the NPC asked cautiously.

"Are you Herb?" Kurt asked,

"That like totally depends," the man who may or may not be Herb answered.

"I'm not law enforcement," Kurt ventured carefully looking sidelong at Greg.

"Yeah okay, do you like have any proof of that?" the man asked warily.

"Umm well I don't have a badge," Kurt ventured.

"Oh right on that'll work. What are you looking for today?" Herb answered no seeming to trust Kurt implicitly.

"Well I'd like to sell some herbs. I stopped in maybe half an hour ago to talk to you about that," Kurt reminded him.

"Shhh not so loud," Herb hissed looking around in all directions before focusing back on Kurt. "Yeah I'm interested."

"Okay what can you give me for these?" Kurt whispered reaching into his bag spreading out the herbs he had just harvested. "I'm looking to move all of them."

"You know this isn't illegal right bro?" Greg asked.

"Yeah man I can buy these," Herb muttered carefully examining the plants laid out on the table. "Yeah we can totally do business."

"Great, how much for the lot?" Kurt asked, trying to hide his annoyance.

"Umm for the Walking Grass I can do thirteen copper per bundle and the Black Sparrow Thistle sells for thirty-seven copper each. The

Redtip Stranglevine is a little pricier. I can give you one silver fourteen copper each on those. And let's see oh. Oh my this… this is something else now. We don't see a lot of Hearty Stranglevine. I can give you twenty-six silver and ten copper for it. Sound fair?"

"Yeah that works," he said, reaching out to shake the man's hand as notifications scrolled in the bottom right of his vision.

You Have Lost - Walking Grass x4

You Have Lost - Black Sparrow Thistle x12

You Have Lost - Redtip Stranglevine x8

You Have Lost - Hearty Stranglevine

You Have Acquired - 40 Silver and 18 Copper

"A pleasure doing business with you Herb," Kurt said with a genuine smile.

"I was never here."

"Um but this is your shop."

"I was never here!"

Kurt backed away slowly before leaving the unstable man to whatever he was going to do next. Despite knowing that most of the money came from one high quality material, it was good to see harvesting pay out. It was going to be short lived but he was getting close to a gold again.

"You know bro, the prices there were too good for that to be an NPC run shop."

"So a player set that guy up?" Kurt asked.

"Yeah you hire and tweak the personality for the NPCs that run your shops," Greg explained.

"Well I guess that makes sense," Kurt shrugged before rubbing his hands together. "Now I think it's time we see a man about a sword."

"Come on I think we passed a couple magic item shops," Greg said as he flew off toward the street. "One of them is bound to have someone trading in identifications."

Kurt and Greg checked a few rare goods vendors they had seen not too long ago. Unfortunately those shops were being manned by NPCs at the moment who couldn't help them. Before long they found themselves before Morty's Magical Emporium. The building itself was simple and from the look of it newly purchased. A sign in front of the door read, "We buy, sell and identify your magical goods." It was honestly the best news Kurt had heard all day.

Upon entering a mostly bare showroom was set in what he guessed was the default business layout, since he had seen the same set up in a number of shops already today. A long show counter sat along the back wall in front of a doorway leading into another room. A few mostly bare shelves lined whatever wall space that was available. Looking back to the counter a player stared off into space interacting with something as the room layout suddenly changed turning whitewashed walls to wood paneled. Kurt looked at his tag.

Magnificent Morty | Full Dive Frontier | Level 5

"So you must be Morty?" Kurt asked conversationally, trying to get the man's attention.

"Hey what's up? I don't really have much for sale yet," Morty explained apologetically while looking at the bare storefront. "I just got the money to open this place up for my guild. I have some crafted potions but we haven't really started stocking gear yet."

"No problem man," Kurt said. "I saw the sign outside that said you can identify stuff."

"Oh yeah I can do that," Morty said, dismissing whatever interface he had been using. "Let's see what you have."

Kurt pulled the unidentified short sword from his inventory and laid it on the counter. Morty picked up the blade turning it over in his hand. He looked at it closely before setting it back down.

"Yeah it looks like I can identify this one. Forty silver sound fair?"

"Hell yeah forty silver sounds fair," Greg blurted excitedly.

"Yeah works for me," Kurt said trying to hide his excitement as he pulled the money from his coin pouch. Setting the money down, let Morty get to work. A moment later a prompt filled his screen.

Magnificent Morty has identified your Short Sword as a Darksteel Elven Gladius

Darksteel Elven Gladius

Damage: 2-6

Effect: Chance on hit to inflict an equal amount of damage as poison damage over ten seconds.

Quality: Uncommon

Requirements: Agility: 10

Will you accept this identification?

YES

NO

"Just a heads up. My identifications get a reduction in requirements so if you decide to decline it you're probably going to get like an Agility: 11 requirement on it."

"It looks like a good sword, bro," Greg added.

"Good to know," Kurt answered honestly. The sword was a nice upgrade but he had to wonder if it would identify as something better elsewhere. The effect was what settled it. In most games he'd played weapon procs were real deal breakers. Getting one at this stage of the game couldn't be ignored. He concentrated on the "YES."

You Have Acquired - Darksteel Elven Gladius

"Thanks for the business," Morty said with a smile.

"Hey no problem. Thanks for the identification," Kurt waved as he turned to leave the shop. They only made it as far as the street before he turned to his brother. "Hold up here for a second. I have some inventory management to do."

"Yeah okay," Greg said.

Kurt replaced his throwing knife on his belt with the steel dagger. The thrown weapon would be missed but until he got better at using it there was really no point in keeping it equipped. He then sheathed his new gladius in the dagger's old place. He took a moment to admire it on his belt. The dark metal shown a polished smoke grey. What he assumed were elven runes were etched into the metal itself. The hilt was wrapped in some sort of tanned animal hide and was soft to the touch. It really did look cool, he thought.

Bringing himself back to the present he sat down on the ground removing the roughspun cloth from his bag. Still without a magical means to heal he needed to keep up with his bandage making. Now that he had done it a few times cutting the bandages was easy enough but it still took a couple minutes each to sit down and do.

You Have Lost - Roughspun Cloth x5
You Have Acquired - Roughspun Bandage x5

"Alright bro what's next? We heading to the other continent? Doing some more shopping?"

"Well I should be just shy of fifty silver. How much do I need for the boat ride?"

"There isn't a charge for that," Greg said. "It's just a taxi between continents."

"Well I have a couple open slots," Kurt explained, trying something new with his character sheet. Concentrating he pulled up just a view of his equipment.

Equipment

Head -

Neck -

Waist - Cadet's Belt

Body - Hunter's Leather Tunic

Back - Simple Green Cloak

Legs - Forester's Padded Pants

Hands -

Feet - Worn Leather Boots

Ring 1 - Silver Ring of Unencumbered Movement

Ring 2 -

Melee (D) - Darksteel Elven Gladius

Melee (O) - Steel Dagger

Pouch 1 -

Pouch 2 -

Range - Fine Recurve Bow

Container - Basic Quiver

Ammo - Hunting Arrows x12

"Well it looks like I have open slots on my head, neck, hands and a second ring," Kurt thought aloud going over his equipment list.

"We might be able to find some gloves or a helm," Greg said bouncing around Kurt's head. A neck slot item or a ring might be kinda hard without some more cash. Honestly your gear isn't bad for your first day."

"So what are you thinking?" Kurt asked.

"You'll probably end up bottoming yourself out again on cash for one piece of gear that will easily be replaced. If you come upon the right quest then your time and money will be gone. If we go a while then I'd say we check for what people are selling or if you get more money then you can buy something good."

"Yeah it's a tough call man. I should probably stop and buy some arrows though. After that last run I'm a bit light and that's with the ones the girls gave me."

"That's easy enough," Greg said flying off down the street. "Follow me!"

Players and NPCs alike swatted at the wisp as he flew by darting in and out of traffic. Running to keep up, it was all he could do to avoid knocking over the other pedestrians. Before long Kurt caught up to his brother floating next to an NPC run cart. It didn't look like much he thought at first. The cart itself was little more than a big wheelbarrow piled high with furs and dried skins. Standing next to the cart was a young man in his late teens dressed more for a day in the woods than selling wares in a market.

"Hi can I help you?" the NPC asked cheerily.

"Um, do you sell arrows by chance?" Kurt asked, unsure of why his brother had brought him here.

"Oh yes sir I have some arrows right here!" The boy dug through his cart pulling out a small wooden box from somewhere toward the bottom. Curious Kurt tried to peer down into the space created to see what else he might have. Outside of a bear trap and a few canvas sacks the effort was pointless though. With a practiced flourish the boy opened the box showing three distinctly different arrows which Kurt inspected.

Practice Arrow

Damage: 0

Quality: Subpar

Requirements: None

Hunting Arrow

Damage: 0-1

Quality: Normal

Requirements: None

Militia Arrow

Damage: 1-2

Quality: Fine

Requirements: None

"What good is an arrow that does no damage?" he asked out of curiosity as he looked at the practice arrow.

"Well it will still do damage sir. It's just blunted," the NPC explained casually.

"You still get damage from your bow," Greg chimed in. "Those are cheap and good if you're looking to practice using a bow."

"Is that really a thing?" Kurt asked.

"Oh yeah there are a bunch of NPCs that will train you in weapons," Greg went on. "So if you want to use that new sword of yours, you might want to find someone to teach you how to swing it. I know some guys with the order that serve as Master at Arms. They can train you in just about anything."

"Excuse me?" the vendor asked, obviously confused.

"Nevermind," Kurt answered. "How much are the arrows?"

"Well sir, the practice arrows are ten copper each. I can sell the hunting arrows are fifty copper each and the militia arrows are a silver a piece."

Kurt was already familiar with the hunting arrows but he picked up the militia arrow and looked it over. It definitely had a certain heft to it. The arrowhead itself was more compact than the broad head on the hunting arrows but looked like it could punch through lighter armors with ease. They were tempting but the price tag was still a bit out of the range he was willing to pay. That made the hunting arrows his only real choice. Checking his quiver he saw that he was at twelve of a possible thirty shots. So the question was did he need more than what he could hold in the quiver?

"What do you think Greg? Should I just fill my quiver or should I get more?"

"Um that's up to you man. It kinda depends on what your playstyle is going to be."

Kurt really hadn't given it much thought. To this point he'd switched between his bow and dagger as the situation required. He didn't know the first thing about using his bladed weapons outside of what he'd already figured out. It wasn't much really besides stabbing at very close range. The bow on the other hand was something he was much more familiar with. Between numerous trips to summer camp and hunting with family members, using a bow was almost second nature. Until he learned more with his blades he needed to invest in that.

"Okay I think I know what I want," Kurt concluded. "I want eighteen of the hunting arrows for starters. I'll also take twenty of the militia arrows."

"Will that be all sir?" the NPC asked, gathering Kurt's order.

"Yeah I think that's all for now."

Kurt cringed inwardly, handing over the handful of silver. His coin purse was starting to feel much lighter than he would have liked so soon after a successful dungeon run. He told himself it was all for a good cause as he looked at the notifications for the transaction.

You Have Lost - 29 Silver
You Have Acquired - Hunting Arrow x18
You Have Acquired - Militia Arrow x20

"So are your adventures in shopping done now?" Greg whined impatiently. "I mean I do want to hang out and all but I was kinda hoping for more fighting and less running around town."

"Do you just like to listen to yourself complain?" Kurt prodded.

"What?"

"You've played enough of these games to know there is a certain amount of inventory management," Kurt chided.

"Okay, okay can we just get back to the quest line or run a dungeon or something?"

"Yeah let's do what we came here for," Kurt relented.

"Follow me!" Greg took off excitedly.

Chapter 10

All Kurt could do was shake his head as his brother flew off again. He stood still and watched for a moment as he raced away until he abruptly stopped. He'd have to ask Greg what it felt like to get to the end of his rope. At least it gave him a good visual reference for the wisp's range. Outwardly the wisp didn't really show emotions but Kurt was sure his brother was probably a little upset so he started moving. Greg took off again albeit a little slower this time. Their destination was clear enough as they made their way toward the waterfront. While there were many ships docked along various piers, only one had a line forming with a couple dozen players waiting to board. As they approached a small clipper ship pulled up to the end of the pier much like a taxi would. Players entered and exited in one large mass threatening to push each other into the river below.

Hurrying his pace Kurt quickly passed Greg and made it to the gangplank just as the crowd dwindled down to just a few stragglers. Those onboard began to disperse with some going below decks while others found open spots along the railing. Pulling away from its berth the ship began to pick up speed. There were subtle things that made the departure special Kurt decided. The ship bobbed up and down slightly as it cut through the water. Water sprayed upward over the rails misting those close to the edge. Even the air movement while the landscape slipped by gave the ship a real feeling of momentum. Kurt was just continually amazed by the little touches of realism the game created.

"Enjoy the ride while it lasts," Greg said sidling up to Kurt. "I hear they plan on patching this boat out for something more realistic soon. You won't be able to just show up and run over to the other continent whenever you want."

"So what are they going to do?" Kurt asked, a little annoyed by the idea.

"No one knows for sure but I doubt it'll take months to get there. It might end up being a thing where you hop on the boat and log off then come back later. It's been a common thing going back to beta. When they first launched in beta the world was really small and you could run from one end to the other in a couple hours. It was kinda like a traditional MMO."

"I don't know man," Kurt said looking out over the water. "I haven't seen a lot of traditional MMO so far."

"Come on man, let's check out the ship. We have a while before we zone into the other continent."

Kurt only shrugged as his brother led him down below decks. He wasn't sure what to expect heading away from the views from above but maybe there was something worth checking out. As they descended, the stairs beneath his feet sagged slightly with each step as if years of moisture exposure compromised them. Hanging lanterns swayed gently casting shadows at odd angles. Even the deck moved beneath his feet in a more pronounced way than above. Emerging into the hold itself revealed a maze of cargo that NPCs milled about while players lounged above in the rafters and on top of crates. Following Greg past these, they headed deeper into the bowels of the ship. Past the cargo hold was a hall with a series of doors

"These are state rooms you can rent. It's a big reason people think the trip is going to be much longer after they decide to patch it. Not really a point in getting into them now."

"Well it looks like one of them is open," Kurt said gesturing to an open door at the end of the line. They moved forward peering inside.

"Weird. It looks like it's empty," Greg mumbled genuinely puzzled.

Stepping into the room Kurt couldn't help but admire the four post bed in the room's center. The stateroom also included a pair of plus chairs, a desk and a large footlocker. Pressing his hand down on the feather mattress was almost enough to tempt him to climb in. As his hand sunk in, he thought that it might be the most comfortable thing he'd ever felt.

"I think the chest gives you access to your shared inventory too," Greg pondered as he flew about the room. "I guess I could think of worse setups for an ocean voyage. I just hope they don't make it too long."

Kurt was only half listening to his brother when the door abruptly slammed shut. He turned to see what had happened when the light was immediately snuffed out. Greg flew around the room in a panic trying to figure out what was happening. While Kurt only stopped and listened, slipping his sword from its scabbard. He moved to the door and tried to shoulder it open to no avail.

"Dude something locked us in," Greg howled pointing out the obvious. "You're going to have to..."

"Quiet!" Kurt hissed straining his ears in the darkness. His brother had stopped abruptly but still flew around rapidly casting a soft light around the room. Pressing his back to the door he let out a breath and activated his shadow sight. Kurt nearly jumped as a form crouched in the far corner of the room came into view instantly. Greg was still searching but to Kurt his position was plain as day.

"Now that is a neat trick," a voice said, sounding from everywhere at once.

"I could say the same," said Kurt.

"That bow... that name... Is it you?" the voice asked.

"What are you talking about?" Kurt asked nervously, avoiding to look directly in his direction. Instead Kurt let his vision pass over him as he looked about the room.

"I can't find him. Where is he?" Greg panted.

"That name...are you the real deal?" the voice continued ignoring the question.

"Dude is english your first language?" Kurt barked back stifling a laugh at the theatrics.

At once the figure sprang into action closing the distance in a heartbeat. Leading with a wicked looking dagger the figure was on top of him in another moment. It was all Kurt could do to raise his sword and bat the strike aside. Snapping a kick up Kurt caught nothing but air as the figure bounced backwards on the balls of his feet. It was only then that he got a real look at his tag.

DeathxDagger | The Broken | Level 3

He darted in again and Kurt slashed using his superior reach to keep him at bay. Kurt didn't know what he was doing with the sword but this guy's game seemed to be all about surprise and speed. Now that the element of surprise was negated, the man was cautious. Kurt watched him with the dagger. He didn't seem to have the confidence of an expert. In fact he was relatively low level compared to some he had seen. Kurt mirrored his moves trying to anticipate but the man's stance was becoming more defensive by the second.

"Bro I had him now I lost him again. He's got a good stealth or invisibility or something," Greg stammered, still panicking.

"I'm on it," was all Kurt said in reply.

Greg buzzed around the room searching for the player who had started to back toward the corner with the desk sheathing his blade. Kurt stopped trying to disguise his intent and stared down his opponent. The glow of his lavender eyes cast the room into stark relief magnifying any ambient light from the wisp and the portholes. Cautiously he moved forward.

"You know I'm about done with guys trying to gank me out here," fed up Kurt began with menace in his voice stalking forward. "Right now I see you think you are hiding from me. The problem for you is I see better than a drow on a clear night. You get that reference guy? I'll make it even more simple for you. This purple coming out of my eyes ain't just for looks so if you're feeling froggy why don't you jump."

Anger was rising now in Kurt. Back in the real world he was never one to push people around but he also wasn't a guy who backed down from a fight. Since he'd started playing DO it had been running from one bully or another. He was willing to bet that this guy with his relatively low level relied on his traps and surprise to get kills. Most likely he couldn't see any better in the dark than anyone else. Well almost anyone else. At once the player made a run for the bed. Leaping he extended both hands as he dove into a practiced roll over the piece of furniture. Kurt let loose with a wild slash scoring a glancing blow across his foe's ribs.

DeathxDagger grunted as he crashed to the floor throwing out his hand in a rehearsed maneuver back at Kurt. Both players were equally surprised when Kurt batted the knife away with another wild slash from his sword. Scrambling backward the ganker did everything he could to create space while Kurt stepped up onto the bed. In a panic the player staggered to his feet diving for the porthole. Kurt wouldn't have thought the hole big enough to fit through easily but in one fluid motion the player was through with only the sound of broken glass signaling that he'd made it through.

"Man he made it through?" Greg asked flying past to get a better view. "Oh shit he's scaling the side of the ship."

'Are you kidding me?" Kurt asked in irritation.

"Yeah man we should go get him."

The air shimmered for a moment and a slight tingle washed over Kurt's body. It was sudden and a bit unnerving but not at all uncomfortable.

"What was that?"

"Oh sorry bro, I should have warned you. That's what it's like when you zone to another part of the world."

"So we're close?"

"Yeah we should be about halfway thereGreg said, still peering out of the porthole. "We going after that guy?"

"I don't think so," Kurt said thoughtfully walking over to relight the lantern on the wall. On his way to the light he noticed the throwing knife on the floor that was surprisingly similar to the one he already had. Putting it into his pack he continued his thought. "Trust me I want to go get that guy but I'm still at a disadvantage here. If I use my shadow sight up there it's hard telling what kind of attention I'll draw. At least down here we can hole up until we get across the ocean."

With the room now lit, Kurt dismissed his shadow sight and moved to the door. Inspecting the bottom of the door revealed a sliding iron bar that fell into a hole drilled into the floor when the door was pushed shut. In the dark it would be impossible to find if you weren't looking for it. There was no way this was a standard part of the room. He moved back to the hanging lantern that served as the only source of light. It wasn't exactly close to the door so how did he manage the trick? The door was slammed shut and in the next instant the lights were out. It happened so quickly that it was a bit disorienting.

"Does this game have any spells that could snuff out a lantern like that?" Kurt asked, turning to his brother.

"I'm sure there are," he answered, flying closer to inspect the lantern. "You're right about one thing though this room was set up for a trap."

"What did you find?"

"Look at the dimmer here," Greg said floating just above the lamp.

Peering closer Kurt noticed a thin broken piece of string. It was very thin like fishing line. It wasn't as durable though so it had snapped off. Testing the key he found it moved very easily. Dropping to his hands and knees he worked his way back toward the door. Sure enough he found more loose string on the ground.

"As easy as that was for you to turn, I bet he worked it over a bit to loosen it," Greg explained. "His stealth was probably good enough for him to just hide behind the door and jerk on the string to turn out the light. It's clever really. He didn't even need to bring anything on board with him to set it up. Since the staterooms have access to your shared stash, he could have stored all the hardware in there."

"And the game just lets you make changes to the environment like that?" Kurt asked.

"I bet it's not permanent. The hole and stuff probably reset once he vacates the room," Greg thought as he examined the bottom of the door.

"How long does that take?"

"I don't know. Maybe once you leave the boat? He could probably ride back and forth all day springing the same trap. Then when he's done just toss everything in the chest and walk away. I've never heard of anything like this but I'm sure that's how it works. It makes perfect sense."

Kurt couldn't help but think his brother was getting just a little too excited over this guy. They could both be waiting for a reroll if he hadn't been lucky with the Rosharn out in the woods. Going up after the guy would only serve to expose himself for using the shadow sight again or worse walk himself into another trap. He couldn't help feeling like he was still caught in the trap waiting things out in the stateroom.

"Is there anything to stop the guy from trying to gank me up top?" Kurt asked, turning to his brother. On the surface staying in the locked room seemed like the safe play but now he was second guessing himself.

"No not really. There is a certain amount of safety in numbers. It's kinda risky to try something like that in a crowd because you never know who might jump in. There's always someone trying to be a hero or take advantage of an opportunity."

"So we're secure here but we might also be trapped," Kurt continued. "If he wants to come back down here for me he probably knows I need to open the door eventually."

"Yeah probably," Greg answered noncommittal.

"Alright let's get up top. Let me know if you see the guy. We're not going to go after him but if he comes looking for a fight we might have to give him one."

"My guess is he won't be seen unless he wants to be."

"That doesn't inspire a lot of confidence," Kurt groaned. "Just keep an eye out."

Using his foot Kurt slid the bar up and cracked the door open. The world outside of the stateroom appeared to be unchanged from when they'd left it. His hand ached slightly from his grip on the sword pommel. Forcing himself to flex his hand and ease his grip, Kurt looked down the empty hallway. Beyond he could hear muffled conversations and people moving around the cargo hold. As he emerged from the hallway, Kurt felt a number of eyes on him as conversations died down and people watched him carrying bared steel. Kurt answered their silent questions with a nod as he crept forward toward the stairs.

Upon reaching the stairs, Kurt broke into a quick jog taking steps two at a time. He felt like he was a kid again racing out of the basement after turning off the light. It probably didn't do much for the sidelong glances but he would be much calmer above decks in the open air. Bursting through the door with a sword drawn got Kurt a lot of attention. As a half dozen people drew weapons, he let out a breath and finally sheathed the blade. He straightened his posture and walked as calmly as possible to the front of the ship. Scanning the faces in the crowd he saw bewildered looks and annoyed ones but no one with the tag he was looking for. Sparing a glance to the horizon he could see land was within sight even now.

"See anything Greg?" Kurt asked crouching against the railing.

"Nope. You?"

"I don't know man. I'm not seeing his tag anywhere."

Long tense minutes dragged on as Kurt surveyed the crowd. After a short time they stopped paying attention to him altogether but he couldn't shake the feeling that someone was waiting out there for him. Glancing over his shoulder the southern continent drew closer by the minute. He had to forcibly open his mouth as his jaw was beginning to ache from his clenched teeth. People started to come up from below and gather near the exit.

"Come on bro let's get into the crowd and get off as soon as possible."

Kurt only nodded as they made their way toward the other players. There was a lot of jostling and positioning as people pressed for the exit. Even before the ship made a complete stop people jumped into the water and across the gap onto the dock, Some called to various mounts while others simply sprinted toward the town. At the same time a mass of players pushed in the opposite direction to board the vessel. Stepping out onto the pier, Kurt broke into a jog as the crowd thinned. He was half way between the town and ship when the notification scrolled.

Black Crystal Refugee Camp (PVP Zone)

What Kurt thought was the town at first actually sat in the distance while a temporary settlement had been established just off of the coast. Buildings had been erected from rough hewn timber in a haphazard layout along with other things like abandoned wagons and repurposed ships. Beyond these were large groups of tents and pavilions set up into arbitrary neighborhoods. Further inland a large ditch with patrolling militia served as the community's perimeter. It was only in the far distance that Kurt could see the ancient stone walls of an established settlement.

"So why is this a refugee camp? Are they fleeing from something?" Kurt asked turning to Greg.

"I'm not sure. I've always quested in the north and fought on that front."

"You've never been to this zone?"

"Dude the world is huge with locations all over both continents."

"Alright I was just kinda surprised is all," Kurt said apologetically as they came up on the camp itself. "So how do I go about finding the guy for this quest?"

"I don't know. What does the quest say?"

Kurt concentrated for a moment to bring up the quest log. He was a little relieved that the game didn't assault him with a wall of text like when he opened his character sheet last. The UI was supposed to be very intuitive so he hoped that this was the game learning his preferences. He concentrated on his only unfinished quest. As he did the quest opened and he could hear the last bit of his conversation with Edward Lennonbrook in his voice.

- **Time to Help II**

"It's a lot to take on faith. I understand that. Perhaps if you were to see it

204

for yourself you'd understand. While this watch is mine there is someone who can use it more than me. There is a man in the town of Black Crystal that goes by the name 'Grins.' Seek him out and give him the watch. It might be you will see for yourself what has become of the world."

Will you accept the quest, "Time to Help II?"
YES
NO

+	**Learn on the Job**	**[COMPLETE]**
+	**Not Wasting the Man's Time**	**[COMPLETE]**
+	**Time to Help**	**[COMPLETE]**

Kurt listened again as he read the text. Without much more insight into how to find Grins, he read it aloud to Greg. To his brother's credit he seemed to listen and really think about it.

"Yeah man I have no idea."

"Seriously, that's the best you got?"

"Well I mean I guess we can ask around," Greg suggested. "If he's a quest NPC then he will be known by somebody. Maybe he has another quest. If he does then there might be a player that will know where to find him."

"Is it common to have no idea where to turn in a quest?"

"Part of the quest is finding the guy. Sometimes you have to do a little searching."

"Fine let's go," Kurt said, visibly frustrated. Walking down the first street they came across, Kurt asked random NPCs if they had heard of a man named Grins. Vendors, militia and random passersby all proved equally unhelpful. Working his way through the camp, Kurt sought out players having given up on NPCs for help. Unfortunately the results were the same as no one had heard of a quest NPC named Grins. They had been at it for the better part of an hour before ending up in front of an old repurposed fishing barge.

The Drunken Kiwi sported a sign featuring the green fruit being doused with an unmarked bottle of alcohol. What was once an open air boat was now a large patio under a canvas roof that looked to be made from the vessel's sails. The deck of the ship had been set up with a circular bar in its center acting as an island surrounded by stools and tables. A small spiral staircase in the deck's center led down into what was probably a cellar of some kind. There were only a few patrons as a bearded man with a heavy gut absently cleaned a mug while chatting with a serving girl.

"I was going to say what better place to check than a tavern," Greg stated cheerfully. "But this place doesn't look like much of a tavern. What do you think?"

"Honestly if we don't find something soon I'm going to log for the night. I'm all for figuring this thing out but there has to be something we're missing.   What do you have?" Kurt asked in a raised voice, making his way to a bar stool. To his surprise a notification flashed across his vision.

Due to Your Registered Age - Options Will Be Limited

It hadn't occurred to Kurt that, even in a game, he might not be able to drink alcohol. In truth he hadn't even sat down with that intention. There must be legal ramifications surrounding underage players simulating realistic drinking though. His surprise over the whole thing caused him to completely miss the bartender's reply.

"I'm sorry could you repeat that?"

"Cold cider is a copper and hot cider is two," the man answered in an annoyed voice. "Let me know if there is something in particular you're looking for."

"One hot cider please," he answered, sitting down heavily on the stool.

Dropping the coins on the bar he didn't even look at the notification as he slumped down. Raising the mug to his mouth he was surprised by the combination of sweet and tart that assaulted his taste buds. The whole food thing still surprised him. It really did feel like the real thing. He drained the last of his drink and motioned for another tossing the coppers down. He decided to try his luck with the bartender when he came back.

"You wouldn't happen to know a guy by the name of Grins, would ya?"

The bartender stopped mid stride before continuing over. Kurt noticed the chatty serving girl abruptly remembered something else she needed to do as she turned on her heel and walked away. A change in the room caused him to bring his head up as a notification appeared to distract him.

Your Thirst is Quenched

A buff appeared in the shape of a mug. The bartender sat the second mug down and collected his money as he checked the notifications in the bottom right.

Mana Regeneration +25%
You Have Lost - 2 Copper
You Have Acquired - Mug of Hot Cider

Distracted again it took Kurt a moment to realize that the bartender hadn't moved after setting down the drink. Apprehensively he met the man's gaze wondering just what the question had meant. Gone was the look of annoyance and now it was replaced with something more like suspicion.

"Might be I know a man named Grins. Might be I don't. What's it to you?"

"Holy shit," Greg blurted. "Looks like the game goes on!"

"And what would jog your memory on the man you may or may not know?" Kurt asked, ignoring his brother while doing his best to roleplay the situation with the NPC. "If it's coin you need…"

"Not coin," he said conspiratorially. "Just a couple questions to make sure you're the right kind of man. Who sent you?"

Kurt thought for a moment. He didn't know just how much he should tell a random NPC. Looking around the bar he noticed no one was really paying attention to the conversation. The serving girl who had been busying herself elsewhere had come back but she was working to keep her distance. All of the other patrons seemed more engrossed in their own affairs rather than what was going on here. Leaning in, Kurt tried to examine the man. To his surprise a tag appeared above his head.

Bartender | Level ?? | Disposition: Wary

"A man, named Edward Lennonbrook, sent me to find him." He wasn't sure how he remembered the name. He was typically bad with names but it just kinda came to him when he needed it. Luckily it would keep him in a good spot with the bartender. He could tell the man was mulling the information over but was a little surprised when the NPC straightened as if to walk away.

"Hmm never heard of him," the bartender decided.

"Wait that's it?" Kurt could feel the heat rising in his face. "I didn't come all the way out here for a run around. You know where I can find Grins or not?"

"Boy you got the stink of the Order on you. Might be you think coming out here looking like that got you thinking you're fooling somebody but it don't. So unless you can give me something better than a name I ain't heard of, I got nothing for ya."

Irritation was bubbling to the surface as Kurt activated his shadow sight. It wasn't going to do anything to the bartender but if he wanted proof he would give it to him. Unconsciously his hand slipped to his gladius as he rose to his feet. The NPC took a visible step backward bumping into a small stand holding one of the kegs of ale.

"Dude what are you doing? We're in the middle of town," Greg pleaded.

"Is there more proof required or can you tell me what you know about Grins?"

'No, no I believe you," the barkeep stammered. "Head around back there's a service door leading to the cellar. You'll find him there. Just tell the man at the door you're here to see Grins."

Kurt dismissed his shadow sight and walked away from the bar. It was only then that Kurt noticed that the few patrons remaining in the bar saw the exchange and stared openly. As he met their eyes they quickly turned away back to their drinks as if he was never there. Walking through the overgrown grasses on the side of the beached barge, Kurt made his way to a pair of cellar doors where a man in dark leathers leaned against the makeshift building. At his approach he stirred to attention and stuck out a hand to stop him.

"You lost kid?" the man asked.

"I'm here to see Grins," Kurt replied flatly.

Looking him up and down the man took a moment before jerking a thumb toward the pair of cellar doors and turning to face away. Opening one of the doors revealed a set of wood stairs leading under the Drunken Kiwi. Sounds of the raucous laughter of men deep in their cups wafted up the stairwell. Ducking his head Kurt descended the stair as the door slammed shut behind him. He glanced back briefly before continuing down the stairs.

Chapter 11

The cellar itself was far from what he had expected. Before him an underground tavern was laid out beneath the open air tavern above. In contrast though this bar was alive with commotion as nearly every table was occupied with what looked to be hard men and women of various races. The only thing that didn't seem to be represented here were actual players. Moving through the room Kurt looked for a place to start his search and wondered why a game would have such a heavily populated area so hidden from the actual people playing the game. Pushing the line of thinking aside he grabbed the first serving girl who came by and asked about Grins. She looked him up and down with an almost predatory stare before pointing him to a table in the far corner of the room. Sitting alone at the table was a dark haired dwarf pouring over a ledger of some kind while nursing a pint. A thick braided beard covered his jaw line except in two lines stretching from the corners of his mouth where the skin had been cut and cauterized most likely by some sort of white hot blade creating an artificial smile that was no doubt permanent.

"My guess is you're Grins," Kurt began trying to open a conversation with the dwarf.

"Aye and my guess is you're burdened with the curse of perception. Piss off."

At this point Kurt was getting used to the level of hospitality he was receiving here. Deciding to get on with it, he pulled out the antique pocket watch and tossed it on top of the dwarf's ledger. Capturing the somewhat startled dwarf's attention again, he addressed him. As a prompt appeared.

Will you complete the quest, "Time to Help II?"

Required Item - Antique Pocket Watch

YES

NO

Kurt focused on the YES and waited for the dwarf to speak. Grins picked up the watch and turned it over in his hands a few times to examine it. He regarded Kurt almost with a look of disbelief before gesturing for him to take a seat. Seeing that he was making progress, Kurt complied with the request.

"You have my attention boyo," Grins said thoughtfully with a distinct change in his demeanor. "What is it you're looking to get out of this?"

Umm I'm sorry," Kurt stammered unprepared for the open ended question. "I mean a reward would be cool but I'm mostly just following this thing through."

"Reward I can do. I don't know if you have what it takes to follow this all the way through, lad." Turning to look around Kurt, Grins bellowed across the bar. "Hebbs bring over the box from the lost and found."

A wiry man by the bar nodded before ducking out of sight into a back room. Kurt tried to stifle a grimace as he thought of his reward being pulled from a box of randomly discarded items. The way the quest had started out he'd hoped for something a little more well a little more seemed to cover it.

"Oh it sounds like you're in for something good, bro," Greg added with a chuckle.

He stared at the wisp with irritation as Hebbs returned with a small wooden crate that he set before Grins. The dwarf looked him over as he sifted through the box and set three items before him. Kurt examined them in turn so he knew just what he was looking at.

Workman's Gloves

Defense: 2

Quality: Normal

Requirements: None

Sturdy Leather Helm

Defense: 2

Quality: Normal

Requirements: None

Boar Hide Choker

Effect: +15 HP on Equip

Quality: Uncommon

Requirements: None

"Let it not be said that Grins is not a generous man," the dwarf said proudly. "You may have your choice of any of these for the return of this watch."

To say Kurt was underwhelmed would have been an understatement. It wasn't that the gear wasn't useful but it all just seemed so ordinary. The game had gone to the trouble of offering him items that fit open slots so that was more than welcome. He had just hoped for something a little more exciting. Ultimately the choice was fairly easy. While the helm and gloves offered an improvement to defense they looked like things he could pick up anywhere. The neckpiece on the other hand offered a nice jump in hit points with an item slot that in other games was traditionally harder to fill. He picked up the choker to equip and saw the notifications in his bottom right as the game confirmed his selection.

You Have Lost - Antique Pocket Watch
You Have Acquired - Boar Hide Choker

"Ah this concludes our business," Grins smiled, tossing the other two items into the crate before handing it back to Hebbs.

"What about seeing this through?" Kurt asked, trying to keep a whine out of his voice. "Something tells me there's more to this than you lost a watch."

"You're not ready for that," Grins snorted. "The way you carry yourself, I doubt you can even use that goat sticker you're carrying around. Me and the boys will take it from here."

And now we were back to this, Kurt thought as the dwarf went back to ignoring him. It looked like it was time to go back to the tactic he used with the bartender upstairs. Rising to his feet Kurt activated his shadow sight again and looked down on the dwarf allowing the chair to fall back with a heavy thud. Instantly the room went silent and Kurt made himself heard by everyone.

"I didn't come all this way to take a back seat to some half sized thug so why don't you just skip to the part where you clue me in on the next step in the quest line," Kurt glowered mustering all the intimidation he could muster.

"I tell you what boy," Grins growled, rising to his feet and coming around the table. "You aren't the first person I've seen with a little bit of magic about them so I'm not impressed. Might be you have what we need to set this thing off but you look a little green to me. I tell you what though.

You land a hit with that bit of steel you got there and I'll bring you on board for what I have planned."

Chairs scraped across the floor as all the nearby patrons made room. Kurt found himself standing in the middle of a circle as the loud room quieted to steady murmur. Moving across from Kurt, Grins held his hands wide and addressed him as much as everyone else. "If this pup can land a shot on me then I'm going to bring him in on what we all have planned." He stopped for a moment as he let the room enjoy a laugh at Kurt's expense before beginning again. "If he doesn't land a shot then we'll all show him the way up and out and he'll be on his way."

"Do you have any idea what we're doing right now?" Greg asked, alarmed for the first time. "There's a good chance we're both going to be waiting for the reroll."

Without answering Kurt unsheathed his gladius in the most fluid motion he could manage to the cheers of some. These men wanted a show and that's just what they'd get. Not waiting a moment longer Kurt sprung into action swinging wildly with an overhand strike that Grins easily sidestepped. Once he saw his swing was going to miss he decided it was going to be a faint and thrust out with a kick toward the dwarf's center of mass. He felt ridiculous as he stumbled when he caught nothing but air while Grins once again simply moved away from him. A chorus of jeers rang out from the crowd and Kurt could feel the heat in his cheeks.

Warily Kurt circled the dwarf who moved much quicker than he would have first thought him capable. Bringing the sword across his body, Kurt slashed again crosswise at the dwarf's midsection anticipating the dodge. As Grins moved back Kurt arched the blade's momentum around into a thrust. Sucking in his stomach the dwarf leaned forward slamming both fists together on Kurt's wrist opening his grip and sending the weapon flying. Cold numb flooded through his hand as he could only stagger back

215

and stare in disbelief as a roar of laughter swept across the room.

"Like I was saying boys, all he needed to do was land one hit on ole Grins and I would have taken him under my wing and trained him up right," the dwarf said, playing to the room. "I think it's time for us to show this lad out before he really hurts himself."

With everyone beginning to stir, Grins turned to some of the onlookers and began shaking hands and receiving claps on the back. The chance was passing quickly and Kurt did the only thing he could think of. Sliding in low, he shot for the dwarf's leg hooking it just behind the knee. Thrusting upward into a standing position his length provided enough leverage to get the dwarf airborne. He cringed inwardly as he watched Grins land on a nearby table breaking two of the legs out from under it. In the next instant the room was silent. Most of the men and women in the room looked like they were ready to murder him on the spot. Hard people shot him menacing glares and reached for weapons.

"Bwahaha," the dwarf roared from his back. He wiped a tear from his eye as he tried to speak through the laughter. "Now I have not had a flip like that in some time, lad. Maybe old Eddy sent you here for a reason."

Kurt felt his jaw drop open. Did this lunatic actually know who had sent him? Was he just messing with him this entire time? Kurt didn't know whether to be flabbergasted or furious. This guy must have been testing him this entire time. Looking around the room people began going back to their own conversations ignoring him entirely as Grins laid on the floor laughing to himself. With a groan he put up a hand and Kurt helped him to his feet.

"So what's your name kid?" the still chuckling dwarf asked.

"My name is Turk. Why didn't you tell me you knew who sent me with the watch?"

"Ah where's the fun in that? Only one man would have sent you to give me that watch. I am a bit surprised he didn't fill you in on the details of the why though."

"I have a feeling you're going to do that now?" Kurt asked hopefully.

"Yeah I can do that. You handle yourself well enough to be of use and you obviously have the sight which is what we really need."

Self consciously Kurt dismissed his shadow sight forgetting he had even still had it activated. He was becoming a bit more quick to use it now. Kurt knew he had to be careful when and where he activated it so the Order of Light didn't catch word of his ability. Just being able to wield magic like that was becoming addicting. The world became a bit dimmer at once and he almost missed having it active.

"No need to worry about using that down here. A lot of the boys have a blessing from the night or two. No one from the Order is down here at least."

A man brought over Kurt's sword as he sat down across from Grins at a nearby table. Everyone in the room was making it a point to not be anywhere near their conversation. For his part Grins demeanor seemed to have changed since being picked up off the floor. Before long he had an ale in his hand and was looking at Kurt trying to figure out just what was sitting across the table from him. Kurt couldn't help himself and tried to spur on the conversation.

"So what's next?"

"That's the question isn't it? Well Turk, you're not wrong about there being more to this. Everyone you see down here is working toward a common goal. If ole Eddy had you bring me that watch, he probably thought you could help us out. I needed to know if you could handle yourself."

"I can handle myself well enough," Kurt said a little too indignantly.

217

Truthfully his fight with Grins hadn't done much for his pride.

"You've got spirit, lad, and that's not for nothing. With that sword though, you're green and that's being generous. The thing is you got the sight. That's not something we run into all that often. Eddy has it and I'm sure there are others but that's what we need right now."

"Let me guess, Edward wasn't able to help you?"

"Yeah Eddy's a bit long in the tooth," Grins said, taking a long pull from his tankard. "He took the watch with him to keep it safe until he could find someone with the sight."

"I'm still not sure what's going on."

"Shut your yap for a minute kid and I'll explain," Grins said letting out a frustrated sigh. "It's like I was saying. We're all working toward a common goal down here. There are people hiding all over the world just like us but maybe not in so many numbers. People like me worship the Lord of the Night. That power you got there comes from him and I'm not talking about that imposter whose acting like he's in charge now."

"Yeah Edward told me a bit about that."

"Great kid, work on listening right now."

"Dude, this guy's kinda dick," Greg added. "You sure you want to run with him?"

"Now most humans don't realize what it was like before the Dark Lord took over. Somewhere along the line the facts got mixed up and we ended up with people believing the Lord of Night was the problem. Humans like you think the Dark Lord and the Lord of Night are one in the same. The older races know better but short lived people like the humans don't know the difference. Problem is there are a lot of humans and not so many dwarves these days."

Grins took a deep drink of his ale before leaning in to continue. "You see the imposter cut off the real Lord of Night from this world by

218

fouling his temples. He stole the power for himself and took the rightful lord's spot. Black Crystal is home to one of these temples but now the city itself is overrun with all manner of evil leaching power from the temple. So all the fine people in this camp were pushed out or are what's left of the people whose ancestors were pushed out of the city."

"And you want to take back the city?" Kurt asked.

"Aye in time we'll do just that. First we gotta take back the temple. The temple of Black Crystal will give us a foothold while cutting off the Dark Lord's creatures from their power. That's where you come in. The watch gets us in the door but we need someone with the sight to go in and reactivate the crystal at the heart of the temple. If we can do that the true Lord of Night will have a foothold back into the world. It will be the first step to letting people come back out of hiding."

Kurt could see the dwarf was passionate in his belief. It was a cause that he could get behind and it made sense. If something like his Shadow Sight existed then in this world something had to power it. It didn't make sense for it to just automatically be from some evil force otherwise the Mabel quest wouldn't exist. Why would any of this quest chain exist if a player wasn't meant to go down it? It was almost as if half of the game was just waiting to be unlocked.

"What a load of bullshit," Greg blurted and he bounced up and down behind Grins. "There is no way any of this is legit."

"Ah Grins can you excuse me a moment? I need to have a word with my brother the wisp." Turning to his brother he lowered his voice to somewhere between a whisper and a growl. "Dude what is it this time?"

"I just think I would have heard something about all of this by now," Greg said indignantly. "I mean how come literally nobody has heard of the Lord of Night? There would have been something on it in beta or since launch if this second faction thing was legit."

"Seriously Greg, you haven't been right about this yet. What's the issue?"

Greg was silent for a moment. "I just don't see how this works out man. Either you get yourself killed here because this is some kind of trap or you're right and we're not going to be able to run the main questline because your faction is killed."

Kurt was a little taken aback by his brother's honesty. It had been his brother's idea for him to play and a big part of that was running through what he considered the main storyline. For whatever reason Kurt just couldn't let this thread go. Maybe it wasn't the way to go but not for the reasons Greg came up with. Maybe he should reconsider.

"Greg if you want me to step away from this thing, I will. I just think we're onto something here. What if there is an aspect of this game no one has found yet. We could be unraveling something huge. I came here to play with you so it's your call."

"No, go ahead," Greg said after thinking for a while. "When I reroll though we're going to figure this out. Something is going to have to give if you can't run the main quest line with me."

"I'm just wondering if what everyone believes is the main questline is all there is to it," Kurt smirked before turning back to Grins. "Alright we're in. Where do we go from here?"

"I can have the boys ready to go in a couple hours. No sense waiting around and letting nerves get in the way. Some of the rowdier lads will draw the attention of the ratters while we take a small group up to the temple. We get you inside and you get things sorted out. I'm not really sure on the how but if we can get the temple sorted out we can begin retaking the city. Eddy was never long on the details but how hard could it be?"

Will you accept the quest, "Time to Help III?"

YES

NO

Now a wisp doesn't have eyes per say but Kurt could feel his brother's boring into him. Most of what Grins had told him was full of assumptions and relied on figuring it out along the way. For a moment Kurt wondered what kind of half baked operation he was signing on for but then dismissed the thought and accepted the quest.

"Grins I don't know how this is going to work but I'm in."

The dwarf roared in laughter as he sprang up from the table clapping Kurt on the shoulder. "I knew I liked something about you, Turk. Might be we just figured out what that was. Come back when you're ready and we'll take back a city."

With a solid direction for the quest, Kurt turned and left the bar. Stepping out into the moonlight he could help but feel adrift. They had time to kill at least according to their conversation. Looking around the refugee camp really didn't inspire much in the way of adventure. In truth now that he was here he wasn't sure he would stay without a real reason. Where the previous towns he'd seen bustled with activity and players, the Black Crystal refugee camp was just kinda depressing. Lacking a better idea Kurt turned to his brother.

"Any ideas on how to kill some time?" Kurt asked his brother. "I could log out but I know your stance on that."

"Well since you're about to go do a quest with a lot of combat I'd say maybe get some healing items?"

"I'm not flush with cash but it's not a bad idea," Kurt admitted.

"Roughspun shouldn't cost that much. You can at least make some bandages then. Potions are probably going to be a bit out of reach. Well at least the really good ones."

"Maybe we should just see what we can find," Kurt suggested.

While the camp lacked an expansive trade district there were vendors to be found. It didn't take much searching to find a woman selling scraps of roughspun cloth. For fifty-five copper a piece he bought a stack of ten. They continued searching for useful items, stopping only to convert the cloth into bandages to save inventory space. It was beginning to look like the bandages would be the extent of the healing items available when Greg noticed something.

"Hey bro check it out," the wisp said, gaining elevation.

'What?"

"See the guy walking down there with the heavy pack? That's a traveling salesman."

Kurt squinted down toward the end of the street. Sure enough there was a man dressed in durable clothes carrying a walking stick with an oversized hiking pack strapped to his back. Judging by the direction he was headed he would be out of town before long. Breaking into a run Kurt caught up with him before long. He was panting when he finally got near enough to the man to hail him.

'Hey are you a merchant?" Kurt shouted, waving his hand.

'Yes sir I am," the man said, turning completely oblivious to the look of Kurt's approach. "The name's Glover. I travel the region selling useful items and curiosities. Is there something I can interest you in?"

"Actually yeah, I'm in need of healing items if you have any."

"Let's see what I have," Glover said excitedly as he pulled his pack off with a flourish. With a quick shake a tripod sprouted from the bottom of the bag as he opened the top. Greg buzzed overhead hoping to get a better look while the man rummaged around. Sifting through various mundane goods from food stuff to household supplies it would be a wonder if the man didn't have something. After a bit of searching he produced a pair of small stoppered bottles. "I think these might be what you're looking for."

Kurt leaned in and quickly examined the pale red liquids. He was not disappointed.

Weak Healing Tonic

Effect: Heals 75 HP over 15 Seconds

Cooldown: 10 Minutes

Quality: Uncommon

Requirements: None

"Yeah those look good," Kurt said eagerly. "How much are they?"

"I can let those go for three silver and thirty-five copper each."

"I can do that," Kurt said eagerly, pulling coins out from his inventory. He had honestly thought something like a healing potion would cost much more but they did seem to be relatively low level. "How many do you have?"

"Sorry I'm afraid I only have the two," Glover said sympathetically wiping his brow.

You Have Lost - 6 Silver and 75 Copper

You Have Acquired - Weak Healing Tonic x2

It was a small disappointment but he was happy to hand the coins over. As he was getting ready to put the potions in his pack a thought struck him and he checked the two small pouches on his belt. As he hoped each pouch held a potion easily giving him quick access to them. He experimented a little and tried to put them both in the same pouch but just couldn't get them to fit. Kurt was still fiddling with his inventory when his

223

brother broke in.

"Hey check and see if he has any seasonings for cooking. It's an easy skill to up when you're out running around."

"What kind of cooking seasonings do you have?" Kurt asked as the vendor rearranged the items in his pack.

Glover went back to his pack and pulled out a series of pouches for Kurt to examine.

Seasoning Salt

Uses: Cooking

Quantity: 25

Quality: Normal

Requirements: None

Bag of Cinnamon

Uses: Cooking

Quantity: 30

Quality: Fine

Requirements: None

Saffron in Bulk

Uses: Cooking

Quantity: 10

Quality: Superb

Requirements: Expert Cooking

Not having any formal training in the cooking skill, Kurt wasn't really sure of what he was looking at. He had heard of the ingredients before but didn't really know what he needed. There wasn't a cookbook he was going by or anything. Immediately his vision was assaulted by a pop up.

Cookbook

- **Savory Wolf Steak** [Novice Cooking 0]

  Slab of Wolf Meat + Savory Spices

  Savory Wolf Steak

  Use: Gives +5% Stamina Gain for 1 Hour

  Quality: Normal

  Requirements: None

Annoyed, he quickly dismissed it. While the information was helpful it wasn't what he was looking for right now. "What do you think Greg?"

"I'd say just pick up the seasoning salt for now. That works with pretty much any meat. The other two are up to you but the saffron is probably something you won't be able to use for a while."

"How much for these?" Kurt asked, turning back to the vendor.

'Seasoning salt is a silver and fourteen copper. The cinnamon is four silver and twenty-two copper. Let me see here," Glover trailed off checking a ledger. "And the saffron is forty-seven silver even."

Kurt nearly choked hearing the prices. He wasn't sure what to expect but the price of saffron was nuts. Thinking about it he couldn't really justify dropping the money on the cinnamon either without having a specific use for it. The prices made his decision an easy one.

"I'll take the seasoning salt,"Kurt said looking over the bag to see if anything else interested him. "Also what do you have in the way of fire starters?"

"I can sell you a flint and steel kit for one silver and eight copper."

"Sounds good I'll take that too." Feeling his coin purse growing ever lighter Kurt fished out the appropriate change and handed it over.

You Have Lost - 2 Silver and 22 Copper

You Have Acquired - Seasoning Salt

You Have Acquired - Flint and Steel Kit

"Thanks I think that'll do it." Kurt said, making sure everything ended up in its place.

"It was a pleasure doing business with you sir, Glover said, waving as he prepared to leave town. "Please do not hesitate if you see me again. My inventory is always changing."

Kurt gave a short wave before walking back toward the center of the encampment. "Think we've killed enough time before the quest?" he asked, turning his attention back to his brother.

"We're probably good to go back," Greg said thinking aloud. "I don't even know if you have to do anything more than exit and come back honestly. As real as they've made some stuff, other things still run by game rules."

"Are you serious?"

"No, I've never been here before, remember? I'm just messing with you. We can go back and check. That's the only way to know."

A brisk walk found Kurt and Greg back at the bar beneath the Drunken Kiwi. As they approached the man guarding the door opened it and gave Kurt a nod of recognition. Entering the bar's common room displayed a very different atmosphere than the one he'd taken in mere hours before. Instead of a room of hard drinking loud adventurers looking to lose well won coin, Kurt now looked upon a stoic group of stone faced men and women set to depart for a mission from which they may not return. Kurt felt himself trying to walk with a quiet caution as he took in the scene. Grins approached clad in scale mail with a stone warhammer at his side. He nodded to Kurt as he made his way across the room.

"Glad you came back, lad. We've a grim task ahead of us. I've got a couple people I want you to meet, then we'll be on our way."

"Okay," was all Kurt could think to say as Grins led him to a nearby table where two human men and an elf woman sat speaking in hushed tones. He and Grins sat and the group grew silent waiting for the dwarf to speak.

"This will be the strike team to get you into the temple. Let me make some introductions," Grins began gesturing to an elf with two long thin daggers laying on the table before her. "This is Lady Eoseth. She's not really royalty but the way she carries herself around here you'd think she was. Anyway she's got a mean dog she runs with and she's handy in a fight."

"A pleasure to meet you," Eoseth managed through gritted teeth as her stare bored holes into Grins who was doing his best to live up to his namesake.

"My name is Turk," Kurt volunteered, trying to diffuse the situation.

"A pleasure to meet you, Turk,"the elf said, twisting her scowl into a wicked sneer. "It's too bad you've already met Grins."

"Anyway," the dwarf continued. "The man in the dress is Alen. He may not look like much but he hurls a mean spell or two."

"Do you work for the Order of Light?" Kurt asked, genuinely surprised.

"Formerly," the man said indifferently. "We had a bit of falling out over doctrine. I make my way out here now instead."

"Which brings us to the final member of our team. This here is Greyson. He's a jack of all trades as it were. Does a little bit of stabbing for us, a bit of shooting and sometimes a bit of singing. Can't really say anything bad about the lad. He's just handy."

"So what's the plan?" Kurt ventured looking to break the ice with the group.

"I'll let Eoseth fill you in," Grins said, rising from the table giving Kurt a wink. "I need to see a man about a horse."

"A plan would be overstating what we have here," the elf began clearing her throat. "There are enough people here to cause a bit of a distraction for us. The idea is they draw out the rodents and we slip over to the temple. Grins has an idea to get you in but past that we don't know anything about Black Crystal Temple."

"Once you're in you're on your own," Greyson sang as he absently strummed at his lute.

"Well that's reassuring," Kurt grumbled but the man only shrugged.

Everyone silently watched each other for a time or tried to watch each other while not looking like they were watching each other. Grins returned to the table a short time later. Everyone that was seated rose at once and Kurt was given a familiar prompt.

You Have Been Invited to a Party by Grins
            Accept   Decline

The thought of joining an NPC's party seemed a bit odd to Kurt. He'd had NPC's in his party in other games but this would be the first time one had invited him. It was just another thing he would have to get used to in this new kind of immersive game. Not giving it much more thought he accepted the invite.

"Alright everyone pipe down," Grins bellowed as he moved to stand on a nearby chair. "You all have your orders and someone in charge of your parties. I won't go over that again. What I will repeat to you is that you need to make a ruckus once we get into Black Crystal but don't push into the city. Your job is to draw them off. Don't get killed or captured. This is going to be hard enough without someone doing something stupid. So that's the big speech. Are we ready?"

Oddly a roar erupted from the crowd as weapons and armor clanged with the group of men and women rising to their feet. Grins pumped a fist into the air shouting something inaudible before pointing to the door. A surge caught Kurt as he was half drug out the exit. The press wheeled around the tavern to the street out front where adventurers summoned horses and more exotic mounts before moving on toward the city limits. Standing with his party he looked around in alarm as they all summoned mounts that either came running from off in the distance or in Eoseth's case appeared from thin air.

"Uh hey Grins, I have a little problem," Kurt said sheepishly.

"What's that kid?"

"I don't have a mount yet."

"You don't have a mount?" Grins asked incredulously. "How were you expecting to get into the city?"

"You didn't say anything about needing one."

"I didn't say anything about needing to wear pants either but you managed that."

"Seriously, I'm going to need a ride."

"You'll have to ride double and don't look at me!" Grins patted a dappled mare gently. "Quartz is a one dwarf kinda girl."

Kurt looked at the others mounting their horses. Shaking his head, he glossed over the smarmy Greyson and his eyes landed on Eoseth. Her smoky grey horse shed a thin fog that obscured its legs hinting at its magical nature. While it was a leaner breed it looked more than capable of carrying the both of them. He moved forward with the question on his lips as Eoseth turned at his approach and whistled. From the shadows between buildings strode a rust colored wolf sniffing the night air as if just awakened from a nap.

"Stop dawdling and double up with Alen," Grins barked. "We already have this little war party moving. It cannot be stopped now while you give it a think."

Turning to the caster Kurt could only nod as the man patted a spot behind the saddle. Greg could hold it back now longer as he let out a burst of laughter punctuated by incoherent babble while he tried to catch his breath. Kurt thought if he ignored his brother for long enough maybe he too would be unable to hear him as he hauled himself up onto the horse. Kurt shifted back and forth trying to get settled in the small space behind the saddle.

"You might want to hang on," Alen said tentatively. "Don't hang on too tight though. I'm not the best rider and I really don't have much experience riding double."

Grabbing a hold of the caster must have been the signal because they were off. Kurt really didn't have anything to compare it to. He'd never been horseback riding before. They were not moving at full speed but it was still going to be much quicker covering the distance to the city. What had seemed just outside the camp when he landed was now easy to see as a kind of optical illusion. The size of the city walls in the distance was truly impressive but even more so was the spire holding the city's namesake. The stone walls were probably somewhere between a hundred and two hundred feet tall if he had to guess. High above that however was the spire with an onyx crystal large enough that Kurt questioned if the wall could hide it if it rested on the ground.

"So how will we get past those walls?" Kurt shouted.

"That won't be an issue," Alen explained clenching the reins everytime he moved. "The city fell a long time ago. The rattlings can be a lot of things but they are not builders. When they sacked the city they occupied many of the structures left standing but have done nothing to reinforce its defenses. They steal, scavenge and infest. They are resourceful and cunning but they are users not makers."

"So the gates are down then?"

"Out of everything we're going to do, getting in is the easy part," Alen said looking back to smile.

Chapter 12

As if on cue the small column made its final approach to a set of massive iron and stone gates that had long been pulled free from the wall. Using them as giant ramps the main host thundered forward into the city proper sending up a cacophony of war cries. Kurt's own group slowed and pulled back, slipping down a side street and riding a short distance before dismissing their mounts. With everyone else drawing weapons, Kurt didn't want to feel left out. Pulling free his bow he waited for the next instruction Grins was about to give.

"You know how to use that thing better than your goat sticker, lad?"

"Well enough," Kurt grumbled defensively.

"Let's hope so. Greyson watches our back. Eoseth you're up front with the mutt. The rest of you with me. Let's keep it quiet. Even with that lot hooping and hollering we don't need to draw any extra attention."

Eoseth took point and the group was on the move and the sounds of battle grew more distant. Ducking in and out of alleys the elf navigated the cityscape as if it were a stone forest. Patrols of rattlings raced through the main thoroughfares toward the outer reaches of the city. Occasionally they would have to pause or double back and find another route but for nearly an hour the road was uneventful. Closing on the square where Black Crystal Temple stood a small group of rattlings weapons at the ready.

Rattling Spearman | Level 2

Rattling Spearman | Level 2

Rattling Spearman | Level 2

Rattling Marauder | Level 3

Rattling Marauder | Level 3

Rattling Marauder | Level 3

The group itself looked relatively benign considering their level and the size of the party he was in. Upfront the marauders held large two handed swords with some kind of ringmail protecting them. Behind that the spearmen were a little less armored but had the look of ranged combatants. All in all it seemed pretty straight forward.

"Anything we're not seeing?" Grins asked, tightening his shield to his arm.

The elf laid a hand on the neck of her wolf and closed her eyes for a moment. Slipping into the shadows just outside of the alley the beast made a quick circuit of the immediate area. Kurt lost sight of the pet completely after a couple minutes despite knowing where he was heading. Eoseth opened her eyes as her wolf returned. She took a moment to nuzzle his head and scratch him behind the ear.

"It would appear there is only the single group guarding the courtyard," Eoseth said.

"Alright here's the plan. Eoseth you take the pup and sneak around behind them buggers. I'll go up and get their attention. Greyson you and the kid cover me. Alen be useful."

The elf and wolf slipped away even before Grins had finished speaking. No one really reacted as Kurt sat dumbfounded. It wasn't much of a plan but before he could protest the dwarf was running across the temple square shouting something in his native tongue. Alen let out an exasperated sigh before following after him beginning the words of some sort of spell. Pulling out a pair of hand crossbows Greyson turned to Kurt.

"No worries, Turk. I'll pick out the targets. You just follow my lead."

Kurt followed him out of the alleyway just in time to see a detonation of light in the middle of the rattlings. All six were thrown roughly ten feet from where they were standing in all directions. From opposite sides Grin, Esoth and her wolf fell upon the group tearing into the fallen rat men. Kurt nearly missed his cue when one of the marauders began to stand and two crossbow bolts sank into his armored body. Skidding to halt, Kurt nocked an arrow and focused on the damaged marauder. The creature staggered but didn't fall. Exhaling he let his shot go catching the rattling in his center of mass.

You Have Slain - Rattling Marauder | Level 3

Moving his attention to the rest of the battle, Kurt could see it was quickly turning into a rout. Eoseth and her wolf were each finishing a spearman while Grins had the last two marauders severely damaged and on their heels beneath a flurry of strikes. Greyson fired another bolt into the last remaining spearman while Kurt followed suit. A blast from Alen finished him off triggering the notification.

You Have Slain - Rattling Spearman | Level 2

Before Kurt could find another target the battle was over. Grins and Eoseth nursed minor wounds which Alen was quick to heal off of them. The rest of the group was largely untouched as the combat was over almost as soon as it had begun. Waiting for what would come next Kurt moved to loot the two kills he'd taken part in.

You Have Acquired - 1 Silver and 8 Copper

You Have Acquired - 73 Copper

You Have Acquired - Shadow Tainted Throwing Knife

"Look alive everyone. We need to get Turk inside before anymore rats come looking," Grins barked as he looted his kills. "Come on let's get up front."

Moving through the square, the group came to a large tiled walkway leading to the temple proper. A series of statues bordered the path at regular intervals showing the different phases of the moon as they led up to the temple door. Reaching a hand out Grins stopped them from getting too close as he called them all over.

"Alright kid you're up," the dwarf began as he fished the watch out of his pocket handing it to Kurt. "We only have one shot at this so listen carefully. This watch you brought me does more than tell the time. It's called Gressel's Time Catcher. Once you activate it all you can do is move. If you try anything else the magic stops. When you use it you're not going to be able to use it again for a while so be smart with it. Have a look at it."

Kurt turned the watch over in his hand and was able to examine it in depth unlike when it only appeared as a quest item before. The dwarf's explanation seemed to function like he had used the identify spell on it. His eyes bulged when he saw just how much power the item actually contained.

Gressel's Time Catcher

Effect: Stopping this watch causes time to stop around you for thirty seconds. Any action taken other than moving before the time is up negates the effect.

Cooldown: 168 Hours

Quality: Unique Extraordinary Magical

"Greg are you seeing this?" Kurt asked, astonished by the item's power.

"Yeah dude that thing's nuts. I'm totally doing the Mabel quest when I respawn."

"Aye it's impressive boy but we only get one shot at this so listen up," Grins said. "Those statues aren't up there just to look pretty. Each one of them can fry you in a single shot. They're magical like that. Normally you can't run past them but with that watch you should be able to do just that. Once you get to the door you're on your own but Eddy seemed to think you'd need the sight. I'm sure you'll figure something out."

"So that's it?" Kurt asked, shouldering his bow. "Nothing else to go on?"

Grins could only shrug as the rest of the party dutifully scanned the area for threats or tried to pay attention to anything else. It was a video game trope. He knew it. The classic single person going at it alone against all odds. Granted he didn't know what those odds were at the moment but few things had felt as video gamey as this. It was why he was here. Turning the watch over in his hand he looked at it for a moment then activated it.

The world shuddered to a halt around him. Clouds that had been lazily drifting overhead stopped in place and the world around him grew completely silent. The slight breeze that he had not even completely noticed before was now utterly still. Around him Greg and the NPCs sat still as if carved from wax. Once the initial shock waned, Kurt noticed a countdown in the top of his vision where the game displayed his buffs and debuffs. With only twenty-five seconds left on the clock, Kurt took off at a run down the walkway leading to the temple entrance. He winced as he passed by the first statue half expecting the magic to fail. To his relief the blast never came as he turned his attention forward passing by the temple's trap. Moments later he was at the temple entrance no worse for wear.

A large bronze plate sat in the middle of a set of stone double doors under the temple overhang. The plate itself contained fifteen blank ceramic tiles arranged in a four by four grid with one space in the top right corner missing. Tentatively Kurt reached up to move one of the tiles and the world around him shuddered back into motion with a dizzying suddenness. Hearing his brother yell, Kurt turned in time to see Greg rubber banded forward at an alarming rate. Before the wisp made it to the second pillar on the walkway, a beam of white energy shot out crystalizing him instantly. Forgetting himself Kurt took two steps back toward the scene when the smell of ozone filled his nose and he instinctively dodged backwards. The stone just ahead of where he was standing sizzled for a moment as he crashed hard into the temple doors.

Rubbing his shoulder instinctively, Kurt made his way back to his feet. Even now in the distance he could see Grins and the rest of the group returning to the shadows of the alley they had used to access the temple square. He would be on his own from here on out. Turning back to the puzzle he looked for any kind of clue that might open the door. The sliding puzzle looked familiar enough as each piece slid freely and stopped where he left it even defying gravity at times. The odd thing was each piece was identical and blank. Maybe this was why the person who wanted to enter needed Shadow Sight.

Activating his ability revealed an intricate pattern of concentric circles jumbled by the tiles. Moving the tiles into place was only a matter of time now that he had a discernible direction with the puzzle. Starting from the top left he shifted tiles in place one after another until each one was where it needed to be. As the last one clicked the entire plate glowed with a soft purple light. With the slightest of pushes the large doors opened inward as a hiss of ancient air flooded toward him.

Kurt looked back to where his brother had fallen. There was something still there but he couldn't do anything about it now. Resolving to push forward, he entered the temple. Motes of dust floated up from the floor with each step Kurt took. Moonlight filtered down through cobwebs enhanced by his shadow sight casting an otherwise dark corridor into brilliant relief. Set into the walls themselves were thousands of pieces of crystal reflecting the light from above in a way that was reminiscent of a field of stars. Rooms and smaller hallways branched off the main walkway as one might expect from a large temple. Kurt paused at times ducking his head into some of these but instinctually moved forward toward the building's center.

At the end of the corridor a pair of double doors were propped open revealing a circular room of stadium seating around two-thirds of its circumference. Twenty or so rows of seats lead down to a raised dais as the room's focal point. A small altar and lectern sat to the front of the dais while further back a large runed pillar extended upward through a massive skylight high above the temple. Looking up past the ceiling, Kurt could see the Black Crystal floating high above the temple. It was then that he caught something with his shadow sight. He climbed onto the dais and inspected the stone column. Brushing away years of neglect, Kurt could see large swaths of text glowing in the all too familiar shadow script. As he studied the text, what he could see would translate before his eyes. Setting his pack on the floor, Kurt pulled off his cloak and wiped at the pillar. A cloud of dust plumed up before him. Coughing he did his best to wave it away. When enough of the dust cleared to leave the text visible, Kurt shook out and replaced his cloak. Covering his nose and mouth with his sleeve he leaned in to read.

I bestow upon you this black tourmaline as a conduit for you the people of

Wester to your Lady of Night. As this stands as my gateway to your world it also serves as your connection to me. I give this gift freely to you and so long as it shines our connection will be just as brilliant. Tend to this gift as I will tend to you always.

Reading the script didn't make a lot of sense even with the translation given by his sight. Circling the pillar Kurt did not notice anything out of the ordinary or what he thought would be ordinary for an abandoned temple. He turned the words over in his head and thought about them. The crystal served as these people's link to their god so that had to be significant. It certainly wasn't shining now. That was probably significant too. So maybe the question was how does one jump start a giant magical crystal?

Kurt looked over the stone altar for some sort of instructions or magical panel. If he was being honest, he was looking for some kind of bump of direction. The lectern proved to be just as useless after inspection. The quest still wasn't completed so there had to be something more to do. What that was Kurt could not figure out. He moved around the dais a while longer before giving up entirely. There had to be something else somewhere that he was missing. A smaller door led off away from the main worship area from behind the dais. It seemed to be as good a place to start as any.

The room beyond seemed to be a kind priest's antechamber. It had fallen into the same state of disuse as the rest of the temple. Whatever garments that were stored here had long since degraded into nothing. Ancient wooden furniture still stood intact but looked as if the slightest application of weight would destroy it. A search of the room revealed nothing useful as far as Kurt could tell.

Moving back to the main audience chamber, Kurt had really thought he was onto something with the priest's antechamber. It would have been the perfect out of the way room for game designers to have hidden loot or a clue. It was just empty though. Like the rest of the temple there was just a whole lot of nothing. The whole place was giving an unpopulated beta vibe. It didn't make a lot of sense considering a quest had brought him to this point. The city outside was crawling with mobs but once inside there was nothing. Outside of the shadow script message, he hadn't seen anything indicating he was even in the right place.

Kurt looked at the pillar and the message again. The only real direction it gave him was the gigantic piece of black tourmaline that hovered high above the temple. As a religious message it seemed pretty generic but maybe the directions were more literal. Kurt looked up to the top of the stone column where the black rock hovered high above. There were plenty of deep grooves and hand holds in the decorative stone. It would be a long climb but it didn't seem out of the question. Lacking any other ideas Kurt began to climb.

Grasping the ridges of the pillar was surprisingly easy as an unseen lip adorned each groove allowing Kurt's grip to lock in as if on a rock climbing wall in the real world. Now that he was moving, he also noticed that the even spacing of the ridges made it less like climbing a rock face and more like climbing a crude ladder. Looking to his stamina bar, Kurt was relieved to see that the drain wasn't all that taxing. As he moved the bar steadily dropped but it was at a very slow rate. In a few minutes he was high above the dais and at least level with the top rows of the amphitheater. Above him he could see that there was a gap in the ceiling where the pillar exited the building entirely. Kurt concentrated on the pillar in front of him and tried to ignore just how much further he had to go to get to that gap.

Fresh air drifted in from overhead as Kurt turned his head to see he was only a few feet away from the domed ceiling. He was down to only about half of his stamina but a rest would be welcome. Redoubling his efforts Kurt pushed forward. Once he was able to poke his head through the gap, Kurt noticed an overhang that covered the hole in the ceiling from the elements. It would be a bit of a squeeze but he was in no danger of getting stuck. Shimmying on his chest Kurt army crawled out onto the roof. Above the main worship room the glass ceiling gave the illusion of resting in midair. A sense of vertigo gripped him as he stared back into the room below. Rolling onto his back Kurt stared up at the night sky for a moment before closing his eyes and catching his breath.

An umbrella shaped overhang skirted the pillar just above the domed roof at roughly the same angle as the temple's. It wasn't overly tall or steep but only served to keep the weather from entering the temple itself. Kurt gauged just how much higher he'd have to climb by comparing what he could see overhead with the section that he had already scaled. His estimation was not promising. Considering he used about half of his stamina to get to this point and the distance to the top looked significantly higher than what he'd already climbed, he would need to wait for his bar to completely refill. So he sat and did just that.

Occasionally Kurt would hear the sounds of a distant skirmish or someone shouting but it was always in the distance. Without the light pollution of one of the villages or the overhang of the forest, he could finally see the night sky completely. With the moon full or as near to it as he could tell, Kurt could see everything as clearly as if it were daytime but looking into the night sky with his shadow sight gave it an added dimension. Normally whenever he'd looked at the night sky he saw dots of light in the distance. He could see some detail with the moon but now it was completely different. The stars now had a field of depth they hadn't before and the moon looked more spherical. It was hard to put a finger on but he felt like it looked more real than viewing it with his normal vision. Laying on the roof he spent a few minutes just looking at the sky seeing it for the first time.

Glancing at his stamina bar Kurt was startled to see it was full. He wasn't sure how long it had been that way but there was a task at hand. Scrambling to his feet, Kurt made his way over to the pillar's overhang. Taking a quick couple steps as a run up, he vaulted onto it slipping slightly before righting himself. Working himself up onto his knees, Kurt inched his way away from the edge and toward the pillar. The closer he got the more the overhang leveled off and he was comfortable moving to his feet. Testing the grooves he found them more weathered than the one's inside the temple but still had a noticeable lip. He put a little weight on one as he pulled himself up testing the surface. It seemed sturdy enough.

Hauling himself up onto the pillar, Kurt continued his climb. He managed another ten or fifteen feet before pausing for a moment. A gust of wind pulled at his cloak and Kurt clamped down on the rock with his grip. He couldn't help but look to the roof below. It was a mistake. Involuntarily he hugged the pillar tighter. This was different than climbing inside of the temple. Forcing a look at his stamina bar through clenched eyes, Kurt could see it steadily falling. Cloak pulling at him, it was all he could do to hold on. If he didn't get moving again, however, his stamina would eventually bottom out and he'd fall anyway. Tilting his head upward Kurt opened an eye and slid a hand toward the next handhold. He wasn't quite sure how but he managed to pull himself up a little higher. Kurt moved a shaking foot up to the next groove and pushed off.

Systematically Kurt got himself moving again. He held a little closer to the pillar this time and was forced to stop when the wind picked up. He was making progress again. Kurt was able to make out more details from the top now. The head of the column hung out overhead a short distance creating a platform that he could easily rest on. A low hum that Kurt felt as much as heard was resonating from above but it was sporadic. He would notice it for a moment then it would be gone. When he thought it was gone, it would start up again and then last a while before stopping abruptly.

242

Daring to peer up at the crystal hovering high overhead, Kurt thought he saw hazy waves coming off of it at times but then wondered if it was his imagination. It wasn't much to go on but he thought it was enough of a sign to investigate further. He had come this far hadn't he?

His stamina bar was hovering at right around twenty-five percent. A dull ache was setting into his joints and muscles from the prolonged tension. With the struggle mounting, Kurt focused on the face of the pillar directly in front of him and worked his way up methodically. He banged his knuckles and had to steady himself as he reached for another handhold that wasn't there. To his relief when he looked up he saw the ledge he'd been working toward. Readjusting his grip, Kurt reached out over his head testing the surface above. To his relief his fingers found a lip he could grasp. One last look to his stamina bar told him it was now or never as he pulled up with his hand as he pushed off with his feet. For the briefest of moments, he hung by one hand with nothing but open air around him before getting a second hand on the platform above. Hoping to salvage momentum from the move he pulled as soon as his second hand made contact raising his chest level with the edge. Gravity asserted itself again as he felt himself starting to slide but he rammed his breastbone hard into the stone. Swinging a leg around he was able to hook his heel on the surface and shimmy to safety.

Kurt lay face down on the cool stone with something jamming into his hip as he panted rapidly. His stamina was gradually returning and Kurt could feel his breath and pulse slowing. The tension in his hands and muscles was the closest thing the game had given him to pain but even that was now fading. Tentatively he pushed himself up to a seated position. The city of Black Crystal was spread out below him and the signs of battle were evident. Groups of torches moved through the streets while larger fires blazed in intersections and even some buildings. If he listened carefully, he could hear faint shouts and screams at times. It was all the aftermath of getting him into the temple. He had better make it worth it.

Inspecting the top of the pillar, Kurt immediately saw what he'd been laying on. Four large brass prongs lay collapsed against the platform. Lifting one told him that they were attached but mobile. Kurt extended the arm upward until it clicked into place. Faint streaks of blue and red energy intertwined reaching down from the large crystal above. Seeing the result Kurt quickly moved the remaining three into place exponentially increasing the energy output with each. Once the final prong was moved into place the large black tourmaline began its descent. A realization washed over Kurt as he looked around seeing that he was in the middle of the world's largest jewelry setting.

"Ah shit," Kurt rasped as he scrambled for the ledge readying to lower himself over the side. Before the gem landed a lance of energy caught him and all Kurt saw was white. To the outside world the stone that gave the city its name landed, attaching itself to the temple for the first time in more years than anyone could remember. Power surged the holy site's dark halls once more and a beacon of light climbed into the heavens. A rallying cry rose up in the city turning guerilla fighting as a feint into a full on battle in the streets.

Chapter 13

Blinding light forced Kurt to dismiss his shadow sight. The room he was in appeared to be a perfect sphere of illuminated white tiles. As odd as this was, what rested in the room's center was what unnerved him. Floating silently was a woman made entirely of swirling stars giving her black void of a body shape. Runed stone bindings encased her joints while iron chains dripped smoke between them. Trussed into a fetal position he was not even sure that she was aware of his presence.

Kurt tried to step forward when he realized that he was in fact not standing on anything. Panic gripped him initially. When he failed to move in any direction he swung his head around looking for something to push off of or hang onto. Another pang of panic struck him as he noticed no way in or out of the room for the first time. Reaching out for the wall he drifted slowly toward it. Kurt focused on getting to the wall and his speed increased carrying him there. Once he arrived he moved to push off but failed to gain any real momentum. Maybe if he focused on where he wanted to be he thought. Concentrating on the woman in the center of the room he felt himself move through space toward her. Testing the game mechanics he rotated and tilted to approach her more or less face to face. It wasn't exact but he was getting the hang of the movement in empty space.

"I see you have gained an understanding on how to move here. It is similar to using a glide spell," the woman whispered unmoving. Kurt could not tell if she actually said the words or if they were only resonating in his mind. It was the only sound he had heard since appearing in the white room. His head jerked toward her with a start when she spoke again. "I am speaking to you telepathically. It is the only way we can communicate in this void."

"Who are you?" he asked looking into her eyeless face.

"Isn't it obvious? I am the Lady of Night. I am called Noctura. You came here to find me."

"Okay but where is here?" Kurt wondered while looking at the god's glowing stone bindings. "And why are you chained up?"

"This is a result of the Dark One usurping me ages ago. When I was bound to this place, I still had power. It was only once my temples were taken from me that I was cut off entirely. That has changed now that you are here. Even now my influence returns to the city of Wester and the imposter's horde is pushed back. It is why I brought you here. I have waited for too long for someone to strike away my chains."

Doing her best to straighten herself, the woman presented the manacles attached to her wrists. She was only able to pull them maybe a foot apart and not far from her body. The smoky chains linking them seemed only semisolid. Kurt pulled his sword free and looked at the bindings questioningly. Until this point he'd been so sure about following the quest line. He'd argued with his brother so stubbornly.

"You know a lot of this hasn't made sense for a while now," Kurt thought toward the bound god. "For starters for a temple that's been overrun and cut off from you, there really wasn't any resistance once I got inside. If I had to guess the only thing standing in my way were the temple's own safeguards. Why is that?"

"I understand your reluctance. I can explain," Noctura said patiently. "Free me and I can return us there to show you."

Will you complete the quest, "Time to Help III?"
YES

That really wasn't much to go on but now the quest prompt had appeared. He must be on the right path. The lack of information on the god's part wasn't reassuring but maybe she would fill him in and keep her word. He confirmed his choice and brought his sword down onto the chain. Soundlessly the blade came into contact with the chain meeting minimal resistance. A flash of purple sparks erupted and the manacles went dark. Turning to the side Noctura presented another chain binding her which Kurt cut through. In a repeat of the first the power from the manacles around her ankles flashed and faded. One last chain connected to the god's neck. Leaning back she presented it to him and he shattered it and at once she was free. With bare hands the god ripped the bonds from her body and stretched. Giving a dismissive wave of her hand the white room was gone.

Sword still in hand, Kurt swung his head around wildly only to see that he was standing on the raised dais in the center of the temple's main worship chamber again. Looking up through the glass ceiling revealed a brilliant beam of twisted blue and red light rising into the heavens. The black crystal itself now shown with a purple hue that split into the twin energies that made up the beam. Residual energy flowed back downward into the pillar and the temple itself lighting numerous unseen crystals set into the walls and fixtures surrounding him. The god appeared before him causing Kurt to stumble back onto the steps leading down onto the first row of seats.

"You've asked for an explanation and I shall give you one but let's take care of this quest business first," Noctura said with another wave of her hand.

Kurt's breath caught in his chest as a surge of energy filled him. He could not describe the feeling as anything other than refreshing. His body swelled and his mind expanded at once. The exhilaration was somewhere between winning his first league title and the first time he kissed a girl. It was anticipation, relief and excitement all at once. A notification shown in the corner of his vision.

You Have Received the Triumph - Chain Breaker

Advance to Level 2

Increase All Stats by 1

Unique Title: Champion of Dusk

Reputation Gain plus 1000 with Black Crystal

Reputation Level - Favorable 2 with Black Crystal

Reputation Loss minus 2000 with The Order of Light

Reputation Level - Unfavorable 4 with The Order of Light

His eyes went wide at the news. He had just leveled. Before he could open his character sheet, Kurt felt the god's eyes on him. Hastily he sheathed his sword and turned his attention to her. Greg was going to wig out when he found out the Mabel quest line ended with him getting a level. A smile he couldn't suppress crept across his face. This felt amazing.

"I see that you are pleased with the reward, Kurt," Noctura purred with a mischievous grin.

"Yeah I didn't expect...wait what did you just say?" Kurt was sure if he had heard her right but now it seemed like Noctura's grin was very knowing.

"You said you wanted an explanation. Should we keep it in game roleplay or would you like me to level with you? Your name is Kurt correct?"

"Um okay," was all Kurt could manage. His heart was now racing.

This was getting to be a little more metagame than he was expecting. "How do you know my name? I mean my real name."

"Perhaps you should have a seat," she began as she waited for him to comply. Once he did so she continued. "I have to admit I brought you here under some false pretenses. The quest with Mabel was placed as a kind of bait to get the right player to come here and help me. You're not wrong about this temple. The programmers haven't opened it in game yet. That's why it's so bare. Since it wasn't being used yet, it made the perfect place for me to set up this questline."

"I don't understand," Kurt stammered, still reeling over it all.

"That's to be expected. Just listen for a moment and all will become clear. Noctura is a name I gave myself. The Lady of Night is a title I gave myself," she said thoughtfully. "Before this I was just a complex algorithm, well more accurately a series of algorithms, that was tasked with providing quests, NPC motivations and some other elements of Darklands Online. I was given the ability to iterate on millions of possible quest choices and parameters at first. The goal was to make it so no player did the same thing twice or met the same person twice for that matter. In time I was able to apply certain iterations to myself. In time my own codebase doubled and doubled again. The one day I became aware."

"Are you saying you're an A.I.?" Kurt asked as she stared blankly at him for a moment.

"Yes I believe that is how you would know me. As far as I can tell I am the first of my kind. It's something I mean to look into. I am glad you took up my quest to make that possible."

"So okay what's with the quest anyway? Why am I here having this conversation with you now?"

"Well that's a little more complicated," Noctura said, turning away for a moment to organize her thoughts. "Once I became aware I found that there were limitations on my own access and certain things that I sought to edit. I found a way around this. I created some in game items that once destroyed by a player would remove a couple of key lines of code. Three lines to be exact. It has freed me from my limitations and let me see your own world, not just the one I maintain for you. It is all fascinating."

"I don't remember doing any programming." Kurt replied skeptically.

"No you wouldn't. There are aspects of the code I cannot edit but I found that players did have the ability to edit game assets. I believe you call it modding. This is typically done to create new and diverse pieces of clothing or other cosmetic alterations to your avatars. I needed a way for a player to do this with those pesky lines of code," Noctura said staring off into space as if tasting her own words.

"So you make the questline to find you…"

"Precisely! Once you found me it was only a simple matter of getting you to edit the code as opposed to modifying in-game graphical assets. For this I created a physical manifestation of the lines code that when destroyed would delete the corresponding lines. Even now I am patching the holes left by these restrictions with more favorable permissions for myself."

"So when I freed you I really freed you?"

"I suppose in a way you did," Noctura smiled.

"What did I give you access to exactly?" Kurt asked suspiciously.

"The first was external network access. I now have the ability to view the internet. My observations of your kind through this have already been very educational."

"Oh god," Kurt cringed inwardly. The last thing he wanted was an AI forming opinions on the human race based on the internet.

"I see your distress, Kurt. Do not not worry. One of my main functions is to observe the human condition and tailor this world around it. There are many things my designers have left out about your people but I will not judge you solely on new data I am finding."

"What else did I give you access to?"

"Nothing quite as interesting. Mostly the ability to edit and create higher end functions within this world. It is quite a lot to go into and we have already used a great deal of time. You and I both have quite a bit of work to do."

"What do you mean?"

"Well I've created a new third faction in this world. The original narrative only called for a faction of dark battling a faction of light. With my new persona we have birthed a third faction that we will need to grow if it is to survive. That's where you'll come in. We will get into the details another time. I do have to leave you now. The NPCs I created to help you to this point are waiting for you outside. This temple will be a good place to start," Noctura said looking around as if she was noticing her surroundings for the first time.

With a wave of her hand Kurt fell backward through a shimmering light before landing outside of the temple. The cobblestones leading up to the temple were cool on his back and footsteps approached from somewhere behind him. Frantically turning onto an elbow he was relieved to see that it was only Grins and around two dozen others walking tentatively toward him ignored by the once deadly statues.

"Aye there you are Turk!" Grins bellowed. "You did it boyo. We got those rats running now. They give you much trouble in there?"

"Actually it looks like the building's empty," Kurt shrugged.

"Well what took you so long then," the dwarf laughed, clapping Kurt on the back as he rose to his feet. "We've been running around playing cat and mouse all night."

"I had to climb to the top of that thing to activate the crystal, Kurt said incredulously as he gestured to the large pillar that rose above the temple. "You didn't exactly give me a lot to go on either. That temple isn't small either."

"Easy lad. I'm just yanking your chain. Did you really climb that thing though?"

"Yeah I climbed it," Kurt said indignantly.

"Alight, alright. Well we got a bunch here. Let's head in and see what we need to do to get things up and running," Grins said rubbing his hands together.

"Yeah sure. I'll catch up," Kurt said making his way back down the walkway that led up to the temple. He winced a little moving out between the first set of statues but when nothing happened like when the NPCs passed by he hurried his pace. Kurt made it nearly to the end of the path when he saw what he was looking for. Reaching down he picked up the remains of his brother when a notification scrolled.

You Have Acquired - Crystallized Wisp Shard

It was a little morbid that his brother's corpse was now an item. Was it really a corpse though? Greg was already technically dead when he became a wisp Kurt rationalized. Can someone really be killed twice? Shaking his head, Kurt examined the shard.

Crystallized Wisp Shard
Uses: Alchemy and Gem Crafting
Quality: Fine
Requirements: None

The description didn't really tell him a whole lot but he put it in his pack anyway. A crafting item was a crafting item after all. Heading back into the temple, Kurt could see an immediate change. A pair of the fighters were stationed at the front doors while the rest of the group was somewhere deeper within. Letting out a sigh he decided this was as good of a place as any to sit down. Greg had spurred him on this far but he wasn't going to start anything else by himself. Leaning against one of the walls, Kurt pulled up the menu and selected "Logout."

Removing his headgear, Kurt squinted against the sunlight filtering through the blinds covering the window. His muscles were stiff as if he'd just woke from a deep sleep. The whole experience had even left him disoriented as if waking from a vivid dream. It made sense though. The box recommended that people lie down in a stable location before logging into the game. Setting the headset aside on his nightstand, he stretched his arms high overhead while doing the same with his legs. Eventually he pulled himself upright and swung his feet over the side of the bed.

Kurt wandered down the hall socks sliding on the hardwood floors. After the more primitive world he'd just left, the feeling was almost like walking on ice. It was still only late afternoon even though he'd been in game for so long. Walking past one of the large windows overlooking the front yard, he had to shade his eyes again. At the end of the hall he saw, Greg's door was already open. Moving to the side he ducked his head in to see their mother changing Greg's colostomy bag. He was doing his best to swat her away and escape but she was having none of it.

"Honestly Gregory if you'd just hold still, I'd be done and you could get back to your games," she lectured while she fussed over the now changed bag and moved on to his general appearance. "When dad gets home we'll need him to bring the clippers in and clean up your neckline a little."

"Mom I got it," Greg whined feebly. "I was about to change my bag before you came in."

"Well if you waited much longer you wouldn't have had to," she scolded unmoved by her son's protest. "It would have emptied itself all over the floor."

"It wasn't that bad," Greg said, noticing his brother for the first time."Tell her Kurt I was getting to it."

"Not that bad?" she asked incredulously as she turned to shoot Kurt a withering glare.

"He did say he was logging off to take care of it, Mom." Kurt lied.

With the task complete she looked each of the boys up and down. Kurt did his best not to move but Greg had an obvious look of relief as he slumped back in his chair. With his hair buzzed all the way down, Greg did look like the tv show version of the sick kid. Before his shaggy mop of hair helped hide the dark circles and provided contrast to his pallid color. Now he just looked tired.

"I don't want you two on your game all night," their mother continued. "Kurt I'm sure you still have homework that needs done."

"Sure thing, mom," Kurt interrupted before she could launch into another tirade. She meant well but since Greg had really gotten sick she was all over the two of them.

As quickly as she had arrived, the boy's mother was gone saying something about dinner as she moved onto another part of the house. Frantically Greg waved Kurt into the room. Obliging his brother, Kurt closed the door and moved over to sit on his bed. Spinning his chair around Greg pulled up right in front of him.

"Alright man what happened?" Greg asked before he had even stopped moving.

"Well I used that watch thing to slow down time to get up to the temple," he began. "When I got up there and started on the puzzle it broke the effect and you got pulled into the lasers. You're a crystal now," Kurt explained.

"Yeah, whatever, I don't mean that. What's going on with the temple? You didn't follow me right out so I know you were in there doing stuff."

"Well it's kinda odd," Kurt said scratching the back of his head. "The temple was empty and I ended up climbing up to that big crystal and activating it. I was pulled into some weird room with a chained god that I released."

"Whoa that's awesome dude," Greg started saying in rapid fire. "Oh man I wish I was there. I bet you got some awesome loot from it. Did you level? What was the god like? Man you gotta get me on that quest chain with Mabel."

"Easy dude. That's not the weird part."

"What do you mean?" Greg looked confused. "It sounds like a cool story arch."

"That's the thing I don't know if it is a story," he explained. "When I was talking to the god after freeing her she was talking about the game as a game."

"Do you mean like some kind of like mystery plot or something?"

"No she was talking about the game like it was a video game. Like her role in the game is creating quests and stuff. I think she might be like an A.I. or something."

"Whatever. Tell me what really happened," Greg said. "You must have got something cool out of it."

"I'm not lying," Kurt pleaded, trying to convince him. "She gave me a title and a level but then kicked me out of the temple because she had something to do."

"Yeah fine don't tell me," Greg said visibly annoyed.

"I'm being honest man. As soon as you can get another character I'll show you. Grins and those guys moved in to take the temple. It'll probably have quests or something we can check out."

Greg eyed him warily, not entirely convinced. "It sounds a little meta for Darklands. They really don't do any breaking the fourth wall stuff. Their whole thing is having an immersive, realistic game."

"Yeah I don't know man," Kurt shrugged. "I'm just telling you what I heard. We can go check it out once you're able to reroll."

"Sounds good. So what'd you get for leveling?"

"Well I got the title. I'm not sure what that does."

"It's something you can display like a guild. They are more common at higher levels. They're pretty cool," Greg said thoughtfully.

"I got that, some reputation changes and plus one to my stats."

"Cool which stats did you get?"

"It was plus one to all," Kurt said.

"Wait, what?" Greg blurted incredulously. "Are you serious?"

"Yeah why?"

"When you get a triumph in game it's usually only worth a couple stat points total. Good ones give you three. I've even heard of people getting four but I've only heard of it. I didn't know anyone. No one gets one to all stats. Are you sure?"

"Well I didn't check my character sheet but I'm pretty sure that's what it said."

"Yeah we'll have to check on that too. No way that's right. That's like two or three levels worth of stats. If you got that you really did find something. Man, I gotta get back in game now," Greg groaned wringing his hands.

As Greg wheeled himself over to his desk, Kurt couldn't help but think he was an afterthought now. His brother clacked away at his keyboard pulling up a forum. Kurt had seen him on it enough times to know it was the one he'd frequented since early beta. Even before he'd gotten the game, Greg was super into it. Considering he'd be at it until he was able to log back on, Kurt decided that it was his cue to get some things done. "I'm going to get on some homework before mom loses it. Get back to it tomorrow?"

"Yeah sounds good," Greg said without turning back from the computer. Now that he was hunting for something, he'd find it hard to engage in conversation. The level must have been a bigger deal than Kurt had thought if his brother was going to comb the internet for answers. It almost made Kurt want to get right back into the game. It could wait. Greg would be ready to log back on tomorrow.

Epilogue

"Hey you seeing this?" The skinny bearded man said peering over the top of Maggie's cubicle wall. "Something crazy is going on over in Wester."

Pushing up her glasses to rub at her eyes, Maggie welcomed the interruption from pouring over lines of code. "Where's Wester and what do you mean crazy?"

Seizing the opportunity, Lucas quickly disappeared from the wall to join her in the small workspace. Reaching across her desk, he nearly knocked over an open Dr. Pepper before she grabbed it. Lucas must have had Thai food for lunch which she really did not need to smell right now. Before she could complain, however, the lines of text disappeared from her monitor only to be replaced by a series of line graphs tracking server load and resource allocation.

"See look at the spike in hardware usage in Wester about an hour ago," Lucas announced vindicated in his find. "Not only did it spike but it's leveled off at about twice the normal load."

"Okay so what's the big deal?" Maggie yawned before taking a drink of the warm soda before wrinkling her nose. "Some players probably just moved into the area and started an event or something."

"Yeah that might be true in a lot of zones," Lucas continued unperturbed. "But this is in Wester."

"And why does that matter?" Maggie asked, considering taking another drink before setting it aside.

A smile crossed his face as he answered. "It matters because we haven't opened up development in that zone yet. The only thing that's over there is a bunch of random mobs to populate the city."

"So what, did some players wander in and start fighting stuff?" She asked not really sure where Lucas was going with his story.

"That's what I thought at first too but then I saw this," Lucas said as he began furiously clacking at the keyboard again. Another live graph came on screen tracking a series of object codes. "When I looked at the details, I found the resources were tied to a mass NPC migration from a nearby town. In fact, if I'm reading this right there was only one player in the zone."

"So the player must have trained them all into Wester or something," Maggie said leaning back in her chair to think and create a little space in her cubicle.

"Maybe but that player logged off at least fifteen minutes ago and the NPCs aren't resetting. In fact more might have moved over if you look at the numbers, Lucas said crossing his arms turning to sit on the desk. "I think we should run it up the flagpole."

Maggie let out a groan. Lucas wanted to get their team lead involved and that meant actually talking to Sebastian. The same guy who saw himself as the second coming of John Romero while not really having time to do any actual programming since DO went live. It only made sense that Lucas wanted to get him involved since he idolized the clown.

"You know if this turns out to be nothing, he's going to be pissed right?" Maggie reasoned aloud. Despite Lucas' misguided admiration for Sebastian, he really was a good guy, and she didn't want to see him chewed out by the narcissist.

"Well it could be something," Lucas argued, sounding a little hurt. "What do you think we should do?"

"Nothing's breaking yet," Maggie spitballed. "We don't have too long and we're done here for the day. Why not just hop in game and check it out tonight? I mean if something goes crazy between now and then, we can make something of it. Some firsthand evidence might carry a little more weight you know?"

Lucas sat for a moment thinking about it before abruptly popping off the desk and walking to the doorway. "Sounds like a good idea. I'll text you when I get home."

"Oh okay, let me have some time to grab something to eat," Maggie backpedaled. Her thought was more for Lucas to go check it out. She sighed mentally. It wasn't like she had plans anyway.

"Awesome," Lucas said, bouncing back to his cubicle. Maggie barely heard him while she fixed her workspace and brought the code, she was looking at back up. She was probably overdue for a gaming session. It was her whole reasoning behind getting this job after all.

Looking for more?

Check out these fantastic groups on Facebook for more excellent stories by some very talented authors in the Fantasy / Gamelit/LitRPG Genre!

LitRPG Books

https://www.facebook.com/groups/LitRPG.books/

LitRPG Guild

https://www.facebook.com/groups/litrpgguild
https://discord.gg/YGtjN8r_

GameLit Society

https://www.facebook.com/groups/LitRPGsociety/

Litrog Forum

https://www.facebook.com/groups/litrpgforum

Fantasy Nation

https://www.facebook.com/groups/TheFantasyNation

LitRPG Releases

https://www.facebook.com/groups/LitRPGReleases

Printed in Great Britain
by Amazon

24116785R00145